Key to My Soul

PROBAL MAZUMDAR

Key to My Soul

PROBAL MAZUMDAR

write · share · connect · publish

Key to My Soul *by* Probal Mazumdar

Published by www.pblishing.com

Marketed by

Maple Press Private Limited
sales office A 63, Sector 58, Noida 201 301, U.P., India
phone +91 120 455 3581, 455 3583
email info@maplepress.co.in
website www.maplepress.co.in

ISBN: 978-81-93324-80-6

Cover, Typesetting, and Book Design by **Flying Trees Private Limited**
Printed in India

10 9 8 7 6 5 4 3 2 1

Dedicated to

Ma for turning the battles in her life into a string of flowers...
Bapi for hiding every thorn in his feet so we could still dream...

Table of Contents

Prologue

24 November 2008

"My love will shine like the moon when the light in the lanterns fade away."

When Siddharth regained his senses for a brief period of time only a few lines from his past kept repeating themselves in his head. "Somebody help...," he tried to say but he could barely speak. His mouth felt dry and stale and tasted of rust.

He sat with his back against the wall. The blood on his left thumb had just about started to clot but the pain was intense. Red blotches of blood covered his white shirt. The back of his head throbbed with pain and his spine was a river on fire.

"Help...help," he tried to say again. He became aware that he was in a tiny room.

On his right, a grilled window framed unfamiliar woods with a patch of blue sky. Through it bars of sunrays streamed into the room. The walls were damp and soot black. Thick cobwebs hung from the ceiling. Few bricks and burnt logs were piled in one corner of the room. And all across the dusty floor colorful paintings lay scattered.

"Water," was all he could mumble. "Water."

At the window, coils of a creeper had snaked inside the room, nodding as and when the breeze slapped them outside.

Droplets of water welled at the ends of the tendrils, before
falling off one at a time. His tongue craved for those drops. But
he could barely move as his hands and feet were bound.

"My love is like ether. It will exist as the fifth element."

He tried to wheel his thoughts back into the past but
something was blocking it. Probably it was the terrible pain in
his head and thumb. He was not in control of either his senses
or his limbs. Unsure of whether he was dreaming or dying he
made a last-ditch effort to shift his hips and legs. But his vision
got blurred.

Before passing out again, flashes of images swept across his
mind, about his first love, his first kiss, the kohl laden eyes, his
paintings, the shocking letters, the locker, the pain, the hurt,
the temple. This was followed by blurred sinister faces flooding
his eyes but they surged past in fast succession.

"If you have lied to us we will come back and chop you off."

An hour later…

A little village boy came running to the village pond in
search of his lost kite. As he looked around his eyes fell on the
small broken house with creepers and vines crawling up the
walls. A smile hatched on his face as he guessed his kite might
have fallen near the small house or on its terrace.

He came closer to the house. The front door was open
partially. Recalling the stories he heard of startling discoveries
of pots of gold and gems from such old dilapidated houses, he
peeped inside expecting some such treasure. His eyes scanned
the small room and he saw the colorful papers strewn all

around. His pulse quickened in excitement.

"Uncle, can I take these?" he asked Siddharth pointing to the colorful papers. "Uncle?"

Seeing no response, he assumed Siddharth was asleep and quietly slid through the narrow gap of the open door. As he tiptoed inside and stared at the paintings, a sudden temptation filled him to make paper boats out of them. He picked up as many as he could and was about to get the man's permission when his eyes fell on the redness all around and the twines that bound the man's hands and feet.

Eyes frozen and legs trembling, the boy turned back and sprinted away as fast as his thin and terrified legs could carry him. Once he reached some distance his mind flooded with dreams of colorful paper boats and rockets. There was in it however, no concern for the silent man or his lost kite at all.

Chapter 1

THE PHONE CALL

15 November 2008

It was an unusual Saturday morning. Siddharth had just disconnected the phone and was trying to face a new reality. He stood at the window staring outside, wondering who the caller was. Why did he avoid disclosing his name? Why had he called from a phone booth? How did he know of a past that was buried in the graveyard of time? Amidst the flood of questions bothering him, parts of the conversation kept ringing in his ears.

"They're trying their best," said the man on the phone.

"How did it happen?" asked Siddharth with a slight shiver in his voice.

"It was a car... near her workplace...it was so sudden..."

"Where's she now?"

"Main hospital. Jamshedpur. In her old hometown. She's been there for two days. Actually I'm unsure how to break this news to you," said the man with deep anguish in his voice.

Siddharth didn't know what to expect. His breathing had slowed down already and he was trying hard to control himself as he mumbled, "Go ahead...I hope...I hope..."

"Her condition is serious. The accident was severe. By the grace of God she's still breathing. But, but..." the man paused.

"But what?" Lines of worry appeared on his forehead.

"She's in coma."

Siddharth felt the sudden pounding of his heartbeats. "I hope …I hope… everything is going to be okay? What do the doctors say?"

"Nothing encouraging at the moment. They are trying their best. I don't know how to say it…or should I say it at all…" The caller paused for a while and then said, "Maybe you'd want to come down here to see her once. We have to be prepared to hear the worst."

There was a dead silence. It was unusually long for a normal phone call to be considered active. But this call was anything but normal. It was odd, unforeseen and upsetting. Yet it was the uneasy silence that bound the two men at each end. There was a disturbing quality about it, a tension that indicated that in spite of the long hush the call wasn't over, that something was incomplete. Something important.

Finally, the caller said, "There is one more thing I need to say. Years back she had meant to share important letters with you. But they never reached you. You must get them now. I have something that would lead you to them. If you come over I'd give it to you."

"Important letters? Like what?"

"I don't know. They were for you. But could you come over?" asked the man eagerly.

"I…I don't know…I'll try." He was neither able to commit nor refuse to the stranger.

"Actually, if you can collect it yourself, I'll feel better. It will ease my sense of guilt."

"Sense of guilt? What was this man talking about?" wondered Siddharth. "Who was he? And what letters was he talking about?" But he stopped himself from asking anything more about the letters. Instead, he said, "I'll see what I can do. Who else is there with her?"

"Her mom. Their friends and relatives."

"How is her mom?"

"By the grace of God she is doing fine. But the accident has torn her."

"And her dad?"

"I didn't see him. I heard he had left the town ages back. But I'm not sure."

"And how are you related to her?"

"As I said I am a well-wisher of their family."

"May I know your name please?"

After a brief pause the man replied, "By the grace of God, you will come to know it eventually. But you must come down. It's important. At least for her."

The conversation ended by 9 a.m. It was time to head for office. But Siddharth didn't feel like going. He wanted to talk to the caller some more. So he dialed the number that showed up on his cell-phone and found that the call was made from a PCO in Jamshedpur.

It was a cold winter morning. The Bhubaneshwar sky was ashen. There were no birds to show signs of life. One could not tell if a cyclone had ended or was about to start. And as he kept staring outside the window the sluice gates of his suppressed memory burst open.

Seventeen years had gone by since he had seen her last. He had learnt to live without her, without her voice, her touch, her little demands, her secrets and stories, her athletic victories, her fears, until she had become a shadow in his life before fading away completely.

It was for her that he had made elaborate paintings, written poems, spent nights watching the moon and even jumped out of the terrace of a three storied building onto a eucalyptus tree, sliding down to the base to escape her father. It was because of her that he understood what sensations a simple touch from a girl evoked in a virgin body and what falling in love meant. She was his first crush, his first love, his dream girl, Hazel.

But that was seventeen years back. And now the sudden news that her survival was uncertain. That she may cease to be. The realization jolted him. Although he had learnt to live without her, the painful thought of living when she was no more had escaped him.

Little later, as his childhood days came drifting back, another incident came unbidden. It was her last letter to him. Was that letter related to the ones the man was talking about, he thought? For he was reminded that the last letter was a little absurd and incomplete. That something was missing. He vaguely recalled a line from it. *"It contains the key to my soul."*

In all the years that passed he had forgotten about it. However, at that moment he was unable to ignore it anymore. It left him restless the whole morning and he paced the rooms hoping to figure out the identity of the caller and locate the last letter from Hazel.

Chapter 2

THE SEARCH FOR THE LAST LETTER

While searching for the letter, Siddharth walked past the bedroom wall-mirror when something made him step back to the mirror and stare at himself. His high cheek-bones and wide lips were dry. So he applied a dab of winter cream over them and then rubbed the sides of his straight and strong nose. His eyes had a downward slant with droopy eyelids and his hair was curly. Tall, dark and dimple-chinned, he stood out in crowds. At thirty-five, he still looked like a college grad.

As he studied his face on the mirror, his eyes rested on the part that Hazel adored.

"Because of that dimple on your chin, I can't stay mad at you for long," she had said.

"I don't give you a reason to be mad."

"You sure do, Sidd. And I cool off only because of your chin and eyes."

"Now my eyes too. That's news. The other day you said you hated my eyes."

"True. That was because I was mad at you. You didn't take me to Ravi's for my monthly quota of *golgappas,*" said Hazel knitting her brows.

"Was that any reason to get mad? I told you I had to go someplace with dad that day."

"Maybe. But forget that. I was meaning to ask you for something for a while."

"I hope that something is not going out for a boring movie."

"What boring movie? When did we go for a boring movie? Last time we went for '*Maine Pyar Kiya*'. And you couldn't stop talking about it for two weeks. Forgotten?"

"As if you didn't talk about it. You were head-over-heels on that Salman Khan and started behaving as if he was your boyfriend. The only thing you did for the next one month, was blabber about him in front of me. Did you ever think why I should have listened to all that? Only about him and his dialogues."

"Oh so this Bengali boy has a bit of jealousy too. That's good to know. But I wasn't thinking of a movie. I was only hoping to see a sketch."

"A sketch? Of that Salman Khan? I won't do it."

"Not of him, you silly. Of you."

"Of me? Are you out of your mind? When did I ever sketch myself?"

"*Chup kar.* You are not in any of your paintings. You have made sketches and painted the whole world: Landscapes, Still life, fruits, water-jugs, streets, railway stations, our school and even monkeys and bisons. But neither you nor I am in any of them. Why?"

"You know Hazel that I sketch those things that inspire me."

"Oh," said Hazel, flaring her nostrils. "Meaning I don't?"

"Hey, it's not that way."

"Just shut up. I want a sketch of yours. Whether you want to sketch me or not I'll leave it to your high standards and taste. But I want your sketch. Period."

"My fingers won't move Hazel. It will be damn boring for me..."

"My foot. Will you or will you not give it to me?" shrieked

Hazel.

"Okay. Okay. But what will you do with that?"

"None of your worry," she said and looked away.

After a little sweet-talking and pleading, she broke her silence and said slowly, "What else will I do Sidd, after we graduate and go to different colleges. It's just another year from now. At least I'll have something to look at."

"Like what?"

"Like your eyes and that cute dimple in your chin."

And then she planted a kiss on his cheeks that left marks not of lipstick but of the long and passionate crush of her tender lips.

Siddharth was still staring at his chin in the mirror, when the city they were born in flashed across his mind. Jamshedpur. He had made a titanic promise ages back to never visit his hometown again. But now it beckoned him to break that vow. He reflected, if he could. Did he now have a choice though, he wondered? How could he not break it for Hazel? The thought that she was battling for life tormented him.

So he called up the travel agent for an emergency train ticket to Jamshedpur. And then he began hunting for Hazel's last letter again.

Siddharth stayed in a company leased three bedroom bungalow. Compared to its size the furnishings were sparse. It had the typical look of a house where a woman did not live; Or had not lived for ages. The taste and touch and smell of a woman were absent from every corner, from every piece of furniture, from every wall of the house. It was anything but neat and tidy.

The only spotless furniture was his bed. The bed-sheets

were always clean and a freshly laundered one was put up each morning. Everything else was neglected, the rooms, the dining table, the sofa, chairs, curtains, shelves, books, the refrigerator and often himself.

The house was disordered. Searching, therefore, for something was difficult by default. As he was prying through the stuffed suitcases and wardrobes Siddharth came across several things he had lost sight of for years, but there was no trace of Hazel's last letter. Clueless, he went on rummaging randomly all over the house, in cabinets, desks and drawers, wardrobes, suitcases and even inside pockets of old trousers which were improbable places to look at.

Yet after several hours of searching he failed. "It can't be. It has to be within the walls of this house," he said aloud. He faintly recalled that he had preserved something in the house but was clueless beyond that.

Finally, late into the night he gave up, determined to resume the search again.

Hazel had besieged his mind. Even when he hit the bed that night he was unable to banish her thoughts away. It carried him back to his school days, to the days they spent time together. Though his feelings for her were erased, to his surprise, her thoughts cheered him up. The seed of a faint longing grew in him to meet her again. He tossed about on the bed and kept his eyes open trying to visualize Hazel's childish face when he had seen her last, until the crows called out the morning. And then, exhausted, he sank into the deep sea of slumber.

The nonstop ringing of the doorbell made his eyes hatch open in alarm. Sleepily he dragged himself to the door to find his domestic help scratching his head with irritation.

"Why are you ringing the bell so much, Babban?" he asked.

"*Bahut kaam hai sahib*," replied Babban looking at him with indifference. He was short and stout and had a round plump face that seemed to have lost all reasons to smile.

"What time is it?"

"*Chai ya coffee*," asked Babban, ignoring his question. He prepared the early morning beverage for him. In Siddharth's assessment that was the only thing he could accomplish which could be approximated to cooking. Long back he had asked him to prepare lunch. After the initial few spoonsful the entire meal had to be dumped into the bin.

"*Chai ya coffee*," he asked him again and stepped inside the room. "*No Time.*"

"Tea," replied Siddharth and fetched his watch. It was 8:30 am. "Can you pull the curtains? Let the light come in."

After a while, as he was browsing through the morning newspaper, Babban came running, "*Sahib*, the gas cylinder is empty." There was a ray of regret in his eyes.

"Is this the second cylinder or the first one?"

"The second one, *Sahib*."

"Let me check." He walked over to the kitchen and after shaking and lifting the cylinder he said ruefully, "It has never happened before that both the cylinders are empty at the same time. I have to book a new one now. It will take a week to get a replacement."

They pondered over the situation and how to deal with it.

"*Sahib*, why don't you get the heater?" said Babban after thinking for a while.

"What heater?"

"The old electric heater you had many years back that your father had got."

"Oh that one. Must be a fossil by now. Will it work?"

"Yes it should, *sahib.*" Babban offering a solution to a problem was rare.

"But I don't remember where we kept it," said Siddharth.

His father, on one of his visits from Detroit to India had brought it. It was an induction heater made in USA and during those days was a novelty in kitchen appliances compared to the gas burners and electric coil heaters.

"It must be in the loft, *sahib.* I remember you had stowed it away long back."

"In the loft? Are you sure?" Babban nodded his head. "Okay let me see."

"No *sahib.* Let me climb and get it.

"It's okay. I'll manage," said Siddharth wondering why Babban was being so helpful. It was surely not out of any sympathy for him. It could probably be for the reason that finding the heater would ensure that his morning tea would not be compromised.

A small folding ladder was soon erected. While Babban held the base tightly, Siddharth crawled up the ladder and into the loft. As he was shoving things around, he suddenly realized that he had missed out the bags in the loft while searching for Hazel's last letter the previous day. And then one by one he started dropping all the old bags and the suitcases.

"*Sahib*, what are you doing," screeched Babban confused by the falling bags. "I asked you for the heater not for bags."

"I know. Here, take the heater." He handed it to Babban carefully and came down holding an old typewriter.

Babban dusted the heater, plugged it and turned it on. And it worked like a charm. As he was brewing the tea, Siddharth went on his rampage again, baring every bag and pulling them inside out. The loft was the only place that he had not searched the previous day.

"What are you looking for *sahib*? Can I help?"

"No. Not required. Here take this old typewriter. Dust it and keep it aside."

As he searched around, an old suitcase which he had used primarily during his years in college caught his attention. It was tattered and torn in places. After opening it he found that it was filled with story books, music cassettes, old school books, unwanted clothes, the college Reminiscences book, a broken piggy bank and a diary. A brown diary.

"This is the diary which had the handful of poems I had written for her," Siddharth said to himself, dusting it. It was yellow and dull with ageing. He had a hunch that the old diary might lead him somewhere. Moving through the pages carefully he found some of his old poems for Hazel. A faint boyish grin appeared on his face. Between the pages he also found two letters Hazel had written for him when they were in school. Finally as he was about to close the diary, a little disheartened, the last page cuffed his eyes. And then it lit up his face.

"*Sahib*. Tea is ready," called out Babban.

After munching few biscuits he sipped the hot tea and cleared the morning phlegm in his throat. He went back to bed with the diary, eager to read it. The last page had obscure lines. Reading it he recalled that he had scrawled them to record where he had kept the entire bunch of Hazel's letters, in case he ever forgot about them. And he was glad he did so, for the lines said that he had kept them in his ancestral home, in Baharampur, in the safety of a trunk that belonged to his late mother. It was likely that the last letter was with that bunch.

"*Sahib*. I am going. All work is done," called out Babban.

"Did you pull the curtains?" Babban was forgetful of pulling the curtains apart each morning. The rooms looked dark and gloomy until Siddharth pulled the curtains himself.

"Yes."

"Did you change the bed sheet?" But all he heard was the door slamming.

Around that time, the travel agent informed him that his train ticket was confirmed for Jamshedpur for the same night. That meant he had to race through the rest of the day to pack his bags and inform his office of an emergency leave for the next few days.

The railway station was a dense forest of travelers and hawkers. Waiting for the green signal to start its marathon, the train hooted and let out lazy hisses of steam. It was dark and about nine in the late evening.

Just before boarding the train Siddharth noticed that he was on the same platform and the same spot where he had once stood, holding a poetry book and waiting for someone to arrive. He paused for a brief second but avoided thinking about that person. It hurt him.

So he chose to think about Hazel instead. He recalled what she had told him once.

"*How can I help not falling in love with you? In that fall I soar.*"

Once inside the train, Siddharth quickly unfolded the bedspread and blanket on the upper berth and climbed up. "Time for some reading now," he said aloud pulling out a pile of poetry books, some new some old, from his bag. He had shoved them in before leaving home.

Poetry lured him in his youth when it proved to be the second useful vehicle for conveying his love for Hazel. Painting being the first. Reputed in school to be a prodigious painter, when he lost Hazel he abandoned painting forever. Gradually, he discovered the therapeutic powers in poetry to help lessen the hurt of life and became a voracious reader.

A lover of Indian poets, Siddharth had a decent collection of post-colonial Indian poets. His office colleague, Mukund Iyenger, was aware of this passion and had gifted a set of books by two writers, Rabindra Swain and Indra on his previous birthday. For weeks he had been stopping himself from opening the gift wrap. But as usual, even that night, after reading a few lines of his favorite poets he closed his eyes without opening the new books.

The train would reach Jamshedpur before sunrise. But although his eyes were shut for a long time, it was not sleep but his past that came rushing to him.

Chapter 3

OPERATION BLACK THUNDER

"A lotus about to bloom," said Vivek staring at the girl at the doorway.

"A light at the end of a tunnel," quipped Sanjay.

"I hope this light and lotus combo is joining our class," said Vivek.

"Buddies, don't be so thrilled," said Sudeep. "I heard about her this morning, when you guys were planning to lock our sports teacher in the common room. She's from the convent school. We know how those girls are. Good luck. I'm not in the chic race."

She stood by the doorway waiting to be noticed, holding a set of books in her left hand and a sleek bag in her right, unsure of what to do next. Doe-eyed, with shiny forehead and long slender eyebrows, she was fair, buttery and beautiful. Her hair was strikingly long and flowed over her shoulders to the hips. There was something athletic about her frame too.

"Ma'am someone is waiting outside," said Vivek to the teacher who was addressing the class. Miss Violet turned towards the door and said, "Oh. Come in child."

"Good morning ma'am," replied the girl walking slowly inside the classroom aware of the sea of eyes on her. She stood quietly beside Miss Violet.

"The Principal told me about you this morning. Welcome dear," she put her arms around the girl's waist and raised her voice and said, "We have a new student in our class. Please welcome Hazel." A volley of claps followed and finally the girl let out a smile. Miss Violet walked her to her seat.

It was the first day in school after a long summer vacation. So stories of travels and treks, summer camps and movies were getting exchanged and made the otherwise quiet students, unusually noisy.

"I need your attention, class," started Miss Violet. "I want to structure the first period differently. I was thinking if each one of us can talk about a subject of our interest."

The students of Eighth Grade looked at each other.

"It can be current affairs, science, history or anything under the generous sun. Anything that interests you. We all can learn from each other," said Miss Violet.

The students sat up in their seats. Doing something like this during the boring Moral Science period every morning was unheard of.

Just then someone tripped at the doorway and stumbled into the classroom, trying with difficulty to balance himself. He was tall, dark and dimple-chinned.

"May I come in Ma'am...?" he asked fluttering his droopy eyelids and flashing an apologetic face as a passport to get in.

Miss Violet snapped, "You are too early for the next class." The students burst out laughing. "Get in now." That Siddharth seldom reached school on time was well known. He covered the length of the room quietly and sat on the empty chair on Hazel's left.

"Tomorrow I'll talk about the basics of my favorite subject, Liberal Arts," resumed Miss Violet. "And from the day after I'd like each of you to volunteer with your topics."

During recess most of the boys introduced themselves to

Hazel. Siddharth wanted to do the same but felt restrained and shied away.

Few days later, during the Moral Science period, Sudeep spoke on '**Operation Black Thunder**'. It was in the same year, in April 1986, when the Indian Commandos had entered the Golden temple in Punjab and had given it that code name. The entire class listened to the narration in awed silence. An impressed Miss Violet spoke about it in the teacher's room.

Sudeep was known for his brilliance and often shocked people with his insight on various social and political issues. It was rare for children of his age to show such grasp.

"Awesome stuff Sudeep," said Siddharth as they walked out of the classroom for a break. "That was some speech. I wish I could speak that well."

"Thanks," smiled Sudeep showing his chipped canine tooth, "I was unsure how it would go. But I had dug up a lot of information from magazines."

The students presented different topics from Black-holes, evolution of the universe to concepts of inflation in economics, privatization and politics. Some even spoke on medical topics like causes and cures for ailments like Jaundice and Diabetes. Then there were narrations of the greatest love stories of all times. Ruskin Bond was quite popular.

It was a winning method especially for the shy who wrestled with stage fright.

Couple of weeks later a Painting competition was held in school. The theme was 'Innocence'. Siddharth won in the senior category. He had been winning every year. But winning that year was different for him. For it was the first time he spoke to Hazel.

"Hey," she called out as they were packing their school bags to leave for the day, "I really liked the way you depicted a baby in diapers holding a kitchen knife. It matched the theme of 'Innocence' so well. Both the drawing and the coloring were terrific. Congrats."

"Thanks Hazel."

"Did you learn painting from anyone?"

"Yes," replied Siddharth. "From a teacher."

"I heard you are a wizard of portraits and still life."

"No, no…that's not true," he said modestly and blushed.

"Can you show me your art books sometime?"

"I am really an amateur, Hazel."

"And I am not going to write a critical review on it for the newspapers you know."

"Okay. All right. I'll try and get them tomorrow," he said sheepishly.

"By the way, how long have you been studying here?"

"All through since kinder-garden. And you, before this?"

"Sacred Heart school," replied Hazel. "Actually, we moved into a new apartment and my parents felt that I should join this school as it is closer to our new home."

They left after chatting for a while. The fact that he was no longer a stranger to her made Siddharth happy and as he walked back home he thought of her and their conversation. A smile showed up in his eyes that spilled out to his cheeks and then to his lips.

Next day Siddharth brought his art books. The pages were long and firm. As Hazel flipped through each painting she was left gazing at the striking colors and unusual brushstrokes.

"They are superb. What I heard was true. You are gifted." Those words made him feel cool about himself. "I loved each painting. Can I take the book home?"

"What will you do?" he asked looking at her curiously.

"Show them to mom. She loves to see good paintings."

"Alright. You can take them. Is your mom into painting?"

"No. Actually my grand-father was a painter apart from being a serious pianist. He always encouraged mom to take interest in such things."

"I hope she likes my paintings."

"She'll love them. And can I keep the Qutub-Minar and the Sugar-cane Vendor? They are so awesome."

"I never tear pages from these books Hazel. But as an exception, I can."

Overjoyed, Hazel thanked him. In exchange, next day, she gave him a 5-Star chocolate bar which he considered so special that he did not lay his hands on it until it became soft and mushy. And then he preserved the wrapper carefully and it remained wedged between the pages of a history book for many years.

Hazel found his simplicity and shyness endearing, so also, his eyes and dimple-chin cute.

Quite often Hazel requested Siddharth to get the new paintings he made. He showed them not only to her but to his friends as well, especially Sudeep and Shankar. Sudeep himself sketched quite well and had teamed up with Siddharth for many inter-school competitions.

Slowly a genuine interest grew in Hazel, not only for

Siddharth's paintings but on the subject as a whole. She observed the styles and techniques, the signs and symbols he used. He used strange symbols like a safety pin on a door instead of a lock, or a fish in the sky, or wingless birds, an axe or a hacksaw at unusual places. No one could quite decipher what to make of them. They intrigued Hazel. So she pleaded him to reveal what they stood for.

And that made him feel extraordinary. Her questions, her interest. Although he won numerous competitions he was never as electrified as he was when Hazel appreciated him.

In the class, there were many who vied for Hazel's attention and tried to find pretexts to talk to her. As a new student, she carried an element of mystery and novelty that stroked the imagination of boys. Moreover, they found her to be simple, straightforward and modest with none of the airs they had believed would accompany a girl, as good looking as her and coming from as posh a school as the convent.

In two months, the annual sports day began with lighting the torch and house parades. The packed stadium resounded with the loudspeaker announcements, blaring of paper horns and the echo of pistol shots triggering a race, the hooting and hoorays, the shrill finger-whistling, ear-piercing shrieks and euphoric clapping. Every house had its own huge tent.

Midway, everyone goggled at Hazel and her unexpected athletic prowess. After winning the gold medal in the 100 m and 200 m run and long jump followed by silver medals in the throwing events like Discus and Javelin, she became a new wonder and bagged the Girl's Champion award for that year.

But her biggest achievement was not the trophies, but the

countless hearts she won.

This was an example of the importance of co-operation in an age of competition.

It was the 800 m run. The race began, and Hazel as usual had taken the lead quickly. But halfway she noticed one of her competitor trip and fall on the track injuring herself. So she stopped, turned and raced back to help her friend get up and laid her on the grass beside the tracks, before sprinting off. She lost the race.

But a special prize was declared for her.

During the awards ceremony, the beaming Principal announced, "We decided to award Hazel Castelino a special prize for her attitude without reflecting on her laurels at stake. This was an example of sporting spirit at such a young age."

The entire stadium echoed with thunderous and resounding applause that did not stop for one full minute. Siddharth couldn't believe what he saw and heard. And for Hazel, due to her participation in the multiple competitions and prolonged friction of bare feet with the ground, the sole of her right toe had ruptured and was bleeding freely. She limped back to her Red house shamiana and sat waiting for help. Before the sports-teacher came with the first-aid, Siddharth managed to enter the tent. He stood in front of her and looked at her with awe.

"Congratulations Hazel. I never knew you were such an all-rounded athlete."

"Thanks."

"You are a star now. I am sure, keeping you in mind, the Principal is already dreaming of a lot of medals coming in, during the inter-school meet."

The open wound on her toe and the beads of blood plopping on the floor distracted him. Immediately he yanked out his handkerchief and wound it over the toe, tying a knot as securely and carefully as he could, to stop the bleeding. The proper first-aid arrived later.

Next day in school her friends swarmed around her, praising her feats. As soon as she saw Siddharth she stepped out of the group. A slight limp was visible as she walked.

"Sidd come with me." She took him to the stairway in the corner and said, "Hey, thanks for being so caring yesterday." She was holding something wrapped in plastic.

"No problem. Is your foot better?"

"Yes, but it will take at least a week to heal."

"Last night I thought of you and the euphoria in the stadium because of you."

Hazel smiled.

"I wanted to let you know that I felt so proud of you."

"Thank you Sidd," she replied and then extended her hands. "I got these for you."

"Oh," he paused and his eyes widened in surprise. "Why did you have to get these?"

"Yours got spoilt yesterday with my blood."

Initially he did not feel comfortable accepting them, but when he saw his name was stitched beautifully with yellow and red threads on the two handkerchiefs, he could no longer decline. In fact he could not stop admiring the cute needlework. It was later he realized that the colors used for the threads signified their school Houses: Her's Red and his, Yellow.

As the days went by, her thoughts poured into the spaces and corners of his mind. When she spoke to him his heart jumped. When she was near him everything else got blurred and became secondary. He wanted to be with her more often, to hear her voice, see her smile, watch her pretty eyes and gaze at the bounce of the shiny sheath of her hair as she moved about.

They did not wait for big events to sneak into conversations anymore. It happened casually in the classroom, in the corridors, during recess, after school, just about any time.

One day as he was getting ready for the Biology class, a paper slipped out of the book and landed on his lap. As he read it, his hands and body shook. Paying no attention to what was being taught in class he read it over and over. It dried up his mouth like a desiccant.

It was a note addressed to him.

Right after the class got over he dashed to the restroom and stood trembling in excitement. He read it once again and felt his heart would explode.

And then with his head lowered, he went back to the classroom. As he crossed her, his eyes locked into hers for a few seconds and his heart thumped wildly against his chest as if a big bird caged inside wanted to fly away.

For the rest of the day his mind was hijacked with the words in the note.

At night his heart heaved like a vessel in a turbulent ocean. His eyes would not close. Amidst his father's snoring sound from next room, he saw the moon slowly traverse the length of the open window, from one end to the other and dissolve at the edge of daybreak.

For the first time someone had shared such fragrant and sweet words, boldly and secretly. They made him feel strangely powerful, brave and wildly ecstatic.

Realizing the futility of trying to sleep any further he got up from bed and pulled out sheets of white paper for a proper reply to the letter of love he got from a girl. By the time his lines pleased him, his father's feet were flopping on the floor in rubber slippers. He yanked out a school book and pretended to study.

Surprised to see his son awake so early, Mr. Banerjee walked over to him. Then he pressed his son's shoulders and planted a kiss on his cheeks. "Good morning *babu*."

In response, he shrank and stiffened.

That morning, for the first time, school looked interesting and he reached before time. But instead of attending the assembly he went straight to the classroom and slipped his note inside Hazel's desk and waited, his face inflamed, as if a crime was committed.

When Hazel came in with the rest of the students he looked at her and then quickly looked away. Miss Violet was surprised to see him in the classroom before time.

"Is this Siddharth or his ghost," she said. The students burst out laughing.

"Maybe he was driven out by the mosquitoes today," joked Vivek.

"Or maybe he saw a ghost," said Sanjay and laughed.

"How come you are so early?" asked Miss Violet.

"I…I…just like that." He could not come up with any reason worth sharing.

While Hazel was settling down in her seat she spotted a piece of paper sticking out of her desk. Grabbing it, she cast a sideways glance at Siddharth who quickly turned his eyes towards the ceiling, aimlessly without returning her look. She began reading it quickly.

"Dear Hazel,

Thanks for your note yesterday and thanks for making me feel special. I felt like a King. I never thought anyone could write such sweet words about me. I hope our friendship deepens with time. While I was watching the moon walk last night, I couldn't help writing a poem for you, probably my first ever:

'Something has grown wings at last
and was flapping within my rib-cage.
I tried to hold on to it fast
but it found its way to this page.'

Actually, I'm hardly in my senses and couldn't sleep last night. So if you find these lines boring, I'm sorry. From a sleepless friend."

All the time, while Hazel was reading the letter, Siddharth watched her in sly, watched her to detect the slightest furrow of disappointment appear on her forehead, or the smallest hurt on her face. At one point he started cursing himself for writing in a hurry.

The moments bored into his temples like a drill.

"Surely she'll think I am stupid. I should've spent more time writing more sensibly."

But his fears vanished when he saw a huge smile flash across the serene expanse of her face. She looked at him without blinking and said, "Thank you!"

And then a sense of relief and thrill replaced his fear. Unable to wait for the classes to get over, he kept asking himself, "What should I tell her next?"

When school got over that day, they walked back home together for the first time. They spoke a lot, uncontrollably, frantically, like the chirrup of birds after a good rain. They talked about studies, their hobbies, recent Bollywood movies, songs, about their lives, about everything under the sun. Except one thing. They did not utter a word on the letters they exchanged. Probably there was no need to for their purpose was over.

At a fork on the road Siddharth asked, "Where exactly is your house?"

"Near the market on the opposite side of the bus stand. And yours?"

"Near the hospital. It is a little away from the bus stand," she replied.

"Nice. That area has a small lake nearby and I am quite fond of that place."

"So both of us live quite near to the school. Walking distance."

As they parted at the fork, they became aware of an attachment deepening each day and in parallel an unfamiliar sense shielding that bond from the world's stare. To hide it. To protect it. For, they felt between them, they were carrying something precious, something meant only for them, something that could not be left exposed in the open. And that was "Love".

It became normal for Hazel and Siddharth to be seen together in the playground, at the badminton court or basketball court, having snacks, at lunch time, during breaks and even after school while they walked back home.

In the cold of November that year, during lunch break, Hazel took Siddharth to a corner near the assembly stage and pestered him to meet her at the Kali temple after school. He had sore throat and was sucking on a mint lozenge.

"Will you come?" she demanded.

"I haven't gone to the Kali temple too many times. Why do you want me there?"

"I will let you know once you arrive. Are you coming?" she asked again.

"Not sure Hazel," he said rolling the lozenge in in his mouth from one side to another making funny sounds.

"Why? Afraid of another Operation Black Thunder in the temple," taunted Hazel with her arms akimbo and nostrils suddenly flaring. She disliked the sounds Sidd kept on making as he sucked the lozenge.

"No. No. Not that. What time Miss Hazel?"

"Around 5 p.m. and stop calling me a Miss."

"I don't know if my father will allow me at that time."

"Tell him that you have come to meet me," replied Hazel, with mischief in her eyes, fully aware of what his response would be like.

"How can I tell him about you? I am not comfortable."

"Okay then take someone else's name," sniggered Hazel.

"He will still not allow. The temple is quite a distance."

"Is it the distance why Uncle won't allow you?"

"Yes. And also because it is getting completely dark by 6 pm nowadays."

"It is just a visit to the town temple Sidd. What are you so afraid of?"

He remained silent for a while and started sucking on the lozenge loudly. That noise irritated Hazel and she said, "Can you stop making that awful sound?"

"What sound?"

"The sound of that thing in your mouth. I hate it. Just swallow it," she demanded.

Siddharth chewed the mint lozenge and swallowed the broken pieces. He asked, "Can we not meet someplace else?"

"No we cannot. Can you not tell your dad that you are going someplace else?"

"No. Why should I?"

"Okay then I will come to your house today and take you out," said Hazel faking a serious attitude and ballooning her lips.

"No. No. Please. Please don't," resisted Siddharth almost whispering.

"Oh so you will not even allow me to your house is it?" she frowned.

"*Arre* it is not that. It may not look proper if you come by to ask me out."

"Really? Are you guys that conservative?" she raised her voice.

"I am not sure what you mean."

"Why can I not come to your house? I am sure Uncle will not have any problem with that. Don't your friends visit your house?"

"Yes they do. But I am not comfortable, please understand, Hazel."

"Okay fine. That's it then. Don't come," she said, pretending to be cross and raising her voice to a squeal. "There is no need to come. Even I will not go anywhere. Let's even stop meeting from tomorrow onwards. No point."

"Okay, okay I will try," he said seeing no other way out.

Hazel continued to look at him crossly.

"Sharp 5 p.m. okay Bengali boy? Else you will see a different side of me tomorrow which you won't like."

"I will try my best Hazel. But it would have been better if I could get someone else along like Shankar or Sudeep. Can I?"

"No. Only you. Solo," she said flatly. "I am not throwing a party for the whole town."

Siddharth arrived there on the dot, unlike his late arrival for school almost every day. He got his dad's scooter and parked it at the base of the temple. Hundred steps above, at the hilltop, he saw Hazel waving at him, flanked by three other girls around her.

As soon as he reached them, without a word, Hazel pulled him inside the temple where the evening 'aarti' had commenced. After the prayer was over, they came out and inspected the huge rocks and boulders bordering the temple.

Choosing the best spots on the rocks that were relatively elevated, flat and polished, the four girls hopped on and sat in a row, side by side, leaving Siddharth to face them. Hazel was on his extreme right and sitting against the temple wall. There was no other place nearby for him to squeeze in and sit.

All the girls, including Hazel, stared at him impishly. Overall it appeared as though he was facing a board of teachers, for breaking a rule at school.

"Okay so what's this all about?" asked Siddharth confused.

"First I want you to meet my friends," said Hazel cheerfully. Before he could say anything she started taking their names. "She is Dimple my best friend. This is Jennifer my cousin and she is Neetu my 'sardarni' buddy. They are all from my previous school Sidd."

Siddharth said a polite hello to all, feeling awkward, nervous and completely out of place in an all-girls set-up where he had no clue of what was expected of him. Although he pretended to look normal, his face gave away his rising sense of discomfort.

"And folks this is Siddharth I spoke to you about. He is my best friend in the new school and I wanted to introduce him to you. He is Sidd for me."

They shook his hands one by one, sitting tight in their places.

Hazel looked the best dressed amongst her friends, shimmering in a puffed-sleeve sequined black top and blue jeans and a pair of ear muffs. Dimple and Neetu looked chic in tight denim pencil skirts and winter jackets. Jennifer wore a velvet shirt and blue jeans, with mittens and a skull-cap. Not knowing that he would have to face so many girls, Siddharth had come attired in the worst possible manner.

"Is he your best friend or someone more special," said Jennifer looking at Sidd directly and fluttering her eyelids in such a coquettish manner that he almost lost his balance on the rocks. He positioned himself firmly.

"At least ask your friend to sit down, Hazel. See how uneasy he is," teased Neetu.

"There is no place to sit here, silly. Where will he squeeze in?" said Dimple cocking her eyebrows at Neetu and looking around.

"I have a better idea. I think we all should stand and make Sidd sit here instead," chirped Jennifer.

"Stop harassing him you uncouth girls," said Hazel. She noticed the blush on Sidd's face, the uneasiness in his posture.

"Who is harassing your friend, Hazel? How could you say such things about us? Did we harass you Sidd huh?" demanded Jennifer with her hands akimbo looking fixedly at him.

Before he could utter a sound Dimple interjected, "You said your friend is a sweet talker but he is not saying a word. Is Painter Babu sick or he didn't have proper lunch?"

"I want Sidd to sit down first," insisted Neetu.

"Yes I agree," chirped in Jennifer.

"Well, to sit beside Empress Hazel and her friends, he has to earn it," said Dimple.

"And what, can your Highness explain, is the way to earn it?" asked Neetu bowing her head like a maid in front of a Princess.

"We will give him a task. If he completes it satisfactorily, only then he will get a seat beside Empress Hazel," said Dimple.

"Shut up you girls. What are you up to? This is enough. Sidd, pay no attention to them," said Hazel, breaking into a plastic smile.

Ignoring Hazel, assuming an arrogant posture and Elizabethan diction Dimple said, "The task is to impress all three of us, the maids of Empress Hazel. It is a fairly difficult task as we have tough skins to please. Only then will you be allowed to be with her."

The girls burst out laughing and started shooting suggestions.

Until that time he did not get a chance to speak. The unexpected ragging loomed on his head like an avalanche about to fall. He wanted to either run away or jump off the hill-top. The girls from Sacred Heart School were known for their snootiness and outgoing attitude. Most of them belonged to well-to-do-families. And the more he thought about it the more he was stricken with nervousness. Only the worst thoughts kept swamping his mind.

He looked at Hazel to save him from the ordeal, but then he noticed that she was not taking sides. In fact, she was enjoying it covertly.

"Come on Painter Babu. Your time starts now," said Dimple looking at her watch.

"But what do I have to do, I am not sure," asked Siddharth managing to put some weight behind his soft voice.

"You have to please us as per Princess Dimple's instructions," offered Neetu.

"How?" he asked.

"That you have to think Painter Babu. I can suggest you sing a song or recite a poem or dance or do anything. And when you act this out for us please refer to all of us as your Highness. You fail to impress us, you go home alone tonight," added Dimple.

Unable to take the hectoring any more, Siddharth started to ask Hazel, "Is this why you brought me here…?"

Looking at his sorry state, Jennifer interrupted, "Be a sport Siddy boy. We are only trying to be your friends. None of us are going to douse you with petrol and strike a match."

Everybody giggled and Hazel had to pinch herself to stop

herself from exploding.

"Is this the way to make friends or scare them out of their pants." thought Siddharth. Then he told himself, "Since I'm trapped anyway I might as well try something." He looked at Dimple and said, "Your Highness, may I recite a few lines from a poem by Byron?"

"Go on." Dimple waived her hands in agreement as if she was signaling a lackey.

He recited the only poem he ever memorized from the school text book:

"She walks in beauty like the night
Of cloudless climes and starry skies
And all that's best of dark and bright
Meet in her aspect and her eyes....."

As soon as he spoke the first lines, Dimple jumped down from the rock and stood in front of him. Then she looked at him with an attitude and walked back and forth several times like a model on a ramp. She swayed and rolled her hips so wide, that her tight denim skirt was about to burst at the seams. The girls went berserk with laughter.

With Dimple's cat walk done, based on the first line of the poem, the girls clapped instantaneously and Dimple patted Siddharth on his back saying, "Nice job Painter Babu."

Siddharth wished that he had ignored Hazel's invitation.

Pointing towards Jennifer, Dimple said, "You may now proceed to the next maid of Empress Hazel."

He turned at Jennifer, "Your Highness, may I sing a few lines of a song for you?"

"Only if it is a great one," replied Jennifer.

Sidd began without thinking, *"Dum maro dum, mit jaaye*

gum..." As soon as he started, the girls cupped their hands like they were holding chillums and took deep drags of air, swaying and swinging their feet. Soon they turned hysterical and started making lurid sounds that attracted the attention of a few temple staff. So they kept quiet for a full minute and then chorused the song together softly.

By this time Siddharth felt more at ease, as he realized, that all the girls were seeking fun. And that he was actually not up against lionesses.

Finally it was Neetu's turn to be impressed and she said, "We have all heard you. We have heard the poem and the song. So I do not wish to hear you anymore." She paused.

"Then what is your wish, Lady Neetu?" pitched in Dimple.

"I want to see. Only see," said Neetu rolling her tongue inside her mouth.

"Oh wonderful. Good for all of us. But what do you want to see?" asked Jennifer.

"I want to see how he is from inside," replied Neetu.

All the girls squealed with wicked delight and clapped in anticipation.

"See what?" asked Siddharth unsure of what was coming and readying himself to run away if the request was outside the periphery of humor. For a moment he felt they would ask him to remove his shirt.

"How much depth you have. How deeply you can perform."

"Ooooh," crooned Dimple. "Can you please elaborate your point to Siddy boy quickly? It's almost dark and we may not be able to see anything at all?"

Neetu looked at Sidd strictly and said, "Okay. I want you to look at the moon and propose to her right now. And no words are allowed. As I said we already heard you."

"No words. Only action?" asked Siddharth, relaxed at the harmless request but equally doubtful if he could enact anything.

"Yep Painter Babu."

It was already dark by then. The temple lights had come up and the moon was shining brightly as a fluorescent silver plate with the stars as silver studs decorating the night sky. Siddharth murmured something and tried to resist but was flatly rebuked by Dimple.

This time Hazel encouraged him, "Sidd why don't you complete it and be done with it? I need to also tell you something important later."

So he kneeled down slowly on the ground and looked up at the moon and extended his arms wide open. Then with his right hand he blew a kiss at the moon and rested the palm on his chest above his heart. On the gravel, on which he was kneeling, he drew a heart sign with an arrow piercing it and placed a brick on it. Next he removed his ring quickly and showed it to the moon and shoved it a couple of times on his left ring finger. Then with a stone, he broke the brick to denote a broken heart. Finally he closed his eyes and opened his arms wide and was back up on his feet again, bowing at the moon.

There was silence for a few seconds before a storm of applause broke out. The girls jumped off the rocks and hugged him one by one and pulled his cheeks and made him sit where they had been sitting and shaking their legs like a pack of royal ladies.

Dimple said, "Sidd it was all for fun. Hazel I pass him. He is a gem isn't he?"

Jennifer in full enthusiasm acknowledged, "Yes. He is Mr. Perfect."

"No he is Painter Babu who does great miming as well," said Neetu smiling.

All of them apologized for their wild behavior.

Hazel was beaming with pride and Siddharth felt it called for a vacation in the hills after a harrowing military training camp. The girls left them together saying they had to run home for their lives as it was already dark and promised to meet again soon.

That a severe scolding from their parents awaited them at home, Siddharth and Hazel were pretty sure of, yet they decided to walk slowly. It was the town culture not to have children loitering on the streets after dark.

They walked down the hundred steps together. Although initially Siddharth felt butchered and embarrassed by Hazel's friends, he realized at the end how quickly, because of them, he was able to develop a cool camaraderie. The one thing that made him happy was that he did not make an ass of himself in front of the girls. He popped a chewing gum into his mouth.

At the base of the temple Hazel paused and asked, "Now I have a question for you."

"Oh. I hope I don't have to impress you now."

"No, not to impress. Do you know why I called you at the temple?"

"To introduce me to your friends?" he said confidently, giggling and bouncing around with joy. He kept shifting his weight on each leg alternately as if he was about to dance. And he started making sounds as he chewed the bubble gum.

"I will give you a tight slap," said Hazel flaring her nostrils

She was suddenly peeved by his excitement and by the sound of chewing. She couldn't tolerate the sound when people sucked and chewed open-mouthed. The sudden mood change and sting of words lowered Sidd's sense of achievement by degrees.

"Did I goof up somewhere?" he asked, biting his right index finger.

"No."

"Then why are you so mad at me?"

"Can you spit out that lousy stuff in your mouth. I told you enough times that I don't like that sound. Throw it out. Right now."

Siddharth obeyed and stood still.

"Don't you know why I called you here? The reason is not what you just said."

"No I don't know."

"Do you at least know what date it is today?"

Siddharth tried hard to recall and said, "It is November but the date…"

"It is November but the date…," mimicked Hazel making a face and pinched his left arm. Then she told him the date.

"Oh yes right I forgot," he relaxed and thought he managed to cross the bump.

"And what happens on this day?" asked Hazel challenging him again.

After thinking about some possibilities like a full moon or an equinox or a winter solstice he gave up and asked innocently, "What?"

"You really need a beating now." Hazel raised her hand.

Siddharth ducked and started running away. Hazel chased him and was right behind him in no time. Siddharth knew that she was a strong runner at school and thought it best not to challenge her on the streets and eventually get overtaken. Also he did not want to provoke and draw the attention of the pedestrians. So he stop and decided to and face her.

"Okay. You tell me Hazel."

"I will not tell. You have to guess it you bum," said Hazel holding his hands tightly.

"Really sorry Hazel, but please break the news now," he pleaded.

"Today is my BIRTHDAY you....you," she screamed on the word birthday and not finding any suitable word to address him, added, "you Painter Babu my foot."

"Oh, really? Happy Birthday Hazel! I never knew it. Why didn't you tell me earlier today," he asked sounding causal. The birthday news did not bring an extra spark to his face which was already aglow with the cool performances he gave to Hazel's friends. And that irked Hazel.

"Few folks already wished me. And you? If they could know how you couldn't?"

"How in the world would I know that Hazel? This is the first time I am ever hearing it. This is your first year in the school. We usually celebrate our birthdays by getting sweets and toffees in the class but you did not do it. So how else would I know?"

"So am I the one who is supposed to get sweets on my birthday?"

"That is how it is here. How did it happen in your previous school?

"Let's not drag my old school. They were much better, at least on my birthdays."

"Hey, I seriously did not know about it."

49

"Then how did your friends know?"

"My friends? Who?" asked Sidd stumped.

"Shankar, Sudeep, Vivek, Sanjay, Mohua, Sheela, Shobana, Ajay, Soumitra and a few others. How come they know about it, your close friends, and you don't?"

Siddharth kept quiet and started wondering. "I'll find out from them tomorrow."

Hazel tempered down her extra sternness, which was purposefully aimed to knock him off the extra enthusiasm she saw in him after he met her friends. That he acted so well for her friends and never did anything remotely as cute for her, was playing in her mind.

But she was the mastermind behind the drama on the hilltop. She was the one who had decided how her friends should play with him and then share their feedback on him. This little secret was revealed by Dimple a year later.

Hazel quickly gathered herself and said, "Hey Sidd sorry for the tomfoolery today. Actually every year on my birthday I visit the temple at this time. You will remember my birthday from now on, right? Give me your hands and wish me."

Siddharth pressed her hands and wished her again, his mind still in a flux on how his friends came to know about the birthday. He swore he would find it out the next day. They walked up to where his scooter was parked.

"I have one question Hazel," he asked with a sudden realization.

"I thought you will have many? But go on."

"Being a Christian why do you visit a Temple?"

"*Shweet* question from a *shweet* Bengali boy. That is because my granny was a Hindu and mom wants me to follow the rituals of both the religions. On my birthdays I go to the Church early in the morning and the Temple in the evening."

"Got it. Wow. Once again, a very Happy Birthday Hazel."

"I kept hoping the whole day that you will come by and wish me. You never came. But hey, I really loved the evening. It was my best ever."

"Your friends really spiced it up for you, isn't it?"

"It isn't because of them, silly."

"Then?"

"It was because of something else, a different feeling."

"Like what?"

"Like us. Just you and me in the temple and this moonlit winter night."

Siddharth gave a ride to Hazel in his scooter and dropped her near her home. They were animated and cheerful. He promised to get her a birthday gift soon.

Next day in school, he found out from Sudeep that a few folks had discovered Hazel's birthday, long back, peeping into her school diary when she was away from her seat!

Slowly they discovered that their personalities were complementary.

Siddharth was shy and introverted. Hazel was outspoken and outgoing. While he became nervous in difficult and tricky situations she displayed fortitude. Being a glib talker and debater she was inducted in the debating club, whereas Siddharth was devoid of oratory skills. While he was studious, she hated books except the ones that offered romance.

Even their hand-writing were in contrast. His was poor and

was attributed to a general observation that artists suffered from bad penmanship. On the contrary she wrote beautifully. She also had a rare ability to reproduce signatures.

However dissimilar both were in nature, they were the blue-eyed students of the Principal as they won medals and prestige for the school wherever they performed; Hazel for athletics and Siddharth for painting.

Chapter 4

THE EUCALYPTUS TREE

In the middle of the winter vacation, in December, in Class IX, Siddharth and Shankar were up on the terrace, chatting under a warm sun and blue sky. They were close friends in school and quite fond of each other.

They were softly singing the super hit national integration song, '*Mile Sur Mera Tumhara*' that was aired on T.V by Doordarshan early that year for the first time. Since then it had gained popularity and was heard on every mouth.

"I have not met Hazel for over ten days," lamented Siddharth breaking out of the song. "I cannot wait for another ten days before school reopens."

"Why can't you meet her now?" asked Shankar.

Shankar was a brilliant student and determined of making it to the IIT. He was also unique in some ways. He was the shortest and thinnest in class. However in contrast to his feather-weight, his voice was uber-masculine. Often people readjusted their perception of him and were forced to treat him more seriously when he spoke. And he spoke fast. It often baffled people too, for they could seldom hear each word distinctly. The words piled up one on top of the other and got shot out together in one cannonball boom.

"I cannot go to her home directly."

"Scared of her parents, *kya?*" asked Shankar.

"Yes what else?"

"Why scared? Do they know about you and her?" asked

Shankar.

"Hazel was saying that they have a suspicion. They have seen us together few times."

Shankar cogitated for a while and then adjusted his spectacles.

"I can suggest one technique for you to meet her," he offered.

"Can you kindly blurt, *Guru-ji*?"

"But I need *guru dakshina*. Tribute," demanded Shankar.

"Like what, you *murga chor* (chicken thief)?"

"Treat at the Chinese restaurant Franks. Agreed?"

"Okay you noodle. But only if it is a success."

"Now tell me, if your dad's scooter is around?"

"Yes it's in the garage."

"Then let us go for a ride," said Shankar confidently.

"And then?"

"We will go to her place now and you wait on the terrace of her building while I knock her door and tell her about it. We go now and come back fast," said Shankar.

"Are you crazy Shankar?"

"Nobody will suspect a guy like me boss."

"What will you do at her house?"

"I'll give a book to Hazel using some pretext and tell her that you are on the terrace."

"And if her parents hear you saying all this?" asked Siddharth unable to trust the plan.

"Just relax Sidd. You always worry too much."

"Have you ever seen her dad, buddy? Uncle James?"

"No. What about him?"

"His personality can be terrifying and largely nightmarish."

"No problem, I will jaw him down in whatever avatar he

appears."

"You are making it sound as simple as a nursery rhyme."

"Maybe I am. But it is Tuesday today and her father won't be home, stupid."

"Hmm," said Siddharth sounding more convinced, "ok then let's give it a try. You wait for me at the street corner while I get the scooter and a book."

They parked the scooter behind the thick trunk of a Kadam tree at a distance from Hazel's house that was safe and not easily visible. Hazel lived in the ground floor of the three-storied building. After making sure no one spotted him, Siddharth ran upstairs to the terrace. Waiting there, holding his breath and a small knapsack, he looked around and made sure there was no one else on the terrace.

In the meanwhile, Shankar smartened up by tucking his shirt inside his baggy pants and stroked his hair in place and then pressed the buzzer.

As soon as the door opened Shankar cringed in horror.

Later he described what he had seen, "Boulder big, charcoal skin and salt-pepper hair. The face was like a garden of weeds with thick side-burns, a black bushy moustache and an unkempt stubble creeping all over. They stood in defiance of scissors and razors. With the large inscrutable eyes, half-shut by plump eye-lids and nostrils like the hollow end of a fire-hose, I felt I was facing a combo of an alligator and a dragon."

Before Shankar could swallow his disbelief Hazel's father rattled.

"Yes son what can I do for you? I hope you are not here selling raffle tickets, are you?" A sound as thin and hollow as an empty tin-box shot through the bushy mouth. And then

KEY TO MY SOUL

he smiled to reveal the archaeological decay of canines and molars.

Hearing the wispy voice behind the devastating presence of the man Shankar gained courage to face him. He decelerated his unusual fast paced verbal delivery as much as he could to a very slow and polite word by word rendition.

"Hello Uncle I am Shankar and I am Hazel's classmate."

"So," said Hazel's father taken aback by the unnatural boom in Shankar's voice.

"I came to hand over this Physics book to Hazel."

Hazel's father looked at the book and his eyebrows rose. He said, "But this is a History book."

Shankar cursed himself for not checking what book Siddharth had given him.

"Oh yes, yes. In fact it is a History book. Slip of tongue Uncle."

"Ok. I'll give it to her. Thank you," said Hazel's father closing the door slowly and looking at Shankar to check if there was anything else he wanted.

They stood like a hut and a skyscraper staring at each other in cold hate.

Shankar was about to turn back and curse the cosmos when a sudden contrast of appearances stopped him, like a sudden bloom of a radiant moon against the backdrop of a prolonged dark and gloomy night. Hazel emerged behind her father.

Hugely relieved to see her, he immediately called out, "Hi there Hazel, how are you?"

"Hey Shankar," exclaimed Hazel with a big smile. "What are you doing here?" She was wearing a flowing floral skirt topped by a tight woolen sweater.

"I thought of returning this book to you Hazel in case you wanted to make use of it during the vacation."

"What book?" asked Hazel unable to recall if she had lent out anything. "Hey come in first," she continued, cutting her way through her father and welcoming Shankar. Her father gave way to them and went inside heaving his shoulders up in surprise.

"I can't stay longer. I have to leave now," said Shankar raising his voice a little to make sure that her father heard it.

"Ok, but do step in for a while. You are here for the first time ever."

"I have an urgent errand to run for. I wanted to give you this book." He shifted slowly and cautiously towards Hazel preparing to tell her about the plan. Just then a woman, attired rather formally, appeared behind Hazel smiling warmly at him.

It was like the rising sun behind the moon.

For a few moments, her looks paralyzed Shankar and set his heart speeding on the fifth gear. Unused to rare sights of wonder, his eyes were unwilling and unable to let go off the ravishing and exquisite face.

"Hello there. I am her mother."

Her eyes were a replica of Hazel's. Her fairness was bordering on pink. Taller than Hazel and broader and fuller, she looked like her elder sister. The blue satin sari heightened her curves and drop-dead gorgeous looks.

Shankar could not to stop gawking. The length of the stare, inappropriate by any standards, did not show up in any way on Hazel or her mom's face. They waited patiently for him so he could find himself back. It struck Shankar, why his friends in school often talked about Hazel's mom and her royal looks.

The dose of contrast after contrast numbed him until Hazel spoke, "Mom meet Shankar. He is my classmate." Hazel sat on the sofa, gesturing Shankar to sit beside her.

"Hello Shankar. What's your full name son?" asked Hazel's mom.

"Shankar … Shankar Iyenger." His booming voice reduced to a purr.

"I keep hearing about you from Hazel that you are a scholar."

"No…actually…nothing like that…actually….," Shankar stammered, feeling shy and proud at the same time, at the praise from someone he could hardly take his eyes off from.

"Why don't you sit down Shankar? I am actually getting ready to go to a friend's place with Hazel. But we have good time in front of us so why don't you two chat. Let me get you some tea." Hazel's mom smiled sweetly.

"Oh no auntie, not at all. I am actually in a hurry and have to leave immediately. Thank you for your hospitality," said Shankar rapidly, unable to determine what to control, his running words or his racing heartbeats. Then he sat on the sofa beside Hazel.

As soon as her mom left, Shankar sat beside her and whispered in his usual high-speed delivery, "Hey listen, look at page fifty right now. I have kept a small note."

Surprised at what she heard, she quickly flipped over the pages and read the hand-written note - "Sidd is waiting for you on the terrace!!! Can you meet him there now?"

Hazel did not take time to realize what was happening and winked at Shankar. "Thanks Shankar, I was actually waiting for this book." she said aloud.

After a hurried goodbye, on his way back Shankar began

appraising his performance at the battle ground he just returned from. He felt although he had batted well against the volleys of Hazel's father, he was bowled over by her mother's sophistication.

On the terrace, she looked around with her hands inside the sweater pocket, the wind billowing her skirt and stirring her hair. As soon as Siddharth saw her, his smile returned. The ten days of separation and restlessness vanished like fever disappears on strong antipyretics.

"Hi Hazel," whispered Siddharth almost running up to her and holding her hands.

"Hey Sidd you guys will land me in trouble *yaar*." She broke into a laughter covering her mouth with her hands.

"Should I leave?" asked Siddharth nervously.

She shook her head and said, "We have some time dear. How are you?"

"I wasn't doing fine until now."

"Let's go to that corner," said Hazel pointing to the section of the terrace which had the huge cement water-tanks. That was a safe spot to remain hidden if people came to that side of the terrace accidentally. She held his hands and led him there.

They sat there for about thirty minutes catching up with the last ten days of the winter vacation and the plans for the next ten. Siddharth had brought a small surprise for Hazel. He pulled it out of the knapsack he was carrying.

"I got this for you Hazel. Merry Christmas in advance." Since Christmas was in a week's time, he had painted a greeting card for Hazel and thrust it into her hands. Hazel's face lit up.

"Oh this is lovely Sidd. I am so touched. "

It showed Mother Mary with child Jesus and a pomegranate. Siddharth painted it based on Leonardo da Vinci's famous painting.

"Your paintings will remain a part of me always. How can I help not falling in love with you? In the fall I soar."

She hugged him dearly and did not let go for a long time. A faint breeze stirred the leaves of the nearby Eucalyptus trees and though the sun was bright and hot it was not enough to beat the winter cold. The hug was more effective.

Hazel asked, "Do you have any plans for Christmas and New Year?"

"Yes I have a grand plan."

"Like what?" Hazel asked curiously.

"Like visiting the terrace in the afternoons and thinking about YOU."

Hazel grinned and said, "Well that is better than doing nothing. An empty mind is a devil's den."

"Please stop. We have enough idioms in the school. What about your plans?"

"We are planning to visit my uncle's place in Ernakulam in Kerala. My parents just decided that a few days back."

"Will it be fun?"

"Yes I will get to see my cousins after many years. From Ernakulam we will visit other places. The rural scenery is breathtaking. You must come with me once." Hazel pulled Siddharth's chin and smiled at him.

"I have seen photos of Kerala. The waters, the greenery really look amazing."

"Yes and the food as well. Mom loves to go there. She has already started making a lot of stuff like sweets and rolls and cakes for my cousins."

"Is your mom a good cook?"

"Yes. Actually phenomenal."

"It must be interesting for you…?" he asked unsure of what he was saying.

"What?"

"… To have your mom … by your side…I mean …"

There was a pause. Hazel understood his anguish. It saddened her to imagine the loss of a mother. She knew that his mother had passed away due to a sudden heart attack when he was seven years old. So she hugged him again while he remained silent with his lead lowered.

They talked some more about general matters and finally it came to Hazel's father.

"Why did you use poor Shankar that way," asked Hazel smiling.

"What do you mean by poor Shankar? He was the one who hatched the entire plan."

"Really? Shankar?" asked Hazel laughing and shocked. "So he's not just good at studies."

"Was there anyone at home other than you when he went?"

"Yes both mom and dad. He met both of them."

"What," asked Siddharth alarmed, "isn't your dad at work today?"

"No he took a day off as he was not well."

"Oh my god. Is Shankar alive?"

"What do you mean?"

"Nothing. I just thought he would run away seeing your dad."

"Why should he run away?" asked Hazel, unable to

understand him completely.

Siddharth did not offer any further comment about her dad's appearance, fearing it might rub her on the wrong side.

Suddenly, Hazel heard footsteps coming up the stairway and almost at the same time she heard her father calling out, "Hazel my girl, are you still here?"

She looked at Siddharth worried. He froze in fright not knowing what to do. But she whispered calmly pressing his hands, "I'll leave quickly. You stick on here, okay? Once I go down with my father, you hit the stairs. See you Sidd."

She pressed his hands and came out of the hiding area, shouting, "Yes I am here dad and on my way back." She hurried to intercept her father on the staircase itself and reached the door of the terrace at the same time as her father.

"Let's go back," urged Hazel to her father.

"You can carry on. Let me get some fresh air," replied her father. "Mom is waiting for you. She is ready to leave." He walked over casually around the periphery of the terrace and then towards the cemented water-tanks.

Shocked and frightened, Hazel watched her father staring at the spot where Siddharth was hiding. She was unsure if he was eye-balling the place or simply gazing at the corner. After a while, her father looked skywards and started whistling.

Seeing no reaction from her father, she questioned herself feverishly, "Why did he not blow up? Where the heck is Sidd? He was right there with me." Confused and worried, as she walked downstairs, she felt a major disaster had either been averted or was waiting to happen. She prayed to Jesus for her friend's safety.

When Siddharth heard footsteps approaching the water-tank he knew he was doomed. But then he saw a sturdy branch of a eucalyptus tree butting on the terrace wall on his left. Praying frantically, he climbed the branch and crawled up on it like an upturned bear. Once he reached the trunk of the tree he slid all the way to the bottom and sprinted away as if a leopard was behind him.

The bark of the eucalyptus tree scratched him all over and ripped him in several places leaving deep red welts.

Shankar was waiting on the scooter and as soon as he caught sight of his friend running towards him, he dragged the scooter to intercept Siddharth midway. He was yet to learn driving. Finally they hopped onto the scooter and sped away with Shankar shooting arrows of questions from behind and reminding Siddharth of the treat at the Chinese restaurant.

"I think it was neat. No one saw us together," shouted Shankar.

"I only hope her dad did not see me."

Though everything went as planned without Hazel's dad and mom seeing him, the slither down the eucalyptus tree did not go unnoticed. Through the dining room window, hundred meters away, a pair of eyes dilated in surprise and resentment.

Hazel had once told Siddharth about someone she abhorred. He lived in her neighborhood few blocks away. Tall, cat-eyed, with massive muscles developed in the local gym, he was generally associated with that section of boys in the town that had low taste for everything: Habits, clothes, kind of friends and such. They had ears pierced, kept thick sideburns, drove bikes at fearless speeds and were indecent, noisy and troublesome.

Five years older to Hazel and quietly possessive about her, he detested anyone getting close to her. He was the son of a close friend of her dad and called himself, "Darryl the jaw-breaker".

Chapter 5

WHERE ART MEETS ATHLETICS

By the time the students reached Class X they discussed advanced topics with their teachers. As with every batch of students, the Physics teacher could not answer all their queries and the Biology teacher stood red-faced at the spray of doubts on anatomy and exchange of naughty glances. And then a downpour of further questions.

The girls and boys grew taller and broader. The dynamics between them changed. They looked at each other with renewed interest.

The high cheek bones on Siddharth's face started to get a rugged look. The dimple on his chin grew deeper. His eyes had a change of character from innocent to not that innocent and he learnt to smile through them. The downward slant of his eyes became prominent. Growing taller by the year, he was threatening to touch six feet. With his dark body becoming muscular and lines of veins emerging, it was fast losing the rounded cherubic look.

Likewise, Hazel was ripening. Her skin glowed. It was hard not to notice her doe-like eyes, which looked stunning when bordered with kohl. Sometimes she wore a plaited pony-tail with a band of hair twisted around her ears giving her a neat look. But mostly her thick black lustrous hair were let loose and they dropped till her hips. She was called 'Rapunzel', the German fairy, by some of her friends because of the long hair. With a 'bindi' on her forehead slightly above the parting of the brows, she looked mature. The boys in the class often cast covert glances at her and day-dreamed about her. Her figure was getting more defined and curvaceous and so when she walked in the school or outside, boys and men equally held their gaze at her a little longer than she had ever noticed before.

The Summer Olympics was almost coming to an end in Seoul, South Korea. It was end of September 1988. India did not win any medals.

One day after school Siddharth and Hazel decided to take a detour from the normal route they followed to reach home. They decided to walk around the stadium, past a patch of jungle that led to the Kali temple and then head home. It would take thirty minutes extra.

As they passed by the stadium, aspiring athletes were already warming up for practice and many more were trickling in. The sun had mellowed down and a cool breeze stirred the leaves. Tiny flecks of grey clouds were gathering above. It was three in the afternoon.

"I am terribly upset Sidd."

"Why?"

"No medals for India at the Olympics this year."

"Yes it was in the newspaper. But why are you upset?"

"Hello Sir, did you ever happen to notice what athletics means to me?"

"No. How can I forget the school Girl's Champion for three years in a row? But what makes you upset?"

"I dreamt of pursuing athletics once. But there's no hope. Look at the folks practicing there in the stadium? Do you see any future for them?"

"May be you are right. Who are your idols Hazel?"

"P.T. Usha and Shiny Abraham, obviously."

Suddenly at that point Hazel squeezed his hands and spoke in hushed tones, "Sidd is there any place we can hide?"

"Why?"

"Darryl is behind us. Not sure if he has seen me but I don't want to run by him now."

By that time they had reached the edge of the jungle. Siddharth said, "You see the steps reaching down to the back entrance of the stadium?"

"Yes. I have been there multiple times for practice."

"Hmm. At the entrance if you take a left it goes inside the stadium. But do you know where it takes you, if you take a right?"

"Yes, kind of. It goes into the jungle, what else," replied Hazel.

"True, but if you walk further up there is a unique spot inside. There are some unusual trees out there that you normally won't see anywhere in the town. You know about them?"

"Nope," answered Hazel pressing her lips hard at the last syllable and then releasing them with a pop sound.

"You will be quite impressed with the variety of trees there. It will help you forget the Olympics and Darryl too."

"Sidd can you hurry up now please? Show me all you want to once we are there."

They ran down the stairs holding hands and taking two or three steps at a time and after walking some distance into the thick woods, entered a large clearing. A trunk of a tree lay in the middle. The branches had been chopped off, possibly by local wood-pickers, but the body remained. A dense cluster of trees surrounded the clearing, hiding it from the world.

They sat on a relatively flattish part of the trunk that was buffeted and polished by the soft crush of buttocks, which meant that it was not entirely an unknown and unvisited place.

Hazel asked, "Have you ever come here before?"

"Oh yes, several times."

"When? Why?"

"Whenever I needed inspiration for my paintings and when I felt like bunking Narayan sir's tuition classes in the evening."

"Really? You bunk classes too," asked Hazel parting her mouth wide in disbelief. And then immediately she remembered something, "Hey, this place is nice for trying something. I wanted to show you this since last week but never got the right chance or place." She brought out a packet from her school-bag and showed it to him.

"You tried this before?" asked Hazel.

"Are you out of your mind?" asked Siddharth, shocked. "Where'd you get this from?"

"Father's pants." She brought out a match-box as well.

"When did you start this habit?"

"To be honest, Jennifer and I tried this a few times last week. It was only last week. And I thought you might like it."

"No. I don't want this."

"Here try one."

Sidd took it and squashed it in his palms. "I said I don't want this."

She ignored his reaction and lit a cigarette. After blowing a few puffs she coughed. "I thought it might be fun."

"Throw it away. It is dangerous."

"Don't worry. I didn't get the kick that smokers talk about.

Nothing happens to me." She blew a few more puffs and looked at Siddharth. "Look at your face. What are you so afraid of? Here try mine." She inserted the cigarette between his quivering lips and made him inhale. He coughed. "See its nothing," she said laughing.

"It will spoil your lungs, Hazel."

"Did I say I am going to make this a habit?"

"Whatever. I don't want it. Can you dump it?"

She didn't press him anymore. She held the lit cigarette between her fingers and occasionally took a drag at it. It was obvious that she was doing it mechanically. Finally Sidd snatched away the cigarette and flung it into the wilderness. She laughed. "Good boy. I hope that cigarette you threw won't start a forest fire. Now tell me, do you come here to paint?"

"Yes. I will show you some of my paintings I made sitting right here."

"Sure. Sure. Now can I ask you, who your idol is?"

"Dali. Salvador Dali."

"Never heard of him."

"He was a genius. Do you recall ever seeing a picture of clocks melting, flaccid and warped, like cheese or cloth?"

"Yes I think I have."

"That's by Dali. He was a surrealistic painter."

Then he explained how arts, in general, imitated life and how artists of different eras looked at their times and the social conditions around. And how they represented their perception through their drawings, paintings, poetry, music and drama.

"But what inspires you Sidd? Any reason you paint so much?"

"What Picasso had said - Art washes away from the soul the

dust of everyday life."

"Don't you want to pursue arts as your profession?"

"I don't think so. I think my problem is the same as yours. Like athletes, I don't think even artists have a future in this country," rued Siddharth.

"Cheer up Sidd. All will work out fine with you. Never give up painting," said Hazel.

He nodded looking unhappy.

"But it looks like this place is where artists and athletes meet. Or rather a place where Art meets Athletics," said Hazel cheerfully pointing at the stadium, at her and then at Sidd.

Then he pointed out what interested him, the trees with their different colors, shapes and symmetries, the hills beyond, the oval of the stadium, the arc of bird-flight, the roots of the uprooted tree, a hopping cricket, the uncertainty of life and the darkening skies above.

She was just listening to his soft voice and gazing at him, without her realizing it; her eyes and ears had shut her off from everything else. After a while, when Siddharth stopped getting any verbal props from her to support his conversation, he paused.

In the silence that continued he rested his right palms over the back of her left hand. And she clasped his hands instantly. They came nearer to each other. So near that they could hear each other's breathing. Siddharth's heart beat became irregular and started its wild acrobatics. He looked into her eyes that close for the first time ever.

Her corneas were clear and strikingly white with a bluish sheen like that of a healthy baby. The eyeballs were large and jet black and sparkled like pearls. She bounced them around with mischief.

For some time, he had harbored a desire to feel her lips. Fearing a bad reaction, he could never disclose it to her. But that day, sheltered by the trees, he felt braver.

"Hazel can I… maybe … one day…?" he started fumbling and stuttering.

"What?"

"No…I mean…I always thought of asking you…one day can I…?" he looked at her desperately hoping to get the right words. But he did not know how to say it. He fell silent. She suppressed a smile and cast a stern look to tease him.

"What? Go on."

"Nothing. I will tell another day," he said backing off and lowering his eyes and head.

"Not another day. Today. Do it," commanded Hazel pouting her lips. "Now." She squeezed his hands.

He was slow to grasp what she just said. He was slow to grasp that she had bored through his eyes into his mind and read his thoughts; his wish was granted, and, there was no tussle, no objection or obstacle.

In fact, she had closed her eyes and was waiting.

And then the trees and the trunk, the birds and the bees, the creepers and the crickets, the greying sky and the receding sun all watched in silent exaltation two young lovers expressing themselves, their love and thirst for each other. The contact was deep and long and naive. It was the first time they came so close. Her lips were tender. They tasted like sugar and salt and smoke at the same time.

The grey clouds seemed to have gathered for a purpose. For

KEY TO MY SOUL

they descended from above like a shower of blessing.

But in the woods, they were not the only ones to get wet. There was someone else lurking behind the trees, staring at them like a fox, with clenched fists. But before he could confront them, they scooted and disappeared in the rain.

For the next couple of days they looked at each other furtively, as a sense of sin played in their minds. It took time to regain normalcy. Once they were comfortable again, they paired up after school like before and often took the detour via the stadium and the jungle to walk home. When they neared the jungle, Hazel would twist her lips and tease him.

"Are you not going to show me the interesting trees anymore today?"

And he would blush and lower his head in embarrassment. However, he did take her there a couple of times more. In fact, more than a couple of times.

About a month later, after a fierce shower had subsided, Siddharth rushed to Azad Bazaar to buy hot 'pakoras', 'samosas' and mutton cutlets. The sun had appeared briefly after the shower but was almost touching the horizon. Few of his dad's friends would visit them in the evening. His dad was still in office and had left some money at home so he could get the snacks before the guests arrived.

While he was walking back home whistling a song, swinging the swollen polythene bag loaded with the snacks, someone spoke to him from behind, harshly.

"So these days you are destroying the purity of this place."

Siddharth turned around and saw a monster figure

approaching him. It was Darryl, twirling a long key chain in his fingers and chewing bubble gum. He continued to walk.

"You can walk or run but you can never hide," said Darryl almost barking from behind. Siddharth quickened his pace. No sooner had he walked hundred feet a roaring motor-bike crossed him, swung around, skidded and screeched to a stop right in front of him.

"What do you want?" snapped Siddharth.

"Answers," said Darryl and continued chewing the gum.

"What answers?"

"Why are you polluting innocent girls of this town?"

"What do you mean?"

"You are spoiling them. Taking them to jungles. Taking advantage of their innocence."

"I don't know what you are talking about."

"Try your smartness elsewhere you lame duck from Bengal. You don't know me. Next time I see you with her so close you'll know why I have been given a bad nick-name." Darryl ran his fingers over his jaws and bared his teeth in cold hate. He chewed on the gum more severely. "Better be with your text books, you lame Bong, and stay away from her."

Without answering back Siddharth walked away as fast as he could. But Darryl caught up with him on his bike and snatched the packet from his hand and rode away.

"Give it back," said Siddharth raising his voice but not high enough to sound confrontational. It was a meek attempt to dissuade Darryl. Siddharth ran behind the bike yelling, "Stop."

Darryl looked behind and grinned and kept driving slowly, "Come take it." He swayed the packet and swung it as if he'd throw it. Siddharth ran as fast as he could. But before he could reach him, Darryl tossed the polythene bag few meters ahead of the bike and directed the wheels towards them.

"Stop it Darryl. Give it back to me," shouted Siddharth running.

In a flash the motorcycle wheels ran over the packet. Darryl yelled back, "Next time you may be where that junk food is." Then he accelerated the bike and zoomed out of sight.

After Siddharth reached the spot where the packet lay squelched and mushy, he picked it up and held it in shock and anger. Slowly, he walked back home. His father was not yet back from office. He stepped into his bedroom and stared at the mirror. His inability to fight back Darryl and counter the attack made him feel cheap about himself. Water streamed down the cheeks from his eyes and fell on his feet.

At the same time, he didn't want to tell his father about the incident. He tried to think of a way of hiding it. There would be questions he knew as the money his dad had left with him to buy the snacks was spent. The only way to cover up the incident was to buy the snacks again. But for that he had to secure money. After searching inside drawers and wardrobes and not finding any, he suddenly got an idea. He broke his piggy-bank.

For the next couple of weeks he avoided walking with Hazel outside school and in public places. The scare of Darryl had taken root somewhere inside him. But slowly she pulled him back to their old ways.

Sitting on the temple rock that monsoon, one evening, watching the people walk up and down the narrow temple stairs like a bevy of ants, they waited for Siddharth to arrive.

Jennifer noticed that Hazel was not in her usual self.

"Is everything all right?" asked Jennifer.

"Why do you ask?" asked Hazel.

"Your face prompts me to."

"Dad is again away for a long time," said Hazel.

"Again?"

"Yes it's pretty bad now. Even this time he said he was going on a business trip but prolonged his stay indefinitely. Mom is very upset."

"It is going on for a long time, right?" asked Jennifer.

"Yes, for the past few years. He quarrels with mom frequently. Sometimes it is loud and I can overhear. Things are not going too well between them. But I don't clearly understand what it is that they talk about."

"Did you ask your mom about it?"

"Yes. But she brushes it away when I ask." Hazel paused before continuing, "I feel a strange distance is growing between dad and mom, between dad and us both actually."

"There. Sidd is coming," said Jennifer spotting him at the base of the temple.

"We'll speak on this again later," said Hazel.

"Did you ever tell Sidd about this?"

"No. I don't feel like sharing all this with him. He is so uncomplicated."

When Siddharth reached them, their conversation had changed, though Hazel's face still retained the gloominess. It was unusual to see Hazel in that mood and so her look stayed with him for a long time. He didn't know that one day he would get to see that same look again.

Chapter 6

THE SHAYARI BRIGADE AND THE DURGA PUJA

1989 was the year when the world saw major upheavals. The Berlin Wall crumbled, China witnessed a deadlock of ideas in Tiananmen Square, the Cold War officially ended, a fatwa was issued against Salman Rushdie for his book, The Satanic Verses, and Dalai Lama was given the Nobel Peace Prize.

The situations around the world never bothered Siddharth. He remained aloof from politics but silently followed the progress of the Soviet Union. After coming across a magazine advertisement of Odessa National Polytechnic University in Ukraine, he bought the application forms for studying Industrial Engineering there someday. It had caught his fancy.

The bright sunshine in the University campus, the colorful leaves during fall, the wide road-walks and mammoth city architectures, the Basil Cathedral, the cold temperatures, their literature, their history, everything allured him. But he never mentioned it to his father.

It was a secret that remained undisclosed.

It so happened that when the students graduated to Standard XI in high school in 1989, they were treated differently by the teachers. The relationship was no longer that of an adult and child. It was one of equals. The students sensed it. Many of them became outspoken and determined. The challenge of doing well in the Joint Entrance exams made them serious.

Books, almost always a repellant, sudo

However, the instinct of mischief a
die down entirely. It was in hiding, und.
And once it surfaced and led them into s.
due to the 'Shayari Brigade'.

In the cold of December that year the .
scouting for the mischief mongers in the   ..ors with a
stiffened tail of teachers behind her.

The boys' toilet had become a museum. Although it was a
hub for gossip during breaks some creative minds saw more
in it than its normal utilitarian purpose. It all started when
the first boy penciled his poetic urges on the wall, for a girl
he was infatuated with. The writing was almost invisible until
he showed it to his friend one day. Then the electrified friend
showed it to another.

And then there were few more lines on the wall by the third
person. Soon others joined and a spark of competition ignited
amongst the boys to outdo each other. The chain propagated
rapidly like a string of kindled crackers.

The walls got a new purpose. It became a springboard
for experimentation, a scratchpad of rhyming poems, haiku,
limericks and free verse pouring from the unchained minds of
budding engineers, doctors and accountants. Majority of the
lines were dedicated to love of the unrequited kind. Slowly the
walls darkened by the marks of graphite and ink.

And then few over-the-edge jokes appeared right above
the urinals. The boys laughed hysterically and shook all over
reading them while using the facilities. All these happened
within three days. A handful of lines were:

"If you ever gave me the chance, I would with you love to

If you ever gave me a smile, I could walk naked across the Nile."

and

"Aaapki aankhon mein basa hai joh
Ek number ka badmassh hai woh".

However the most loved one was:

"Buland bharat ki Buland tasveer."

This was based on the Bajaj Scooter advertisement that flashed across national television and was inscribed just above the urinals.

The endeavor became a tiny sub-culture, almost a secret movement. But before the walls bore bigger ballads, the toilet cleaner reported on the changing landscape to Sir J, the High school Class teacher. Furious and embarrassed at what he heard he rushed to the school Principal, who in turn set up an urgent meeting with the management. After the meeting was over, the teachers stormed out of the room led by the Principal and marched into the boy's toilet. Even the lady teachers jostled along for a glimpse.

Half an hour later, everyone came out with their cheeks smoldering as the flat of an overheated clothing iron. They hurled phrases like "never seen this in the History of this school", "the worst set of students we ever had", "this is what the new generation is like", "undisciplined rascals" and many such.

Sweating and panting, Sir J addressed his students inside the classroom. He was trying to isolate the guilty and his eyes bulged out like those of a bullfrog.

"I cannot believe what I saw," thundered Sir J. "The Principal is devastated and will take severe action on those students who showed their smartness on the walls." While he was shouting few girls giggled. This infuriated him further.

He roared back, "Girls, I don't think this is funny. I expect you to remain quiet and not support this deplorable act. The boys have brought utter shame to this class. To my class. Now those of you who wrote those nasty messages, please raise your hands."

There was no action. No hands moved. There was pin-drop silence. Only Sir J could be heard breathing like a dragon about to discharge his next volley of scorching words. The boys faked ignorance on their faces.

Vivek asked, "Sir how do you know if it was our class students who did this?"

"Who else uses that toilet? There is only one class and one toilet on this floor. You are lucky to have a dedicated facility. And look at what you have done to that privilege."

There was silence again. At this point Hazel looked at Siddharth. She questioned him with her eyes if he knew anything about it. He did not pretend that he was unaware.

"I repeat, can the guilty raise their hands, please?"

Still silence. And then Sanjay volunteered, "Sir, I think someone else has done it and I don't think the students from this class have anything to do with it."

"We will soon find it," Sir J said with gritted teeth and hurried out of the room.

The bell rang for lunch break and everyone dispersed in hushed conversations. After lunch break, Sir J entered the classroom with a foxy look. He eyed his students in disgust.

"Boys please submit your English and Hindi Essay notebooks right now," said Sir J.

"Sir, essay notebooks?" asked Sanjay as if he didn't know what that was.

"Yes. We have decided to compare the handwriting in your notebooks with those shameful writings on the walls. Since none of you are cooperating, we have to take this step. Please make it fast as we have to complete a lot of work on this today," said Sir J.

Slowly everyone started getting their notebooks and kept it on Sir J's table. The pile soon grew to sixty books. Two books per boy.

"We will go through each of them and it will probably take the rest of the day today. So the Principal asked me to inform you that the class is dismissed for the day. Everyone is in a bad mood. Come back tomorrow at the regular assembly time."

The students packed off for home. That day Siddharth asked Hazel to go home on her own saying that he needed to talk to some of the boys regarding the issue.

Next morning when all the students assembled in the classroom, Sir J announced two points that rocked the entire class.

"Based on the handwritings we have come up with a suspect list of the culprits. Second, the Principal has announced that there will be no further classes for you until the culprits are identified."

The students were shocked to hear the second point as the final exams were just a few months away and if the classes were interrupted, it would affect their studies severely.

"I will give you fifteen minutes so that you can decide for yourself what you want to do. One option is for the culprits to step forward. The other option is interrogation of each student from the suspect list by the special squad set up." With these words Sir J left the room.

The boys gathered at the back of the classroom to discuss. And during that discussion, the different characters and personalities of the boys got revealed. Few students chickened out, while few others threatened to spill the beans if no one owned up. They did not want the exams to be affected. Some others shouted that their unity was being broken by Sir J's politics. Some of them tried to bind everyone. However, they concurred on a decision.

Fifteen minutes later when Sir J walked in, Shankar volunteered and said, "Sir, we agree to be honest and not impact our studies. We will give you the names."

"Good decision boys. I will request the Principal to minimize the punishment."

"But we have a request, Sir," said Shankar.

"What is that?"

"Can you assure us to keep the names only with you and the Principal?"

"What do you mean?"

"We do not want any other teacher to know the names," replied Shankar.

"I can request that," said Sir J. "Please write down the names and give it to me."

Out of a class of thirty boys there were ten names. They were summoned to the Principal's office. She was appalled to see the faces. Siddharth was also present.

"You are the brightest students I have in that class and all this had to be from you?" said the Principal. Beyond that she could not bring herself to speak anymore and looked helpless and let down.

All the boys apologized frantically and vowed never to do anything remotely close to what they did ever in their entire lives. They stood with their heads drooping, almost touching the floor. The Principal, actually fond of those students as they were amongst the best, could not bring herself to punish them severely.

"I need a handwritten apology letter from each of you by today. You will also be on special duty after school till your session for this year ends." She left them with a warning.

The toilet walls were all cleaned the next day and all the feelings and emotions so tenderly penciled on the walls, got buried under the disregard of layers and layers of fresh paint.

The boys' toilet lost the short-lived status of a museum. The classes resumed.

The 'Shayari Brigade', as the group of ten students came to be known as later, stopped the toilet cleaner trotting by, one day. They asked him why he had to report about the writings to Sir J, instead of warning them. Smiling sheepishly the toilet cleaner avoided a good explanation. But he revealed something interesting that the boys could never have imagined.

"All the teachers were madly laughing while reading the toilet walls. And Sir J. was the loudest amongst them all," he said.

September 1990. Autumn was transitioning into winter. The flowers of Kans grass spread a sheet of white over a bed of green. The wind carried elements of romance. Suddenly the sleepy town woke up. It was in a grip of festivity and looked youthful and vibrant. Women and girls swarmed the streets and shops. It was time for Goddess Durga to step down to earth again and fight the demons. The countdown for the four day Durga Puja had started.

Siddharth made plans with Hazel for the first two days of the Puja celebration as the last two days were ruled out due to family get-togethers. On the first day they quarreled over the two hit romantic movies of the season that were running in the two best cinema theatres in the city, Payal Talkies and Basant Cinema.

"I want to see *'Aashiqui'*," pestered Hazel.

"I want to see Madhuri Dixit, in *'Dil'*," protested Siddharth.

"Oh, so you like her more than me, is it?"

"Hey listen. I don't want to complicate matters. Can we watch both?"

"But first *'Aashiqui'* in matinee. *'Dil'* in the evening show."

They sat in the dress circle glued to the theatre screen and to each other, holding hands, popcorns and cold drinks and holding back the tears. Both movies left them dazed and their songs remained etched in their souls forever. After the evening show, Hazel led Sidd behind the cinema hall. It was desolate except for the occasional movie goer who'd go there to release their bladder.

"Can I?" asked Hazel, pulling out a cigarette from her hand bag in excitement.

"I can't believe it. Have you gone mad?"

"It's only once or twice a year *yaar*. I am so happy today. Don't say no."

He didn't argue. He watched her in mirth as she coughed desperately and finally gave up consuming only half the cigarette. He blew a few puffs too just for the heck of it. They spoke about the movies, the dialogues, the romance and drew closer until their lips locked.

The second day turned out to be a major episode in their lives.

The one 'pandal' that stole the limelight that year was built as a replica of the famous Dakshineswar Temple, near Kolkata and was incredibly beautiful. It was made entirely with a zillion hand-fans and got rapturously reported in the newspapers. People from all over the town and the outskirts queued up. It was also the nearest one from Shankar's house.

"We must go there," said Siddharth.

"Yep. I just wait for this Bong festival," replied Hazel. "It's such an experience."

When they turned up Shankar was already waiting to welcome them. He was attired in traditional kurta and a shawl. They had planned to go 'pandal' hopping together.

Siddharth was dressed in a white traditional kurta and pajama while Hazel was wearing a tight black top, laced on the neck and sleeves and a deep red velvet skirt that stopped at her knees. She framed her eyes with thick black kohl and painted her lips red. And with each step the hoop ear-rings bounced and her long pony-tail swayed across her waist.

After entering the 'pandal' Siddharth prayed to the Goddess Durga. Then he observed the pandal construction with its intricate designs and marveled at the craftsmanship of the artisans. They spent some time watching the jostling crowd, the drum players and their roaring drums, goddess Durga and her posse. The roll of drums was magical.

"Hey, let's go to my house now for some South Indian filter

coffee," said Shankar.

"It is okay here Shankar, I like watching crowds," said Siddharth.

"But it's difficult to hear what we are talking. Let's go Sidd," he insisted. "My parents are away. Let's chat there for some time and then we will move on."

In his house Shankar prepared the coffee. While they were chatting and drinking, the landline phone inside the bedroom rang. After attending the call he came back hurriedly.

"Guys, I have to go right away."

"What happened?" asked Hazel.

"Dad just called. Our car broke down in the outskirts of the town. I have to immediately get the car mechanic there. But you guys stay till I come back okay."

"Hey it may take long for you to come back. It is best we move," said Siddharth.

"No, wait here. It will take about an hour to pick up the car mechanic and get back. And if I start locking the house now it will take more time for me to get there. I really want to spend the rest of the day with you guys. Please."

Although it meant that it would delay their entire plan for the rest of the day, Siddharth and Hazel agreed to wait for him.

"Thanks buddies. In case I get late, I will ring this phone," said Shankar and left.

The drum beats had stopped for a while. Siddharth and Hazel stood at the balcony to get a view of the pandal which was about a hundred meters away. They watched the people in their glittering dresses, romping in and out. The air carried the sacred fragrance of flowers and joss-sticks, drifting from the pandal. They felt elated and carefree. The four days of the puja was supposed to be that way.

After fifteen minutes they came to the drawing room. Siddharth fetched a water jug from the dining table and saturated himself. Then he sat beside Hazel on the sofa holding her hands, explaining the mythological stories of Durga Puja. Hazel rested her head on his lap. He slipped a chewing gum into his mouth.

After listening to him for a while she put her forefinger across his lips playfully so that he could not talk anymore. Then she ran her fingers across the curls of his hair on his forehead and brought his face down near hers. She looked deep into his eyes.

"Sidd can I ask you something?"

"If you want to," he said chewing the gum, making the characteristic sound.

"For heaven's sake Sidd can you stop making that cheap noise? I told you infinite times that I can't bear that stupid sound. Spit it out now."

He had no choice but to remove the gum, "You are too mean with me sometimes. What was your question?"

"When we grow up, will we be as affectionate to each other, like we are now?"

"I think so. Why?"

"Suppose we end up going to different colleges will things remain the same?"

"We will meet during the vacations, no?"

"Won't distance matter? You keep harping about the Ukraine University."

"True. I have that aim Hazel. But I'm not sure what will happen."

"That is so far. Why don't you look at the Indian colleges for engineering?"

"I am preparing for them as well. And anyway I gave you the sketches of my face already. You can look at those as long as you want. I remember the way you bullied me into giving you that."

"What do you mean bullying you? It was after months of pleading you. By the way what about your promise to make a sketch of mine?"

"Hmm. I will do that soon Hazel."

"Still not getting enough inspiration to sketch me. Is it?"

"Nothing like that. I will do it soon. Can you cheer up now?"

"It was just a feeling ...," said Hazel.

"Why don't you say something good?"

"Like what? About what?"

"Like love...about our love for instance?"

"Like what about our love?"

"Maybe what was it that you found good about me. Which aspect?"

"Okay," she said clearing her throat. "But you go first."

He began readily. "First it was your ocean big eyes, then your face, your long hair and then everything else. The way you talk, walk, run, your voice and lately the way you push me around to get things done your way." Hazel pinched him and giggled. "Now your turn."

She began rolling her tongue inside her mouth and her eyes, "Honestly, it was your quiet nature. Your artistic side. Then it would be your eyes and dimple-chin." She paused and added, "Also my belief that I can push you around to get things done my way."

"Don't worry about the last part. Your belief might change with time."

Hazel wagged her tongue at him.

"Now can we create one liners that define our love?" he asked.

"Give an example."

Siddharth thought for a while and then grinned as if he found the perfect line.

"My love will shine like the moon when the light in the lanterns fade away."

"Will the light be there twenty years from now?" asked Hazel.

"Yes, if you agree to all I say and stop pushing me to get your things done."

"Stop joking."

"Ok. How about this one…I can give up my life for my love."

"Not impressive. It's much easier to end one's life for love, than to sustain it."

"Ok. Ok. I give up. Now, your turn," he said.

Hazel thought for a while as well and then slowly uttered each word.

"My love is like ether. It will survive winds or fires, flooding waters or a barren earth. My love will exist like the fifth element."

"Hmm." He took a moment for the lines to soak in. "That's a deep one."

"After we marry, when I arrive wherever you live, I know you and your family will welcome me. But can you greet me with something I have in mind. Something special?"

"Wow you are thinking too much into the future. Greet you

with what?"

"Roses," she said biting her lips. "Big red roses."

"Big red roses? Why?"

"I love roses. They are the keys to my romantic soul."

"Big deal. No problem."

She clasped his hands and looking at him tearfully, said, "Sidd I love you."

"Hey what's the matter?"

She paused and spoke with her fine nostrils dilating, "I need to tell you something."

"What?"

"Something that I am unable to keep to myself. I need to share it with someone. Sometimes I don't feel like being at home," she said ruefully. Her face suddenly got the same look she had when Jennifer and she were at the temple top one day, waiting for Sidd to arrive.

"What?" Instantly he recalled the unusual look he had seen on Hazel's face.

"Actually mom and dad are having problems…," she blurted out.

"Like what?" asked Siddharth, straightening up, surprised.

"They quarrel and quibble over simple matters."

"It happens with every couple. Don't worry," said Siddharth trying to brush it off.

"No it's different. I can't explain it, but it's not normal. I don't understand what they talk about and argue. Dad drinks way too much these days."

Siddharth kept quiet unable to offer any assurance. Leading a simple life with his father had never opened up any conflicts at home and he didn't know how to respond.

"They talk about their past and mom often cries. I feel terrible," she said with her eyes going moist again and the kohl smudging the sides.

"I am sorry to hear that Hazel."

"No I am sorry," said Hazel, pulling herself together, "I should not pollute you. You are innocent. I feel good having said this much. Actually I was miserable for the last few days for some other reason and I guess, this came up because of that."

"Some other reason? What was that?"

"It was terrible. Do you want to hear it?" asked Hazel.

"Nope, if it is scary or about ghosts."

Hazel smiled and her lightly painted lips shone like her jet black eyes. She paused.

"Actually I saw an awful dream one night."

"A bad dream? Everyone sees such dreams Hazel. I think I know what it was about."

"What?"

"It's about your handsome dad who'd never agree to our marriage. And you wanted me to fight back. But I didn't, obviously, as I am not that type. For I can be a lover, not a rebel. And you woke up dejected," he said lightheartedly. "Am I right?"

"Shut that crap, will you," she said pulling his hair, half cross and half in smiles. "It wasn't that. It was terrible...of things going crazy between you and me. I wept in sleep..."

Hazel tried to go on but he cut her short. This time he brought his fingers on her lips and pressed it lightly. Then he pulled her hair a little and tickled her armpits and poked her ribs sideways. Hazel jounced.

"Stop it," she pleaded, breaking into a laugh.

He was in no mood to hear her woes and continued to tickle her. She kept on twisting and laughing and tried to loosen herself from him. In the tussle she almost fell off the sofa but he held her tight and brought her closer to him. They studied each other's eyes. When their lips came dangerously close her taut muscles slackened. He smooched her gently.

The songs of 'Ashiqui' were playing on some faraway loudspeaker.

He carried her to the bedroom in his arms and lowered her on the bed like she was an angel. They held each other for a long time. Her hands were soft, slim and firm. She pulled him towards her until his chest felt the soft crush of her bulging breasts.

They turned him wild. Cupping his palms over them, he squeezed on them gently. But he quickly moved his hands away as if they had sinned, as if they had touched fire.

She brought them back to where they were.

They had little awareness of what was happening. Their hearts raced and their lips felt a fatal pull. They looked at each other like two creatures rapidly turning mad. Bound by nothing but an unusual warmth in their bodies, detached from happiness and sorrows, they were overpowered by lust and an explosive hunger for each other and finally surrendered to the designs of nature.

Outside the drummers had picked up their sticks and were frantically beating the taut hide of the drums creating thunderous sounds and vibrations of euphoria.

The last time Hazel and Siddharth were that intimate was on

the following Valentine's Day in 1991. It was less than a month before the board exams for High School commenced. Little did they fathom that fate, from that Valentine's Day onwards would bend their dreams into another direction, another story, another reality.

Chapter 7

THE COLLAPSE OF THE SOVIET UNION

The High School board exams were in-progress in March 1991. But to everyone's surprise, Hazel did not appear for her exams. It created a flutter amongst her friends.

"Hazel has measles," said Miss Violet. "Her father informed me. So she cannot appear for the exams. He also said it is contagious and none of you should try to visit her."

The High School board exams completed by end of March. The graduation was completed with a grand farewell organized by the Principal.

The start of competitive entrance exam was just a month away. Hazel was missing. Siddharth was deeply concerned about her. But being busy attending mock exams by a private coaching center and burning midnight oil, he was unable to visit her. Also measles meant he had to keep away from her for some time.

During those days the telephone was not yet a common household utility in Jamshedpur and the cellphone was unheard of. So a week after the High School exams, when a virulent story started spreading by word of mouth, it stunned the entire neighborhood.

And then rumors abounded.

That she was careless and indisciplined. That children were no longer moral and innocent and society was crumbling. That people from her community are unrestrained. That it was her own classmate, with whom she went astray. And therefore she got pregnant.

Siddharth was bewildered and shocked to the point of disbelieving what he heard. His embarrassed father, for the first time ever, lost his nerve. At first, some people in the locality did not accept it. But gossip alters belief rapidly.

Mr. Banerjee tried to vehemently deny the allegations. But he had to temper his outcries when his son gave confusing answers.

"But dad, I heard it was measles. Miss Violet confirmed it to all of us."

"But that's not what we are all hearing," said Mr. Banerjee raising his voice.

"I...I...don't know what to say *baba*." Siddharth denied everything.

"Were you two having a...," started Mr. Banerjee, but checked himself immediately. "This is so shocking. So shocking."

With fear banging inside his chest he went over to Hazel's house a few times. However, the door was either locked or never opened. So he managed to get Dimple, Jennifer and Neetu together the next day at Dimple's house. They sympathized with him.

"We heard it was measles earlier. Now we are hearing rumors," said Dimple.

"We can't even meet her Sidd," said Neetu.

"You won't believe, being her cousin even I am not allowed to meet her," said Jennifer. "Her father, Uncle James, is acting strangely. Yesterday he turned me away saying that she will not meet anyone. It was so mean of him."

"Sidd we are all surprised with what is going on with Hazel," said Dimple.

In less than ten days another news spread like a dust storm. That Hazel and her parents left town for her abortion.

Since school had already closed, Siddharth was spared the rain of questions from friends. Yet, he would often get a second look from neighbors, as if they were trying to judge him or solicit answers.

He was broken and could not find a single soul in whose bosom he could dig his face and weep. He knew he could not hold himself much longer that way. Amidst his desperation to meet Hazel and the wind of ugly rumors against him, he hardly had the mind to appear for the entrance exams.

One day while Siddharth was returning from a coaching class four boys in motorbikes screeched to a halt beside him.

"Hey smartie," said one of them.

Siddharth turned to face them. They wore bandanas around their head and neck. Only one of them was wearing a helmet. They looked coarse and aggressive.

"We are here to educate you," said the boy with the helmet.

They hurled incestuous abuses and charged him of hurting Hazel. Siddharth tried to protest but received a severe blow on his face from the boy with the helmet. He was tall, muscular and white-skinned and got off his bike for a showdown while the others circled Siddharth in their bikes so he could not run away.

"You see these eyes. They have seen it all. In the woods by the stadium, in the rain, in that circus show down the eucalyptus tree, during the stupid Bong Pujas. Today we shall end it all." He removed his helmet and said, "You will never forget me. I promise."

It was Darryl. The three of them started fisting Siddharth. Barring a few times when he ducked to avoid the rain of blows he mostly stood there receiving them, somehow convinced of the inevitability of a backlash from Hazel's community. Then the two boys held him by his arms in a vice like grip while Darryl slapped and punched him on his face. Blood trickled out of his mouth. Tears welled in his eyes. He was almost at the verge of crying.

"You will remember me as Darryl the jaw-breaker."

A brutal kick on his shin brought Siddharth down on his knees. He cried out in pain.

"You see this," said Darryl pulling out a sharp knife. "We will put this in your head." He was aiming his right leg to launch another brutal kick when a loud clamoring from behind arrested his attempt. It was familiar voices of Sudeep and Shankar.

They were running towards them.

When the boys realized that Siddharth was no longer alone, they quickly delivered a few more blows and slaps and then jumped on their bikes and sped away.

"We will hunt you down again," shouted Darryl and fired another salvo of slangs. "Better leave this town for good. Else the worse is yet to come."

Siddharth hurriedly went home, shaken and embarrassed, without even properly thanking Shankar and Sudeep. The taste of blood mixed with shame and fear inside his mouth was unmistakable.

Somehow he managed to appear for the state Joint Entrance exam and then a sudden change occurred within him. He felt negative about himself and harbored mixed feelings about Hazel to have left him so abruptly without informing. And he couldn't bear to see his father's embarrassment who, in few months, would move to USA on company work.

So he decided to go to Bombay and stay with his cousin until the results of the Joint Entrance exams were out. Mr. Banerjee agreed to it. Bombay put his life back in first gear and relieved him of his immediate fears.

That year the Prime Minister was assassinated on 21 May. Siddharth learnt about the word 'suicide bomber.' He learnt other words like Perestroika and Glasnost. For the Soviet Union economy collapsed the same year. Talks about disintegration of the Soviet Union into different countries were heard. The cost of bread and tomatoes shot up ten times in Russia. Siddharth's dreams of going to Ukraine University became muddy.

Luckily, that year he got admission for engineering in NIT Trichy.

When he returned from Bombay he found the windows in his room stoned and cracks radiating out of the gaping holes. He knew it was the handiwork of Darryl and the biker boys.

"I came from office one day and saw the window broken," said his father. "I have lodged a complaint with the police."

"Were you hurt?" he asked.

"No. But amidst all this, it was nice to hear about your

results. We must start preparing for your new life in college. I will travel with you for the admission procedures."

The rest of the days were spent packing clothes and bidding goodbye to his friends. Couple of times he sensed Darryl stalking him on the streets and so he took detours to avoid him. There was still no news of Hazel or her family. The rumors did not fizzle out from the mouth of the townspeople. The neighbors had firm opinions on the matter. Word had escaped that Siddharth was a decent guy in disguise and in few circles that he was a serial offender.

Unable to defend himself or lift himself up from the sludge of allegations he kept wallowing in it with shame. And a persistent threat of being assaulted by Darryl frightened him. Estranged and embittered in his own town he wanted to escape.

That was when Siddharth swore that he would never step on that soil again. He had to bury Jamshedpur forever.

As for Hazel, he remained confused. His fears out-weighed his concern for her. The lack of news, each passing day, left him anguished. He forced himself to treat her absence with indifference, even to suppress her thoughts. And in front of his father, who had spent a lonely lifetime trying to bring him up, he felt diminished in worth and reduced to rubble.

That propelled him to breakout and forge ahead into a hazy future, without Hazel, with the vestiges of love, against all odds, against his wishes. And the admission to the engineering college gave him the desired escape route.

The night before he left for college, he slipped out of his house in stealth and walked about half a kilometer and stopped. That area was dark as most of the streetlights were unlit. Occasionally the bulbs were stolen or broken by the town urchins. It was a moonless night. He stood behind a Coromandel Ebony tree that was surrounded by large rocks and stared at an apartment in the ground floor about two hundred meters away. It was in total darkness. His heart wanted to leap out into the house and hold someone close to his chest. But he realized the futility and the dead-end of his desire. That was the last time he saw Hazel's house.

Then he turned to his left and looked at another building in disgust. After waiting for two minutes and making sure there was no one around he put on a monkey-cap and wrapped a shawl across his shoulders and walked briskly towards the building. When he reached there he tip-toed towards the door of a ground floor apartment that was well lit. He felt his shirt pocket and then bent down.

He brought out a small piece of paper from his shirt pocket and slipped it underneath the door. Then he turned around and quickly walked away. After he had reached about fifty meters someone shouted at him from behind. He turned halfway to see who it was but other than a dark outline of someone rushing at him he was clueless.

"Stop right there," shouted the person again. It was not a voice Siddharth recognized yet he quickened his pace. But the man behind started shouting and running.

Siddharth panicked and was about to run when he tripped on a rock and toppled over. He fell on his face and his hands touched a few hard and wet objects. Stones. His hands quickly felt them and in no time he grabbed a few large ones and rose up. The man was getting closer to him.

With trembling hands he flung the first one at the dark

shape but missed.

The person barked and sprinted towards him, "You'll regret this once I catch your neck."

Siddharth hurled the second stone with force and by the sound of the contact he knew he had hit the bull's eye. The man let out a cry and dropped to the ground. Siddharth broke into a mad run and didn't stop till he reached home. He had taken a detour to avoid the possibility of being followed.

He couldn't sleep the whole night fearing he'd be trolled and stoned. He wondered who the man was who chased him and where the stone had hit him. Next morning he left for college with his father. Although he maintained a stoic face, his teenage heart screamed and wept and each beat carried with it muted sounds of hurt, fear, shame and melancholy.

Throughout the journey, the handwritten note he had slipped into the house the previous night, repeatedly played itself in his mind. "Hazel hates you. Forget her. She is not the types who will give in to a bully like you. You can go on breaking jaws. But one day God will teach you a lesson."

Chapter 8

JAMSHEDPUR MAIN HOSPITAL

"Which way is the ICU?" asked Siddharth to the lady at the hospital reception.

"Upstairs. You'll find the directions there," said the lady. "Who are you looking for?"

"Hazel. Hazel Castelino."

The receptionist looked at the computer screen and said, "Yes, she's in there. Just moved from the Critical Care Unit to the ICU. But do you have a pass, Sir? It's only ten a.m. And it's outside visiting hours." He ignored the receptionist's query and moved on. When he was stopped by the security standing just before the stairs leading to the ICU, he managed to get past with an imploring smile.

Once he was upstairs the thought of seeing Hazel quickened his blood and made him nervous. Each step he took he felt like turning back. The seventeen years of disassociation confused him in what capacity he was visiting Hazel. In what right? What would be her mom's reaction when she saw him? He fretted over what to talk, what not to talk and such.

The hospital corridors smelled of disinfectants and trauma.

Twenty feet away from the ICU he saw a circle of people around an old lady in the center. Uncertainty and sorrow hung in the cold air and on their faces. The old lady was wearing a long skirt and a woolen cardigan over a shirt. All black. Her face was ageing and her hair was whitening but the regal looks were still intact. She was Hazel's mom.

As soon as Siddharth recognized her, his flame of purpose started flickering.

He wasn't sure if he could face her. A peculiar turmoil had set-in, in his abdomen and he had to almost double-up to allay the discomfort. It was the same sensation he had had on his first day in pre-school when his mom's fingers slipped away from his and he had to walk on without her, with the line of boys, into the unknown and uncanny spaces of the classroom.

He turned back, took the stairs down and bolted out of the hospital building. After walking a few yards he spotted the hospital canteen within the premises next to the main gate.

"Perhaps hot tea and snacks will make me braver," he told himself.

An hour later when Siddharth was about to leave the canteen when he saw Hazel's mom step out of the building. He quickly turned sideways to hide himself but did not take his eyes off her. She was flanked by people. They walked slowly. One of them led her by her arm.

After they went outside the main gate, Siddharth immediately hurried into the hospital building and towards the ICU. There he saw three ladies sitting right outside the ICU. They were wrapped in winter shawls. He quickly approached one of them and asked, "Is a patient named Hazel inside?"

"Yes," said one of ladies. Curiosity crept into the somber faces of the other ladies.

"Are you related to her?" asked Siddharth.

"We are their neighbors." At that point the other ladies nodded their heads wrapped in winter shawls and woolen scarves.

"I am her school friend. Isn't her mother here?" he asked deliberately.

"No. She just left for home to eat. She's been starving for a few days now."

"Oh I see. When will she be back?" asked Siddharth.

"We told her not to come back before evening. We will be here until then."

"I've heard only bits and pieces of her accident. Do you know how it happened?"

"Oh yes. She was at her office waiting for important cargo to be delivered. Her office is located on the east of the circular road opposite to a small cinema theatre."

"Cargo? What kind?"

"Sculptures." replied the lady and continued, "Once the truck arrived, the unloading started using a large crane. On normal days the area stays crowded due to the cinema theatre. But that day the traffic was sparse. I am told, a car came speeding from the north and took a left on the circular road. It did not expect the truck and a crane planted mid-way on the road. When it saw the loaded crane swing in its direction it swerved and braked suddenly. Then it skidded on the road and went hurtling towards the office."

"Was she the only one to be hurt?"

"No. The car hit a staff and her before ramming on to the office wall. In the crash her head got injured and she collapsed. People rushed over to them. The staff guy and the car driver were moaning and trying to move. I heard, they were still conscious but she was not."

A sudden silence fell on the corridor for a few seconds.

Siddharth moved to the ICU door. Through the circular see-through portion of the door he watched the outline of Hazel. She was on the ventilator and all covered and closed to the world like her beautiful eyelids. A shiver passed down his spine. He could not bear to see her in that condition. "Oh Hazel, is that you there?" he almost cried out. After almost two decades of separation his eyes could hardly accept the sight that fate was forcing him to see. After staring at her for a while he stepped back to the ladies.

"What is the doctor's opinion?" asked Siddharth to the lady again.

"To wait and watch. They are monitoring. But aren't saying much. I hope God is watching the plight of such a beautiful girl and will show some mercy," said the lady with a grief-stricken voice. "Such a tragedy for such lovely people as she and her mom."

Siddharth stood near them and periodically walked up to the ICU door to see Hazel. He was reluctant to believe that it was she inside. An attending nurse was noting something in a register beside her. He stood watching a few nurses come and go.

Expecting to meet the anonymous caller who had informed him about Hazel, he waited there for a couple of hours. Surprisingly, no one turned up to identify himself as the caller. It was still a mystery. But whoever the man was, he hadn't lied.

But who was he? Whoever he was he must have known Hazel and him closely.

After a while, sitting near the ICU, he felt out of place and almost like an alien. There was no one in the hospital, he knew. There was no one in the town amongst his friends who he knew lived there anymore. Nor was he in touch with anyone after he left school. So he thought of walking around his old hometown. It was a place with beautiful lakes and hills and manufactured trucks. After all, it was the place he was born in, fell in love with and then was forced to abandon.

Chapter 9

THE STREETS OF JAMSHEDPUR

"Hello Sir, take these fresh apples, you won't get such anywhere," said a fruit-seller waving from his cartload of fruits.

"Sir come here. These gooseberries are the juiciest. And these oranges, cheapest in town and of best quality," said another holding plump oranges in his hand.

At the bus-stand on the periphery of Azaad bazaar, ignoring the fruit-sellers, Siddharth kept looking intently in a particular direction. Over a dozen shops away his eyes rested on the familiar saloon that stood moldering. A soggy lane meandered through rows of grocery and hardware stores, sweet shops, pharmacies and costermongers before fading into the saloon's doorstep.

"I can't believe it is still there," he told himself in wonder.

Behind the glass swivel door of the saloon, a barber was seen busy at his trade. A pair of scissors and comb inched up and down together over the thick hair of a portly man sitting on a high chair, motionless and rigid.

"Is it the same barber?" he asked himself.

It was a bright winter afternoon in Jamshedpur. The roadsides were lined with wild marigolds and petunias. Riding the gentle wind was the sweet smell of marigolds and peeled oranges. From the bus-stand a warren of narrow lanes led into the heart of the bazaar, which was an integral part of the small township. Although the crowd was thin, a few construction machines sputtered creating enough noise to raise the general drone in the area.

"What was his name?" he tried to recollect as he neared the saloon.

Seventeen years is a long period. Changes in a small town that has seen its youth are not subtle anymore. Houses turn somber, smoke-stacks erode across the haggard skyline, the economy in general changes marked by a shift in habits and values of the populace.

And yet many things still remain the same. The old streets, the smell of seasons, the temples, churches, mosques, schools, the views of nearby hills and certain people who are still entwined with the town and its ways, its character, its warmth and would never abandon it in spite of the lure and pull of bigger cities.

"Will he recognize me after so many years?" A trickle of doubt crept in his mind.

Right outside the saloon he unzipped his brown suede jacket mid-way and eased the muffler firmly wound around his neck. To avoid hitting his head against the lintel of the doorway he bent his six feet frame. As he pushed the door the barber's name struck him.

"Hello Aarif-ji."

Peering through the thick-rimmed glasses the barber paused and tried to place him for few seconds before replying with a casual indifference, "Please come in, Sir. It will be about fifteen minutes before I can attend you."

The clicking of scissors continued.

The barber had the same unhurried diction. His hair was now a mat of white over a dark bony face. The nose was still distinctly flat and it had always provoked him, as a child, to reproduce the plateau on his own nose by pressing it with his thumb.

"It's his friendly nature that gets him his customers," his father had told him once.

"Please sit on the sofa Sir. Sorry for the wait. I just started with this gentleman."

The smell inside was a mixture of cologne, shaving cream and dust. Cut-hair was spewed all over the tessellated floor. Mirrors and glossy posters of Bollywood actresses covered the walls. A pedestal fan by the window weakly whirred and wheezed and moved its head in an arc, at one end of which it stirred clumps of hair in a bin and at the other end it startled the pages of magazines into a flutter. In the cold it served as an exhaust fan.

"No problem please take your time. I will wait."

Before sitting on one of the high chairs, he picked up one of the film magazines he was fond of as a child. Stardust. The cover page showed a leading Bollywood actress holding her arms close to her naked torso in a strategic way.

After a while, unable to restrain himself any longer, Siddharth blurted, "Aarif-ji, you have forgotten me. But do you remember Mr. Benoy Banerjee?"

Hearing that, the barber turned back instantly.

"I am his son, Siddharth. As a child, I always got my hair done by you."

"*Arre*, Banerjee Babu's son?" he asked instantly, apologetic. His eyes gained a sudden sparkle of old marbles polished after a long time. He came over hurriedly and hugged him. "You look quite different."

"Yes it is over seventeen years. How are you?"

"Seventeen years?" Aarif-ji was chomping betel leaf for some time and in his ardor to talk, almost spilt the chewed leaf. A little spittle trickled at the sides of his mouth. Plodding to the corner of the room he emptied his mouth into a spittoon and wiped the sides with a towel that was counting its days to be disposed. "I am doing well son. How is Banerjee Babu?"

"Dad is fine."

"When did you come?"

"Early morning today."

"After so many years? What brings you here?"

Siddharth thought if he should tell the true reason for his visit and decided against it. "My company sells grinding wheels to the factory here. So I came in connection to that."

Their conversation seemed to have hit the dozing customer like a stream of pebbles out of many catapults, as he came out of his stupor quite startled. After reassuring himself that a war had not broken out, he dropped a look at the mirror.

"Please cut it carefully," he said and slowly went back to his state of reverie.

"*Ghabraiye nahi,*" said Aarif-ji comforting the man. He resumed his work after striking the comb against the scissors a couple of times to get rid of cut hair stuck between the comb teeth. "I will take proper care. Don't worry."

Siddharth quickly viewed himself on a large mirror kept at an elevation in front. He needed a shave too, he felt.

"So you came to sell wheels here?"

"Yes. And also to meet a friend of mine."

"Hmm. You must be a big man by now."

"No. No. Aarif-ji. Nothing like that."

"How long are you here, son?"

"Maybe a few more days."

"Hmm. I am so happy to know that you still remember me."

"Actually I am quite excited to see your saloon where it used to be."

Aarif-ji seemed to be done with his job with the sleeping customer and shook him awake. The man hitched himself up and then twisted and turned several times in front of the mirror at various angles. Satisfied, he left quickly on his short and outwardly bent legs.

"Ahh, now I have you completely by myself. Time flies by so quickly that you hardly notice the changes around you. You may not know but I have two grand-children now. I also bought a house nearby few years back."

"How wonderful," exclaimed Siddharth.

Talking about the various changes in the town in the last two decades, Aarif-ji shared a lot of anecdotes along with news about the current honchos at the truck factory. Being an old barber in a small town and flocked by its people all the time, he had remained a focal point of gossip and was naturally brimming with stories, new and ancient.

In a way he was the town's historian.

One thing led to another and Siddharth asked him about his school chums and their fathers some of who were of repute in the town in those days. Disconnected with his friends as much as he was with the town, he was eager to gain any morsel of information. He suspected that Aarif-ji might have had some knowledge about them as well.

The grandfather wall-clock gave three dongs.

"Did you ask about Dr. Mitra, the one who is a pediatrician?"

"Yes."

"Oh, he is still practicing here. Was his son in your school?"

"Yes. In the same class. Do you know about him?" asked Siddharth anxiously.

"Of course. Very much. Actually Dr. Mitra still comes here for his haircut."

"And his son?"

"I don't know much. But Dr. Mitra often grumbles about him."

"Why?" Siddharth asked a little alarmed.

"He says his son has not earned either name or money and has wasted himself. Sometimes I hear of his son playing in the local musical events. *Wohi gana bajana.*"

Siddharth was unhappy to hear that about Sudeep as he was such a brilliant student. He recalled the stunning speech he had given in school on Operation Black Thunder. They had often bunked classes together trailing up the hills trapping tadpoles, insects and wild flowers in small bottles to impress the biology teacher. Once they had found a human-skull near the lake and earned the wrath of the Lab Assistant by placing it on his table. Sudeep had a remarkable flair for Biology and politics and excelled in playing the *tabla*. They shared a common passion for painting too.

Lost in such thoughts, Siddharth winced, when his head was sprayed with cold water. "You have not lost much hair I see." Aarif-ji continued in the same slow pace and asked, "Son, are you married?"

"Yes."

"So you must have kids by now. Isn't it?"

"No."

Siddharth's mouth became dry and he tried to ferret a smile.

Talking about his past pained him. Aarif-ji started humming a tune and he was lost reminiscing about his school days and especially his moments with Hazel.

After a while Siddharth asked a direct question, "You remember the Castelinos?"

Hearing that Aarif-ji stopped humming, "You mean James Castelino?"

"There you go. So you know them. The daughter recently met with an accident and is hospitalized in serious condition."

"Yes I heard."

"You already know about it?" Siddharth was stumped.

"News comes to me from all around like wild wind."

"I am planning to visit them today."

"It is tragic…for all their family went through," said Aarif-ji clicking the scissors.

"What do you mean?"

"The daughter and mother had disappeared for many years before returning back."

"Really?"

"Yes. The father was a real bastard. *Bada harami.* They left because of him."

"And then what happened."

"After few years even he had to leave town for some police case against him."

"Police case? What kind?"

"Some business scam. *Hera pheri.*"

"Where did his family move to?"

"I don't know what happened after the daughter and mother left town or where they moved to. But they returned after many years."

"Can you tell me whatever you know about them?"

"I don't know much. But I heard they have set up a small business in the city."

"And do you know if she got married."

"I heard some stories. But they can't be believed. I don't know."

"Oh I see."

"And then the daughter had this accident recently. Very unfortunate people. But it's all written here. *Naseeb apna apna.*" Aarif-ji pointed at his forehead indicating the fate lines. "Anyway tell me more about yourself. Now that you are married and settled don't delay having kids, else you won't become a grand-father in time, like me."

Aarif-ji laughed and nearly choked on the betel leaf he was chewing. Thin red roadways trickled from both ends of his mouth. He grabbed a water bottle and drank. The mirror showed the curves of his Adam's apple bobbing up and down.

Once the haircut and shave was over, a head and shoulder massage followed.

"Now you look like a celebrity, son," said the barber patting his back for the last time.

Rising from the chair Siddharth thanked him effusively. "Your magic with hair is still visible, Aarif-ji."

"Do extend my greetings to your father, a very kind gentleman. Your dad had helped me once financially, to stabilize my business. Did you know?"

"Is it? He never told me about it," said Siddharth pleasantly surprised.

"Yes he did. I can never forget him. Do visit again. *Khuda Hafiz*", said Aarif-ji holding him close to his chest for a while.

"Take care Aarif-ji, *namaste*," replied Siddharth extending a hundred rupee note.

Biting his tongue, Aarif-ji refused to accept any payment for the haircut.

While bidding him goodbye Siddharth felt sad. From the time he stepped in his old hometown he had been feeling like a total stranger. But the casual conversation with the barber sparked the lost kinship with the soil. He was happy to have visited the saloon.

Outside, the sun was on its way to kiss the horizon and the breeze was gentle on his face. He drank the cool air and felt refreshed and young. "Let me walk around and see the old places," he told himself.

Taking a right from the bus stand, he walked past the rows of houses and couple of streets that led to the flat where he had lived until the end of his school days. From a distance, he stood staring at the apartment, remembering the old days, his gentle father, his late mother, his precious room, the terrace. The building had the scars of time on it and badly needed a fresh coat of paint. His childhood flooded his mind like a strong breeze gushing across a room unlocked after many years.

"I can never leave this house *baba*. Is there a way we can live here forever?" An echo of an old conversation with his father, flashed across his mind. He was nine years then.

"This is a company flat, son. We have to leave it one day."

"When will that be?"

"When I retire or maybe if we move out earlier."

"I don't want to move out of this house. This is mom's house. If we are gone, when she comes back how will she find us?"

"We are not going away now itself, *babu*."

"I don't want to leave this place ever, *baba*. Never."

His father had held him close and kissed his cheeks and calmed him.

"Ok. You will stay here as long as you want."

He wondered how many families would have moved in and moved out of the apartment since they vacated. He gave a last look at the walls and the windows before moving on. There were other places he wanted to see.

Crossing a small field that led to the main road, he walked up to his old school – Little Flower School. The faces of his teachers and friends, the voices in packed classrooms and assembly, the fear of cane and the mischief in spite of it, the smell of cosmetics on concert days, the tumult of the annual sports day and the tearful last day in school, came back to him.

He watched a few students loitering around the school corner, talking and laughing, carefree and unconcerned.

"Education is, what remains with you when you leave school," he recalled his brilliant Geography teacher telling the class once. "And if you remember me twenty years later with a smile, I know my job was well done." Siddharth could not help smiling.

"There are no ladders to climb Mount Everest. You will face hardships to reach your goal," said Mrs. Violet on the last day of school. The school and his teachers had always made him feel proud.

Circling the school boundary he came across the stadium where people had started their daily practice and the patch of jungle where he often sat and painted in isolation. And then as he walked past, his eyes got fixed on the hill top about half a kilometer away. Something stirred inside him. It made him unsure whether to move forward or turn around.

He stood rooted staring at the temple on the hill.

A stream of words floated up from some recess within him like bubbles surging from the bottom of a pond and exploding softly at the surface.

"My love will shine like the moon when the light in the lanterns fade away."

Pushed by his past, he moved on. Goose-flesh pimpled his skin. The Kali temple on the hill had a climb of hundred steps from the base. It had always been a safe hideout for the hole-and-corner meetings of young lovers. Walking up the slope his mind raced back in time.

"I can be a lover, but not a rebel."

After reaching the top he sauntered around the premises before entering the temple. The priest was chanting the evening prayers and swaying a number of earthen lamps in front of the goddess. A huge gathering of devotees milled around the priest chanting along. A man behind the drums gave a steady beat while another clanged the cymbals. Once the prayer was over, he shouldered his way through the crowd to the open spaces of the hilltop.

The air was colder and his cheeks started to redden. To get a better view of the general scenery he clambered atop a huge boulder. The view was sweeping and spectacular. He could see most parts of the town. Looking sideways, hundred feet away, his eyes hovered around the temple gate. People were coming out of the gate in throngs.

"Just you and me in the temple and this moonlit winter night."

The sky was darkening. A little later he started climbing

down the boulder. Then he looked at his watch and briskly walked down the temple steps. He had to check into a hotel for the night.

Early next morning Siddharth rushed to the hospital. A few people had already gathered there. Their faces reflected deep concern and worry. But they were not the ones he had seen the previous day and neither was Hazel's mom present.

"She will be in anytime now," said one of the men when he asked about her.

"Is there any improvement?" asked Siddharth. "Did the doctor say anything?"

"They had repeated the CT scan on her followed by a brain MRI. It showed multiple clots and edema and fractures in the skull. It seems that we need to wait until the swelling subsides and the small clots get absorbed on their own. Only then will they be able to operate and remove the big clots."

"So will a surgery happen?"

"Not until the small clots vanish. Which won't be for a few days now. But the doctors are not sure if the clots will subside. And that is a grim possibility as well. They are just waiting to see what happens. But in case the small clots disappear a surgery is likely."

As he was discussing with the group someone tapped his right shoulder from behind. He turned around to see a pale-skinned, tall and muscular man. He had sharp features and thick light hair with a hint of golden strands. His face was friendly and he had a warm smile. The neck was as thick as a tree trunk. And his body was rugged like that of a bouncer.

"Excuse me. Are you Siddharth?"

"Yes."

"I have this for you," said the man extending a packet with his right hand.

Siddharth held the small packet and examined it quickly and asked, "Are you the one who called me few days back?"

"No. I am Shane. Shane Gordan. A gentleman asked me to give this to you."

They shook hands.

"Who was that person?" asked Siddharth.

"I am not sure."

"Isn't he here?" said Siddharth, his gaze lingering on Shane's bulging biceps.

"He was. But it seems some urgent work has kept him away for many days."

"How is he related to Hazel?"

At that point a petite and pretty woman came up and stood holding Shane's hands. She had curly hair that reached her shoulder and she looked not more than in her late twenties. She smiled at Siddharth and said, "Hi."

"She is my wife Helena," said Shane. "To your question on the man's relationship, he told me that he was Hazel's family acquaintance. And said that an old friend of Hazel, named Siddharth, would arrive here and that I should deliver it to him. Don't you know him?"

"Umm…actually no," said Siddharth. "What was his name?"

Shane scratched his head and said, "I kind of forget. It was something like JD or DJ. I didn't ask him to elaborate. It was a brief meeting and he said he had to leave urgently. I never saw him after that."

"I am surprised. Even you don't know him or his name."

"Actually I have never seen him before. I hope there is nothing dangerous in the packet," said Shane winking at Siddharth.

They laughed. Siddharth did not feel it appropriate to tell them about the mysterious call he had received and why the caller had insisted him to visit the town. In his mind the incident had shaped itself into a private matter. But another question was burning inside him and he finally asked them, in as indirect way as possible. "How long have you guys known Hazel?"

"Many years now."

"It must be hard on Hazel and her family. Does she have children?"

Shane and Helena looked at each other and then at Siddharth and shook their heads.

"She is not married," said Helena.

That made Siddharth restless. It was something he did not expect. But he did not show his surprise. He asked them some more about her accident and health and after a little while told them that he had to leave.

"Have a nice day," said Helena smiling, holding on to Shane's arms tightly.

"Good day Ma'am. Thank you very much Shane for handing over this packet to me." He noted that Shane and Helena were a cheerful couple. One could judge by their physical proximity to each other that they were married not long back.

Back at the hotel where he was staying, the first thing Siddharth did was to open the packet Shane had given him. It contained a box the size of a cigarette packet. Inside the box was a key and a note that was folded four times.

"Siddharth – This is the key that would lead you to the letters Hazel had left for you long back. As promised on the phone I am leaving this key with you now. When you get time please do visit the locker. I think you have the locker number with you. I don't have it. It was mentioned in the letter she sent you when you were in college. Regards."

"The locker number? Is in the letter Hazel sent me in college," wondered Siddharth.

Siddharth called up his travel agent immediately to book tickets for that night to Baharampur, about 200 km from Kolkata. Since Hazel's surgery wouldn't happen in a day or two he decided to travel to his ancestral home to fetch all of Hazel's letters especially the last one that he faintly recalled had more details about the key.

He phoned his father after the ticket booking was confirmed. "Hello *baba*."

"Hello son, I was trying you on your landline yesterday," said Mr. Banerjee.

After working in the factory making trucks in Jamshedpur for most of his professional life, Mr. Banerjee was deputed in Detroit, Michigan in USA for few years. Finally, to support his aged mother, he moved to his ancestral home.

"Yes I was not at home. How is *thakuma?*" asked Siddharth about his granny.

"Not too well *babu*. We did a quick check up last week."

"Any new issues?"

"No. Same observations. Blood sugar, cholesterol and

pressure is perfect."

"That is very good."

"But it's her arthritis that has blocked her movements. She was asking if you could come over once."

"I am actually planning to visit you. It has been a while since I met you both."

"That's good to hear. When?"

"Tonight."

"That's good news. But so suddenly?"

"*Baba*, actually I am in Jamshedpur right now."

"Why?" asked Mr. Benoy, surprised.

"Sales related company work," he said, hiding the real reason. "So I thought I will visit you on my way back home."

"Oh I see…" said his father. "That's surprising. You finally went to Jamshedpur after all these years? Did you get to see any of your old friends there?"

"Not exactly. Actually yesterday I went to Azaad bazaar and to the old barber's saloon. Do you remember Aarif-ji?"

"Oh sure, I do."

"He was very excited to see me. We chatted for some time and he gave me details about Sudeep and Vivek. Looks like Dr. Mitra is still practicing there."

"Really? Remember, the number of times we went for your health check-ups?"

"Yes I do. By the way, Aarif-ji told me that you had helped him monetarily once?"

"Oh that was nothing." Mr. Banerjee didn't say anymore. "Did you get to visit Sudeep or your school?

"No. I didn't have much time. But I did take a stroll around the school, our old apartment and the nearby areas."

"How was the town in general?"

"Pretty much the same I guess, few things better and few things worse."

Chapter 10

THE TRUNK

"Split the head in two. The eyes should be intact."

"Okay *saar*."

"Belly and back should be separate. Square them up into equal pieces."

"This will be an excellent buy."

"Better be. You are charging me such a fat amount."

"No *saar*. The season is over, so the prices have shot up. Elsewhere it is 700 rupees a kilo but I am charging you less."

"Alright. Make sure the scales are removed completely."

"All done. Here let me scrape some more."

"I hope you have cleaned the insides well."

"Yes. Yes. Is anyone special coming home?"

"My son. If the taste is flat then I'll return it."

"Don't worry *saar*. It is from the Ganges. Your son will ask for more. Guaranteed."

Mr. Banerjee picked up his son's favorite fish, cut and sized and cleaned and hurried away. As instructed by his mother, a whole list of things had to be purchased, like pumpkin creeper, pumpkin flower, drumsticks and its leaves, Malabar spinach and tiger prawns. Fresh and always in limited supply, they would sell out fast in the market. The jaggery and Bengal basmati rice could wait.

Although it was just 6:30 in the morning, the local market was abuzz with buyers haranguing over the price and quality of everything being sold.

"I will cook what he likes best. After all he is coming after a year," said Mr. Banerjee's mother the previous evening. She was beaming with anticipation.

"Okay Ma, but don't burn yourself out."

"Don't worry. Sheela will help me with everything. I will only move the ladle. What else can I do these days other than stirring the cooking pot?"

When Mr. Banerjee came back with the bags loaded with vegetables and fish, his mother had already started her preparations. She was supervising the house maid Sheela who was busy mixing and grinding spices on a big stone slab. A few neighbors kept enquiring about his son's arrival from outside the compound gate.

"What time will the train arrive, Benoy?" asked the neighbors.

"Eleven is the right time."

"Okay we will come back later once he is back," the neighbors said and went away.

"Benoy come here," called out his mother.

"What is it Ma?"

"I wish his wife was also coming. I have seen her just once during their wedding. Why didn't you insist him on getting her as well?"

"Her father isn't well. So she had to go there to look after him," said Mr. Banerjee. That was a lie. She was not appraised of her grandson's marital condition. It would cripple her.

"Hmm. That is good. She should spend some time with her father. By the way, Sheela caught some crabs and small Tilapias from the pond. Did you get the Hilsa?"

"Yes Ma," said Mr. Banerjee washing his hands. "And

everything else you asked me to get. I think I got the entire market today at your doorstep."

The house was aglow with excitement and his mother, in spite of her old age and bad health had planned for an elaborate lunch. As she got busy with the cooking, Mr. Banerjee grabbed the morning newspaper and slid into the armchair.

After a while, although his eyes were glued to the newspaper, he wasn't reading it. Transported to a time when his son was young and motherless he reflected if he was able to successfully accomplish his duties as a father.

One regret that shadowed him was that he could never befriend his son.

In front of his wife's pyre, as he watched the body shrink to nothing, he felt the stab of grief deep inside. Without his wife anymore his hook to the world was lost. As the flames sprung up and slowly died, the woodpile and the smile on his face turned to ash.

He stepped back home that day, withdrawn, as if no one else existed or mattered. His son grabbed him wanting to know what happened to his mother and for a long time sat beside him clinging to his arms, bound by the common thread of sorrow, waiting to be embraced and spoken to. But his gaze was fixed at the horizon and he remained stiff and unresponsive.

Finally, unable to ignore anymore, he put his hand over his son's shoulder and spoke. But he stopped, fearing his cracked voice would show how splintered he was from within.

As the days went by, he saw his son playing with his toys alone, aloof from his friends, lonely in his infant world. And he could do little about it for he himself had built a brick-wall around himself.

One Sunday afternoon, two years later, when his son was with his toys, he tried to strike a conversation with him, "Want to play with me *babu*?"

"Hmm."

They played for a while.

"What do you want to be when you grow up? Pilot, doctor, engineer?"

"I don't know," said his son peering into the toys, distant, quiet.

A notepad lying next to the toys caught his attention. As he casually turned the pages he gaped at them with his mouth wide open. There were at least twenty drawings of his wife. In some of them she was sailing alone in a boat, in some she was sailing in the clouds, in others she was with Lord Krishna and Shiva in outer space.

"You drew them *babu*?" he asked in disbelief.

"Hmm," his son nodded, peeping inside a toy he was particularly fascinated with.

"They are so beautiful." He kissed his son on his plump cheeks and soft forehead and hugged him several times.

From the wall that he built around him, a brick of sorrow dislodged and fell permanently and a ray of smile escaped.

The following week itself Mr. Banerjee had arranged for a private drawing teacher entrusted with enhancing his son's exceptional drawing skills.

About a decade later, when he was deputed to Detroit from his company, his son had entered college. So every summer he made him travel to USA to stay with him.

He recalled his conversation with him once during sunset, as they were trailing along the lake in the Elizabeth Park in Detroit that was surrounded by flower beds and maple trees.

"*Babu*, you may think that I am seven seas apart. But I am just a phone call away."

"Sure *baba*."

"I will fly over immediately in case you need me, okay? It is just for a few years the company wants me to be here and then I will go back to India."

"This is working just fine *baba*. In summers I wait to be here with you. And during the winter break, I look forward to be with *thakuma* in Baharampur."

"Do you like to travel to Detroit every summer, *babu*?"

"Very much. Quite an escape from the summer heat in India." And after pondering over something for a while he added, "There will be an exception though in my third year."

"Why?"

"I need to stay back in India during the summer vacation for the mandatory summer project for college."

"Oh I recall that I need to arrange for that. I think it will be best that you complete the summer project in my company in Jamshedpur itself."

"*Baba*, I don't want to go back there. And you know the reason."

"Hmm," Mr. Banerjee paused for a while. "Okay. I have some contacts in Hind Motors near Kolkata. They make the Ambassador cars. I can try and get you there."

"That will be much better."

"Babu, on your point of not going back to Jamshedpur, I

keep forgetting to ask you a question. Did you hear about the Castelinos?"

"No, I did not," his son had replied in undertones. There was a visible lack of interest and hurt in his voice when he answered that question, which Mr. Banerjee fathomed immediately.

That was the closest he ever spoke to his son about the Castelinos. Knowing his son's relationship with Hazel, he never pried deep into that past, unwilling to upset him.

Lying in the armchair he ran his hands around his waistline and felt the healed scar that ran almost as a semi-circle from the navel to the spine. It was smooth and swollen like an embossed line. He remembered how he had fought once for his son on a desolate street on his way back from office. The punches, the knife, the police station, the hospital. But his tongue was sealed on that event and he never mentioned about it to anyone.

Once again the question bothered him, "Have I done enough for my son? I wish I had tried harder to be a better friend."

After folding the newspaper he kept it on his chest and closed his eyes. A rare smile appeared on his face and his heart pounded like the pistons in the train's engine that was carrying his son to him.

His childhood memories of Baharampur were vivid. The countless ponds, endless fields, a neighborhood without walls and neighbors untouched by the city venom of competition had planted a deep-seated sense of intrigue in his young mind. It created an image of a parallel world of wonder.

At that time, in spite of more than half a dozen rooms, the

ancestral house seemed crowded due to the joint families of his uncles living there. During vacations, when his father and his aunts poured in with their families, it turned into a pen of overstocked hens. But it was fun. From sunrise the gang of cousins created a riot in the courtyard with their games and sibling fights that ended with dinner when they had to be dragged to their beds by their ears.

However, as the years passed by, each room started becoming empty one by one when his Uncles migrated to the cities. Finally after his grandfather's demise, the only member left was his grandmother. So his father, Mr. Banerjee went back to Baharampur to live with his mother after he got his retirement. And then the house regained its former glow, at least in one of the rooms.

It was nothing less than a celebration, when Siddharth reached there at around eleven in the morning. His grandmother hugged him and shed tears of joy and made him sit on her lap. That was how she greeted everyone when meeting them after a long time.

"You weigh so less, *babu*," said his grandmother. "Are you fasting?"

"No not at all *thakuma*. In fact I have gained weight," said Siddharth. Although he sat on her lap, he did not rest his entire weight on her, fearing it would hurt her thin and aged legs. He took most of his load on his knees and feet.

"Doesn't look like it, babu. And I have a complaint for you for not getting your wife."

"*Baba* told you about it right?" asked Siddharth exchanging glances with his father. They were in sync, as far as the excuse and story was to be presented to *thakuma*.

"Yes he told me and so I am pardoning you. But next time you better get her here. Even last year you didn't get her. I don't think I can ever visit you all again in the city *babu*," she said in a feeble voice.

"Don't say that *thakuma*. You will surely be able to visit me soon. *Baba* was saying that your health has improved a lot in the last few weeks."

Satisfied with seating her grandson on her lap, she slowly got up and walked towards the bed. She was permanently bent from the waist and walked around with a long stick for support. Her face elongated and flattened, in cycles, as her toothless gums continuously worked on the betel leaf and ground areca nuts.

"Your dad always tells all that to keep me happy. Anyway, here take this," she picked up some coconut 'laddoos' she had prepared with the help of the maid.

"Oh my 'laddoos'," exclaimed Siddharth gobbling a handful in one go.

Due to the arthritic fingers she could no longer knead the raw mix of grated coconut and sugar. But once the mix was ready she was able to roll them between her palms into tiny spheres. She knew if there was anything her grandson could never say a no to it was her coconut 'laddoos'.

"When are you planning to become a father, *babu*?" she asked him suddenly.

Siddharth nearly choked on the sweet balls. "Not immediately, *thakuma*."

Mr. Banerjee passed a low chuckle.

"I don't know why you are delaying it so much?"

"It is okay *thakuma*. There is time."

"Next time if there is no news, I will talk to your wife directly."

"Okay, okay." He was lost in the rich taste of the 'laddoos'.

"How did you like them?"

"Just as always. Every time they taste better."

She laughed, contented that her grandson was happy.

"And what about my gift?" she asked, her drooping eyes widening into a sparkle.

"Here," said Siddharth, pulling out a frame from the suitcase. "This time I did not get a baby Krishna stealing butter from the pots."

She looked at the large picture framed and saw a baby Krishna drinking milk directly from the udders of a holy cow.

"Beautiful. This is so nice *babu*," she kissed his cheeks and looked at the walls, contemplating where to hang it. "But will I ever get a painting done by you again, huh?"

Mr. Banerjee was listening to his mother and son animatedly and spoke little, wishing not to break the fine conversation. Few neighbors started pouring in to greet his son. They lived there for decades and were almost like family members. Whenever Siddharth visited, they flocked together and shared stories for hours. A profusion of invitations for dinner and lunch would follow for the rest of his stay.

Finally, Mr. Banerjee looked at the clock and said, "Take your bath, *babu*."

"Yes and come back fast. Lunch will be served soon," announced his grandmother.

"I'll be back in a blink of an eye," he said tossing another 'laddoo' in his mouth.

At lunch, he stuffed himself as much as he could on the fried fish and crabs hauled from the pond. His favorite Hilsa was baked in plantain leaves and every other dish was seasoned with freshly grated coconut. The taste was unmatched and unbeatable to any other food he ate in cities. Cooked in mud-oven using jute sticks it carried a distinct smoked taste.

In the afternoon Siddharth grew restless trying to identify the trunk where he had kept Hazel's last letter and the box. As per the diary he had kept it in his mother's old trunk. He realized that in the big house it would be impossible for him to locate the right trunk, without rousing suspicion of his father and grandmother, as there were so many of them he had to pry open. So he tip-toed to his grandmother's room for help.

She was busy cutting thin slices of areca nut using a steel cutter and was chewing a freshly made *paan*. The tiny iron mortar and pestle used to grind and paste the *paan* was lying beside her.

"*Thakuma.*"

"Hmm? Did you not sleep yet, *babu*?"

"No. Can I grind some betel leaves for you?"

"If you want to. I won't need it until evening though."

He sat down on the floor and stuffed two betel leaves and a mixture of cut areca nut and sweetener into the tiny mortar and started grinding them with the pestle. As a child he had always loved to do it. Since she had lost all her teeth early she could not chew the leaves and nuts without turning them into a fine paste.

They chatted for a while about his uncles and cousins and the neighbors. Finally he told her, "Can I ask you a question?"

"*Bol na.*"

"I wanted to have a look at the trunk which has *Ma's* memories."

"Why all of a sudden?" she asked, propping herself up on the bed.

"Just feel like it. It is many years since I have even seen it."

"Okay. It will be in that room. Come."

She picked up the walking stick and slowly took him to a room that was mostly empty except for piles of iron trunks and boxes stacked on top of each other. There were rows of low wooden stools, called *pidi,* a bunch of jute mats, coconut husks and copra. She pointed at a trunk that was kept underneath two trunks.

"That one. It is not locked. Be careful when you hoist the trunks, they can be heavy."

"Sure *Thakuma.* I will be back with you soon."

"Let me know if you need anything more. I'll fall asleep the moment I lie on the bed."

Squatting on his haunches Siddharth opened the heavy iron trunk. It was over ten years since he had last opened it. The articles his mother loved were all there, the old urns, pretty dolls in dozens, picture albums, song-books, a lorgnette, a hand-fan, pashminas and colorful scarves. As he stared at the contents a tidal wave of sorrow rose inside him.

He remembered her easy love for him. The faint and incomplete memories of her loving embrace, of her warm laughter and sweet looks, touched him in gentle ripples.

Holding the objects in his hand he looked closely at them. It was as if each of them conveyed a bit of her, her beliefs, her likings and her nature. The bits collectively outlined a whole and sharpened an image that was blurred by the fog of time.

Flipping through the books of Tagore and Saratchandra, he found some of them were gifted to his mother by his father on their marriage anniversaries. He recalled his father selecting the items his mother was fond of and storing them away in the trunk. He was seven years old then.

The only other time he had opened the trunk was ten years back when he had to drop Hazel's box in it. Immersed in old memories about his mom, he became oblivious to everything else around him. He dusted every item with a piece of cloth, with care.

He also spotted many of his old painting books from his school days. He opened them one by one and flipped through them. Before he kept them back he thought of carrying them with him to Jamshedpur.

"Age has certainly brought me closer to her," he thought. While he worked through each of the objects, lifting, inspecting, dusting and keeping them back in the same way they were kept inside the trunk, he came across a white packet, wound by a thick rubber band.

That would contain all of Hazel's letters including the last one.

He quickly thrust the packet under his armpit, closed the trunk, prayed for his mom and got up. As he turned around he saw his father standing at the door watching him.

"What were you doing?" asked his father casually.

"Oh…nothing…I …was actually…going through mom's trunk just like that," he said making it sound as casual as he could.

"And dusting them too?" asked his father smiling.

"Yes. I thought they needed a bit. Were you watching me?"

"Not for a very long time. I just came by hearing the creaking of the iron trunk." He walked in and took a look at the trunk and said, "I have not opened it for a long time myself."

"*Baba* do you still miss her?" he asked walking over to his father.

"You can never really forget someone who was that close to you. Can you?"

"Never." He thought about his mom and then about Hazel.

"She was a great woman," said his father staring at the closed trunk.

"Yes, she was."

"Leave all that *babu*. How about some tea?"

"Sure."

"Then come to the verandah. I will meet you there in ten minutes."

After tea Siddharth planned to take a walk nearby. As he circled the houses adjacent to theirs, he reached a bunch of berry trees and a bamboo thicket few feet away from the edge of the pond. Two large jack-fruits trees towered on his left. The thick roots of the berry tree jutted above the ground and he sat on them under the bosky shade. Picking and plopping fallen berries and stones into the pond, he watched the ripples smoothen.

Then he brought out the packet and tore the seal and pulled out the last letter from the bunch of letters.

The pond was serene. A flock of ducks came paddling and quacking and as soon as they spotted Siddharth they glided away in the reverse direction. A school of fishes broke the surface of water like drops of a drizzle and vanished under the water hyacinths.

He began reading the last letter once again after fifteen years.

"Dear Sidd

This is a voice from your past. I had hoped that our paths would cross again some way or the other but I have come to believe that it no longer will.

Although I don't live in Jamshedpur anymore, our school, the temple, the stadium, the market place and the town we spent time together, keep coming back to me. I always hoped, some morning when I open my eyes, you will stand in front of me. But it never happens.

The lake, the forest areas and the hills on the outskirts of Jamshedpur, the very places that I loved, are fading away. I am learning to live without them, without you.

However Sidd there are some things you need to know about me, which is hidden from the world. There are reasons why I could not connect with you earlier. This letter is not the right means to tell. There may be a right way or a better way of doing this but at this time I can think of none other than the below.

I am enclosing a small box with this letter. **It contains the Key to my Soul.**

The key in the box is of a Locker. I own that Locker in SSBI bank in Jamshedpur. The number is 873. I have added your name as a joint holder of the locker along with me. I have the original key and now you have the duplicate.

You will know how my days went after the axe of fate had split us apart.

In your thoughts. Hazel."

When he had read the letter for the first time and then ten times the same day, he found it strange that there was no box with the letter. Reading it after so many years, it struck him hard again on why the box was missing. It puzzled him.

Then he told himself, "It must be referring to the box and key that Shane gave me at the hospital. I wonder who the guy actually is who gave it to Shane? And assuming it is the nameless caller who gave it to Shane, how did the key reach the caller in the first place?"

After reading the letter again he was also filled with a sense of loss and sadness. The words made more sense now than he made of them fifteen years back when he was still in college. The short note disturbed him, especially the last line.

When he stepped into college in 1991, having got separated from Hazel, he felt as if one of his limbs had been amputated. The new life was oppressing to deal with. The revolting canteen food, the strangers he had to share his hostel room with, ragging by seniors, nagging by a humorless warden, hard discipline and the sudden ejection from a protected life.

Like all the students he too had landed there without a clear goal in life.

But soon the hostel-life sucked him into its unique churn. The very things he hated later endeared him. For he found means to shroud his dislike and his past. By making friends to roll over the crisis of loneliness, smoking pot, drowning his angst in rock songs of G'n'R, Pink Floyd, Eagles, in excursions, in cultural fests. He went easy on studies, easy on life.

But, with all of this, the anchor of his soul was lost. The motive to paint.

With a single sweep, fate had tossed away the only coin of true love he had, with Hazel embossed on one side and his enormous gift of painting on the other.

Couple of times he tried to sketch her face but gave up even before he reached mid-way. After that he rarely picked up a pencil to sketch or a painting brush again.

To ignore the stubborn memories of Hazel that came crashing like waves from time to time he had forced himself to believe that she was no longer a part of his life. He wanted to live life and not face a death-like void that life was fetching him in daily installments. Though he had stamped out his feelings for her slowly, he could not forget her.

And then he got a letter from Dimple. It was a few months after the shocking series of bombings in Bombay in 1993. He was in his third year in college. Dimple was studying Economics, in Fergusson, Pune. The news blew him to bits like a bomb-blast. It said:

Hello Sidd (Painter Babu),

Trust you are doing fine. I am sorry for dropping a letter after six months. How time flies. Can you imagine so many years have already gone by since we joined college?

Recently Jennifer dropped her first letter to me ever. You may not know, that she and her family had moved to Australia soon after we entered college. Even I did not know until now. That explains why she never responded to my initial letters to her.

*I got her second letter yesterday and with it some shocking news about Hazel. I thought it best to let you know about it. Jennifer mentioned that Hazel has decided to be a **Religious Sister** and lead a life of obedience, poverty and chastity.*

It sounds odd but even Jennifer doesn't know the reasons.

This news was relayed by Hazel's mom to her close relatives and Jennifer learnt about it, through their family network. But there is still no news of where Hazel and her mom live. They are not revealing that yet.

Take good care of yourself Siddharth and make sure that you hold yourself tight and strong even if the wind blows against you.
.............."

The sudden update from Dimple re-opened his tenderness for Hazel. It provoked his guilt and prodded old wounds. He considered himself the reason behind her unnatural desire to become a Religious Sister.

At the same time, he was unable to accept her decision to lead a life of celibacy and break all ties with him. He felt helpless and angry. Every time he thought of her he was invaded with thoughts of betrayal and injustice. He was unable to love her or hate her and certainly unable to forget her. He smoked pot and sometimes drank codeine to forget her.

It was exactly a year later, during his final year in college, while he was watching the repeat telecast of the Miss Universe Show with his friends in the hostel common room, when he had received the last letter from Hazel.

The boys sat huddled near the television. They ogled at the visuals, of what was preserved so long underneath clothes, of what was considered private, made public so suddenly, so boldly, so flamboyantly.

Sushmita Sen had won the crown that year and an argument had started over it.

A few students from Palestine, on scholarships, were

bantering the others in the room.

"All this is an eye wash friends," said a Palestinian student.

"What do you mean?" asked an Indian student.

"The cosmetic industry want their products to have a bigger market. So they chose a winner from India this time. Next year it will be another country," said the Palestinian friend. "This is only a business gimmick. Don't you guys understand?"

Some of the Indian students, who found pride in the achievement, took offence.

"They are jealous because India is doing well," whispered a few Indian students.

It was in the middle of the altercation the postman announced a courier for Siddharth from the stairs that had the last letter from Hazel.

Right after finishing college he had a month in between before joining GrindGood Company in Bombay. As his father was in the USA at that time, he had come to Baharampur to keep few of his belongings, along with the letters.

He never visited Jamshedpur, not only because he vowed never to go there again but also for losing the only anchor in the town, his father who no longer lived there. Then he got busy with his job in Bombay, frequent tours in other cities and finally got bound by marriage. It was also true that the letter and the missing key had vanished from his mind.

He spent the rest of the evening, plucking and tasting ripe berries, breaking bamboo branches and beating the blue water gently with them, until the sky banished the sun and slipped into its black night gown.

The two days went by quickly. But he did not tell about

Hazel's tragic accident to his dad. In the company of his doting father and grandmother he felt much relaxed. His neighbors often saw him sitting by the pond, immersed in thoughts, in the tranquility of the surroundings, amidst the coconut, jackfruit, jute, mango, guava and berry trees and the blue enchanting skies that seemed to always have a colony of birds flying freely. Little did they know, that he was constantly abraded by thoughts about Hazel and her tragic condition.

The night before he left, in a conversation, his father spoke about his old passions.

"Did you pick up the paintbrush again, *babu*?"

"No."

"You have god's gift with you," said Mr. Banerjee. "You must not stop painting."

"I don't feel like doing it anymore."

"Don't just leave it. Try to paint occasionally, at least." Mr. Banerjee knew the reason well enough on why his son's interest had faded away.

"I still love reading poetry though."

"That is good too. Who do you read these days?"

"Mostly Indian poets." He thrust his hands into a bag and fished out the new books. "My colleague, Mukund, gave these poetry books by Rabindra Swain and Indra. He said that he had read about them somewhere and thought of gifting them to me. But I haven't had the time to browse them yet. Maybe one of these days I will. Have you heard of them?"

"No." Mr. Banerjee nodded his head.

"You can try reading them as well."

"Hmm. Oh by the way I forgot to ask you, what time is your train tomorrow?"

"Afternoon. But actually I am going back to Jamshedpur."

"Why. You just came from there."

"True *Baba*. But there is some urgent work. You know the usual sales stuff."

"Hmm. And is there any news from Kiran or her family?"

"No. They don't bother."

"Did you reach out to them anytime?"

"No. But I am being fleeced all the same. I am thinking of changing my lawyer."

"The law and its lecherous ways," said his father sarcastically. "Don't take it too hard on you, *babu*. You have done all you could to save your marriage. But they are trying to drag this for too long. There must be some way out."

The same night he also brought out the starting points of his intimacy with Hazel – a bunch of his old painting books she had seen and admired. He had seen them in the trunk. Secretly he desired to be appreciated all over again for his paintings by Hazel like he used to be in school. The same anticipation filled within him. He wanted to give them to Hazel. But for that she had to open her eyes. She had to survive the blow she received by the cruel hammer of fate. So he prayed for her in the prayer room so that she comes out of the coma.

To place the painting books in his bag, he removed the poetry books that Mukund had gifted him, hoping to put them back once all his art books, clothes and shoes were stuffed in properly. But later, somehow he forgot to put back the poetry books in his bag. They lay in a shelf near his bed until Mr. Banerjee spotted them a day later. But by that time he had already left for Jamshedpur.

Chapter 11

KIRAN AND
THE BASKET OF MANGOES

The journey back to Jamshedpur from Baharampur was a long one. As the train cruised the countryside, it was not the landscape but the image of Hazel in the ventilator that flashed across. Siddharth wondered if Hazel's condition had improved. He shunned the thoughts that crept in time and again of hearing a tragic news. Intentionally, he avoided calling Shane to find out about her health. No news was a better gamble than a bad one.

Instead, he thought about the letters, what they contained. Why was the key missing along with the last letter she had sent him? How did the nameless caller got the key? At the same time his guilt of never making a serious attempt to meet Hazel in the past, kept bothering him, almost hurting him. The pain grew in intensity as the wheels brought him nearer to his childhood hometown, closer to his bedridden old beloved, closer to a reality whose uncertain possibilities he wasn't sure how to face.

Towards the end of the journey something else was also trying to tear into his thoughts. It was the conversation he had had with his father the previous night about his wife, Kiran, who had deserted him four years back. And then at one point, when the train was gathering speed and swaying like a cradle, he dozed off. Hazel's childish face blurred and faded away and got replaced by Kiran's.

The first time he met her, it was in a train for six minutes. It was a unique incident. Kiran was travelling with her parents from Kolkata to the Puri sea beach, on the Orissa coast, for a short vacation. They planned to meet him on the way as he lived just one station before Puri. A few days before the meeting, his father rang up Kiran's father from Detroit, USA.

"Thank you for your detailed email Mr. Bose," said Mr. Banerjee.

"It is my pleasure Banerjee babu. Actually our travel to Puri was pre-planned. I thought of writing an email to you beforehand and check if you'd be okay for us to meet your son on the way," said Mr. Bose.

"That's a great idea. Your daughter and my son can meet and decide if they connect well," laughed Mr. Banerjee.

"Ha. Ha. Yes in this age both girl and boy must meet and be satisfied before getting married. It's no more like how it used to be in our times," supported Mr. Bose and chuckled.

"Mr. Bose, I will inform my son to meet you at the station."

"Excellent. Thank you Banerjee Babu."

"Can you please send me the details of the coach number, the seat number, date and time of travel? So it will be easier for him to locate you."

"Sure, sure. I'll email it. It would have been great to meet you as well."

"I am sorry I cannot be present there Mr. Bose. Being so far away from my country makes it so difficult."

"Oh don't worry Banerjee Babu. I understand. It is still good that we could connect through the newspaper matrimonial. And lucky that your son is not with you in US, otherwise the meeting would have been quite impossible, I guess."

"True, true! Alright then, I'll inform my son. Enjoy your trip to Puri Mr. Bose and hope things turn out well."

"Thank you Banerjee Babu. I too hope that things turn out well. Goodbye."

Siddharth had met Kiran on the insistence of his father. Mr. Banerjee knew about the turmoil in his son's life and wanted to help his son move on. So right after Siddharth completed college and joined his first job in Bombay, Mr. Banerjee had started searching the Indian matrimonial columns through his relatives, although he was in Detroit, USA.

He knew only love could replace love. And only the wave of fresh love could wash away the sad debris of lost love. After a year or so of Siddharth joining his first job, he started hinting about marriage and regularly spoke to his son from Detroit.

"Son, we have to eventually settle down in life. It is right time for you to start thinking about sharing your life with someone."

"What are you proposing, *baba?*"

"Nothing unusual. I was hoping to see you get married soon," said Mr. Banerjee.

"What? It's just one year since I am into this job. I am not ready."

"I am not asking you to do anything now. Just to start thinking about it."

"What's the hurry?"

"No hurries," bluffed Mr. Banerjee. "Eventually it will happen, so thinking about it will not kill or harm anyone. It takes time to eventually find a compatible partner. And think of *thakuma*, how thrilled she'll be to see her grandson's wedding in her lifetime."

Though Siddharth was unconvinced, he could not argue too much with his father as Mr. Banerjee did not pressurize him in any way. It was a casual request.

Or at least Mr. Banerjee intentionally made it sound casual, so as not to incite his son's resistance. After two years, with many such discussions, Siddharth finally gave a nod.

Actually, in the end, his granny nailed him, "Your dad has spent most of his life without your mom. Think of how happy he will be when you have a child. Only a newborn's giggles can fill a lonely man's heart with infinite joy."

And then Mr. Banerjee started razing all the matrimonial columns in leading dailies and came across Kiran and her family.

The day when Siddharth met Kiran for the first time, it was quite windy. He was waiting eagerly at the railway station platform for the train to arrive. Wearing a white T-Shirt, blue Jeans and sneakers he looked calm and casual. The pictures he had seen of Kiran and her short bio-data, along with the information about her family and lineage, appealed to him.

He kept his right hand behind his back all the time. It had a poetry book.

As the train slowed down his heartbeat quickened. He saw an elderly man craning his neck from the door of the coach where Kiran and her family were supposed to be in. As the train came to a halt, the man jumped out and smiled at him.

"Siddharth?" asked the man, trying to confirm his conjecture.

"Yes Uncle I am Siddharth." He quickly passed the book he

held in his right hand to his left and shook hands.

"Excellent. Actually I recognized you by your pictures I had seen." Mr. Bose shook hands. "Please come inside quickly son. I guess the train won't stop here for long."

"Yes Uncle, it stops here only for six minutes."

"Excellent."

Inside the coach, Kiran and her mother were waiting, a little more decked up than normally people would be, while travelling in a train.

"Hello *kakima*," said Siddharth addressing Kiran's mom and then he smiled at Kiran.

"Hi," said Kiran sweetly.

"Please sit down son," said her mother pointing towards Kiran's right.

As he was about to sit Kiran's father intervened, "Sit here. Sit here. This side," he said indicating the seat in front of Kiran. Siddharth chuckled as he switched sides and sat in front of Kiran. They both smiled at each other.

"Have you ever visited Puri earlier?" asked Siddharth.

"Oh several times," said Mr. Bose. "You must have been there yourself, correct?"

"Plenty of times. It is so close to Bhubaneswar. And the sea beach is so tempting."

"True."

Although Kiran appeared shy and was unable to talk freely, her parents noticed the instant approval in her eyes for Siddharth. Slim and dusky with interesting features her smile was hypnotic. She had a retroussé nose that made her look unconventional. Her hair was curly and shoulder length and she wore a blue silk scarf as a headband that revealed a neat forehead. Siddharth was relieved to find that the pictures had not given an exaggerated view of her looks, in fact they had hidden a great deal.

"I heard that you are a good singer. Did you learn music?" asked Siddharth.

"Yes. Hindustani classical. I have completed till the eighth grade," replied Kiran.

"She is a very good singer," added Kiran's mother.

"And how far did you study?" asked Siddharth although he knew it from her bio-data.

"I completed Bachelors in Computer Science."

"She was working and recently left her job. We made her quit," said Kiran's mother.

"Why," asked Siddharth.

"She was losing her skin tone and becoming so thin. There is no point of working so hard if you lose your health. But I told her to first settle down and only a year or two after marriage she can look for a job, if she wants to. Not before that," added Kiran's mother.

"Son, since how long have you been in this city?" asked Kiran's father.

"About three years Uncle."

"Excellent. Do you like the place?"

"Yes Uncle. It is a quiet city and there are a lot of interesting places to visit from here like Puri, Konark, Gopalpur sea beach and numerous temples in the city. Even the movie tickets come very cheap."

"Excellent," said Kiran's father.

"Do you watch movies," asked Kiran's mother.

"I do every week. There are quite a few decent theatres here."

"And how do you manage your food?" asked Kiran's mother.

"We use a tiffin service," replied Siddharth. "Sometimes I cook, *kakima*."

"Really. How did you learn?" asked Kiran's mother surprised.

"I learnt few items from dad first and then added on to the list by experimenting."

"Excellent," said Kiran's father. "I myself cannot make anything except tea."

"What about you? Do you like to cook?" asked Siddharth smiling at Kiran.

"Yes I can manage," she replied blushing.

"Oh she does it quite well. All my sisters praise her for it," said her mother.

"How long will you be in Puri?"

"About five days. The sea is so beautiful and relaxing there. One feels like staying there forever. But we all have to return to our nests, isn't it?" said Kiran's father.

"Yes that is correct Uncle."

The taut air of formality was just about loosening when the thread of conversation snapped abruptly with the jolt of the coach. The engine had tugged forward.

"You must leave son, the train is moving," said Kiran's father. "We had the pleasure of meeting you. God bless you. I will speak to you father. Here take this. Just a token of love from our side." He handed a basket full of luscious mangoes and dry fruits packed with thin plastic.

"Thank you. And I got this poetry book for Kiran. I hope you like it." He quickly handed the book to her and they smiled at each other. Then he hurried towards the exit and jumped off the moving train, holding the basket of mangoes in one hand and waving at Kiran who was waving her hands, and her parents with the other.

Kiran stared at him through the window till he was reduced to a blur. Her eyes had met their match.

Chapter 12

HONEYMOON

"A honeymoon must be like a block-buster hit."

Mukund Iyer, a deeply introspective person, was Siddharth's closest colleague in office. With an unusual command over Shakespeare and a self-taught admirer of Jungian psychology, his erudition endeared him to many. Although he was like the reserved types, a pitcher of beer set his tongue loose. Psychology, Shakespeare and even accounts of the most private parts of his life would tumble down his mouth.

Mukund was five years into the company when Siddharth joined as a trainee and they developed an instant liking for each other. On Friday nights they paired up at pubs.

"Honeymoon is the key to a special lock called wedlock. If you turn it right then you enter the bedroom of a happy married life. Like me." He thumped his chest. "But Chief, believe me, if you fail to turn it properly then it will lead to a different room. The restroom. Restroom of woes."

The beer pitcher on the table was empty and he ordered for a refill.

"I am sure your tip will be valuable," said Siddharth. At that time he had just joined GrindGood Company and was learning to be patient with his drunk senior at the pub.

"Chief, it is just a tip of the iceberg. My experience is deeper. Honeymoon has to be played and savored as if the end of the world is near. As I said, a honeymoon must be like a block-buster hit. You must keep a minimum of five nights for it. The longer the better."

"Five nights? Why?"

"Because that's the only time when couples are ignorant of each other. Simple."

"Ignorant?" asked Siddharth puzzled.

"Yes. The less you know of someone, the better you feel about the person. It is the only time in your marital life when a genuine grin will show on your face. Trust me Chief."

Siddharth laughed. But Mukund was not joking, he was dead serious. The beer in the pub had unlocked him. There was no stopping. His bleary eyes shone under the strobe lights.

"You need to keep two things in mind for your honeymoon. First, never choose a hot place. Heat destroys determination. It defeats purpose. That's why the Americans and Russians are ahead of us. They live in cold places. Choose a cold place. The colder the better. Second important thing is planning."

"Planning?"

"Yes Chief, honeymoon requires meticulous planning. Else it will be like a picnic. You eat and play silly games and return without achieving anything. It's all about planning."

The wedding was grand. December 1998.

The planning for the honeymoon was actually done by Kiran. Before the wedding Siddharth and Kiran had met few times in Kolkata and discussed about their honeymoon location. Katmandu in Nepal was dropped because of the political turmoil there. The other option proposed by Siddharth, Dalhousie in Himachal, was rejected too because it would involve a lot of travel time. Finally she decided on Lachung, near Gangtok in Sikkim for its proximity to Kolkata.

Five nights, five days. In the coldest of cold places. In peak winter.

And so they started on their maiden voyage together without the lingering presence of anyone else, dreaming, fantasizing about locked desires that always craved escape.

At the hotel lobby in Lachung, an attractive receptionist presented them with two complementary bottles of brandy, a small memento and electronic room keys. She escorted them to a large well-furnished room that dazzled with the shimmer of satin and velvet all around. Two red roses lay snugly in between two pillows on the bed.

Before undressing, to keep herself warm, Kiran drank most of the brandy in one go. Siddharth washed, sprayed cologne all over his body and put on fresh clothes. As he was combing his hair, facing the mirror, Kiran started complaining.

"My head is spinning. I can hardly stand."

"You need rest. It must be the travel fatigue." He told her looking at the mirror.

"I think I need to lie down." So he helped her lie on the bed.

She did not know that it was the brandy that made her tipsy. She drank it like water. Until that day she had stayed away from alcohol. Neither did Siddharth realize the real reason for he too was not a habitual drinker and unlike his friends who tanked at every other party, he merely took perfunctory sips to provide company.

"The first night is the most significant night. The keyword is restraint. It's easy to jump and hump all about, but you must hold on to civility and gentlemanliness. You must not frighten the poor girl. Go slow, go easy." Mukund had told him in the pub.

But for Siddharth the first night was like any other. His mounting eagerness was nipped in the bud as he watched his newly wed wife collapse beside him in slumber, drunk.

The second day was well spent, touring historical sites and looking at the breathtaking views of the hilly terrain, the snow-covered mountain peaks, the pine trees and polished boulders along speeding streams and rivulets. They had hired a jeep for the daylong tour.

At one point they saw a snow covered hillock, white and smooth like candy floss. They decided to slide on its slopes. So off they went holding hands, rolling over one another to the bottom, the cold searing their eyes. They laughed and canoodled. Then they clambered up the hillock and again slid and rolled and kissed. The sequence was repeated at least ten times, until the bored jeep driver asked them if they had any other plans for the day.

They felt happy that finally their honeymoon had taken the right turn.

In the evening, a bon fire was lit up in the Hotel backyard. An old Hindi song was playing out of a radio. The guests sat around the bon-fire in a circle, singing and sipping the local cereal based drink called 'Chaang' out of a bamboo container with a bamboo straw.

"Looks exciting stuff," said Siddharth looking at others swigging merrily. Fascinated with the novelty of a bamboo straw and a bamboo container he refilled it multiple times.

"You are not used to it. Don't drink too much dear," warned Kiran. She avoided the drink based on the effect the brandy had on her the previous night.

But he ignored her words. He glugged it like a child

charmed with a new beverage. And then in no time he threw up, some of which went straight into the bon-fire and doused a few burning sticks.

"I told you not to over indulge, but you did not listen to me," cried Kiran.

He vomited some more.

Taking his load on her shoulders, she helped him walk over to their room. She laid her hubby on the bed exactly the way he had helped her the previous night.

Siddharth's ears were echoing Mukund's advice as he started dozing off. "The second night is one of celebration. The keyword is freedom. Of the body. You become free to unlock the flood-gates without fear of looking clumsy or scary. So let the night roll with you."

But the second night proved to be equally disastrous. In no time, vanquished by a local drink, he was snoring. Kiran forced herself to sleep without proper dinner, patiently enduring his sudden snores that startled her at times in the dead of the night.

The third day onwards there were repeated power failures. The lights came up just for a few hours each day. The tiny electric room heater turned into a useless showpiece. Due to the high altitude and cold, Siddharth developed flatulence and consequently lost his appetite.

"Let's get out of this cold storage," she told him in the morning.

So they went sightseeing in the jeep. Sunshine flooded the hills that day.

Down the hills, in one place, they located a patch of grassy area that was not covered with snow and was flanked with deodar trees all around. As soon as they reached there, they kissed reflexively and he could not resist fondling her breasts.

"If that damn room is jinxed, we will utilize this place," he whispered.

"Yes, at least this is warmer than the freezing hotel room."

"This is the moment we came here for. At last."

She burst out laughing at his words but he silenced her with his lips, swallowing the rich red lipstick. She tightened her grip around his waist and brought him closer to her. The cold did not stop them from removing their leather jackets, woolens and the shirt until the flesh was covered just by thermals. Then placing his palms over her buttocks, he lifted her so her face was at the same level as his. She crushed his mouth with hers.

And then as suddenly as they had started it all, she shrieked and fell to the ground.

"Look," she screamed and pointed behind him.

Siddharth turned around and shouted in shock, "Run."

They sprinted towards the jeep, shivering, half-dressed, holding the jackets and woolens in hand. The driver was looking at them with mirth and chewing the end of a twig. Cursing, they jumped into the vehicle barely managing to slip into the outer garments. As the jeep passed by the wooded patch, they saw the two black, bulky, furry, horned animals standing close together in the same place they were hoping to gain a worthy time.

"Deadly. They looked like phantoms out of nowhere," cried out Siddharth.

"What are those?"

"I have no idea."

"Do you know what those are?" Kiran asked the driver, shivering.

"Yaks," said the driver grinning.

Warm in their furry coats the yaks stared at them while they trembled in fear, the chatter still loud and prominent in their teeth.

Back at the hotel the electricity played hide and seek. They had to spend their nights tucked inside layers of blankets, in spite of the woolen sweaters and jackets. The cold had become merciless.

The grand plans of experiencing romantic conversations and exploring each other had to be abandoned. Mukund's words rang continuously in his mind.

"The third night is the night of imagination. The keyword is choice. You choose the positions and the place, the bed or the floor, the bathroom or the balcony, terrace or tree. The more bizarre the choice the more the thrill multiplies."

After saying this Mukund had brought down the beer-mug on the table with a bang, as if he had said all he had to say and all that was there to say on the topic of honeymoon.

However, in the hotel on the hills of Lachung, the five nights were more like an ordeal to be done away with quickly rather than savoring it. Every night they waited for the night to end and the sun to rise. The notion of honeymoon as an endless romantic dream was shaken if not shattered.

The expert advice from Mukund was not weather-proof. In the end, Siddharth rued, "How expensive can a trip be. We come all the way here only to earn a few kisses."

Apart from her beautiful voice as a singer Kiran had expert hands of a cook. Siddharth noticed it a week after they were back from their honeymoon. He was away on a two day tour to Rourkela Steel plant. When he was back at noon, he was surprised with what he saw.

Kiran was at the door, dressed in a green silk sari bordered in red, with her face touched-up and her hair decked with strings of fresh jasmine. She flashed a big smile at him.

"Welcome back dear," said Kiran holding his hands.

After he removed his shoes and dropped his bags, she stood on his feet with her entire weight, hugging him while he slowly moved around the drawing room with her, embracing and kissing her. They wouldn't let go of one another.

When he stopped walking, she said, "Walk some more. It feels good to get a foot ride like this." So he walked some more.

"Finally I am back with you. The two days were like two years."

"Same here. How was your trip?" asked Kiran.

"Bad and boring without you. Are we going out?" he asked.

"No. Why do you ask?"

"You look dressed to go out."

"So you've noticed. I thought men are blind to such changes. But we are not going anywhere." she said twisting her lips into a mischievous smile.

"Something is brewing inside your head? Huh? What's the story?"

Kiran stepped off his feet and helped him unbutton his shirt. Then she whispered and crooned such sounds into his ears that made him squirm.

"The Geyser is on for your hot shower. The towels are on the rack where you keep them. Your bathrobe is on the hook and fresh clothes are laid out on the bed."

"Whoa. How did you know about these things?"

"I know your habits by heart, dear. Now go and come out fast." She pushed him into the bathroom and went to the next room to fetch a bunch of tuberose stalks.

After the shower, once he was all dry and powdered up, he slipped into the pajamas and a T-Shirt kept on the bed and went straight to the drawing room. Kiran was already sitting on the couch smiling and ready with her battery of questions.

"So how did you find Rourkela?" she asked him.

"It was hectic and I kept missing you."

"Next time you must take me wherever you go okay," she said seriously.

"I'd love to. But you know it is an official trip so..."

"I don't know all that. You must take me along. Staying without you was horrible."

"Okay. Okay. I'll try," he said laughing. "Next time I'll try to club my tour with some place of travel."

"Did you visit any fun places in Rourkela?"

"Plenty. I was inside the plant the entire day and had meetings. At night I walked up to the nearest restaurant for dinner. Those were the fun places I visited. Happy?"

"Actually, I love travelling. In fact, as a kid I travelled across India with my parents and dreamt of traveling abroad. Doesn't your company send you to those places?"

"Rarely. Sometimes to France as the headquarters are there."

"So what is your work like with grinding wheels?" asked Kiran.

He explained the business his company was in. And before she could ask another question he said, "Hey let's talk more later on. I am hungry. Shall we order something?"

"Go ahead. The waitress is by your side."

"Meaning?"

"From now on I will take your meal orders sir."

"Did you cook today Kiran?" said Siddharth laughing.

"Yes. We had enough of the so called Chinese and Continental food. No more."

"That's really awesome. It is indeed a special day. Actually I thought the aroma is from our neighbor's kitchen."

"It is from our kitchen, you stupid," she pinched him.

They laughed and went towards the dining room hand-in-hand. The moment he saw the spread of dishes on the dining table, his eyes popped out.

There was steamed Hilsa fish, fried Chicken, long strips of eggplant fry coated with sesame seeds, sautéed mixed vegetables, Moong daal with a strong seasoning of fried cumin seeds and dry chili in oil, rice, green salad and a smattering of sweetened tomato chutney. The aroma of Moong daal seasoning was all around the house.

His gustatory senses were rarely so stimulated, except when the cooking was done by his grandmother. At the table he behaved like a cat, lapping up everything as a cat would from a saucer of milk. It was either years of starvation since he joined college, or lack of fine cooking, that made him look like an unfed animal. He made such sounds while eating that it distracted Kiran.

Kiran ate modestly like a lady and watched her husband with satisfaction. And why not? She saw his cheeks remain swollen throughout, as he kept stuffing his mouth with more food than it could hold at a time.

"There is magic in your hands," he said at last, licking his fingers.

"You make lot of noise while eating. But I will take it as a compliment. Don't chew off your fingers though."

"*Thakuma* would be very proud if she ever ate this."

"Thank you dear."

"How did you learn to cook so well?"

"Mostly from mom."

"Hmm. Looks like it wasn't an unsound decision to marry an engineer who also knows cooking," he said nibbling at the last grain of rice.

They quickly cleared the table and stacked the plates and bowls in the kitchen sink. The maid would arrive shortly to clean them.

After a sumptuous meal, the path of least resistance is the path to the bed. And when it is covered with satin sheets and strewn with tuberose flowers, the pull is gravitational, the allure heady. Siddharth hopped on it and waited, inhaling the scent of the flowers, running his hands over the smoothness of the satin cushions. A smile of content flashed across his face.

Minutes later Kiran stepped inside and closed the bedroom door behind her. She raised her arms and jingled her armful of glass bangles and biting her lips looked at him like a restless she-wolf.

Chapter 13

THE KNOT BREAKS

Two years into their marriage, life had changed somewhat.

An IT company had advertised for a walk-in interview in the newspaper. She had appeared for it and found herself a job as a software programmer. The pay and the possibility of travelling abroad in near future tempted her.

The equilibrium of the house had started to alter. Yet for two years it went fine until Kiran was asked to travel to USA for project work. Siddharth's initial excitement waned when he heard that she would be away for three months.

She failed to read his wavering mind for it was an unusual opportunity for her. At one point when he refused to let her go she lost her cool. But he cuddled her. They argued and she wept. Then they made love. And that way the advancing crisis was clipped.

Finally she went. But she came back after six months as her assignment got extended.

When she came back he could hardly recognize her. The black curly hair was straightened and brown and longer than he had ever seen her grow it. The make-up, the dress, the sunglasses, the handbag and other accessories reflected a style that seemed alien and demanding legitimacy. A decisive boldness settled on her face and expressions that almost hinged on arrogance. It showed when she spoke to cab drivers, to vegetable vendors, to the milkman, the maidservant, to her neighbors.

Six months later, when she was asked to visit the US the second time, she was thrilled and agreed to it without discussing with her husband. She asked her company to process her spouse visa as well. But Siddharth disagreed to travel with her.

"Why not?" she asked.

"What will I do there? Just sit idle without a job?"

"So what. Once there you will find one. Everyone is travelling to USA these days."

"True. But it is mostly people in IT who are going."

"You can also try and change your job. It is a matter of few months."

Although during those days hordes of engineers were joining IT, many switching over from unrelated professions, her insistence did not have the desired effect on him.

"I don't want to change my job. Computer work doesn't fascinate me."

She tried to persuade him and show him the life that was waiting to be lost. She stated her dreams of settling abroad with him. But he was adamant. It was her dream, not his.

"You can at least go for a vacation with me and see the places yourself."

"You know I have been to the US few times already when dad was there."

"So are you saying you will not come with me?"

"All I am saying is that I don't want to switch my job. I can go there for a month at a stretch but not more. You go ahead, if that is so important for you."

The talk ended abruptly. She saw a taunt, a challenge in last line. They spoke on the same topic night after night and ended their conversation in the same way. Their differences widened, but not without rousing the interest of their neighbors. Few of them overheard their arguments and inched closer to their windows.

One night as she was putting away his office shirt in the laundry basket something caught her eye. Few strands of hair. They were long. But not hers as they were longer. She stared at them at length and was unable to dismiss her thoughts about them.

Then she remembered what she had seen in the second year of marriage in an old bag. It had surprised her that she was kept in the dark. In fact it hurt her. But she never told him what she saw. Instead she placed indirect questions like, "Did you ever have a girlfriend? Did you have any breakups just before we married?" Siddharth had negated all her questions. That made her weave hair-thin threads of doubt into a tiny ball of suspicion.

But when she saw the strand of hair on his shirt, the ball grew in size as did her temper. Yet she did not open her mouth. Instead she chose to dwell on it and use the deliberate flame of rage to blacksmith her ambition further.

There were other reasons that kept stoking her inflamed mind. Books, she had observed, frequently snatched him away from her. His silly poetry books. The respect and love they commanded over him, sometimes, made her feel tiny in comparison. And the baby he had been hinting at often made her lose sleep.

And what about her dreams? Of settling abroad, of travelling to countries, going on long drives on the spectacular highways in the US, basking in their progress, the easy living, the flashy cars, the glittering malls. There was no other profession that could carry her as far and as easily to those places. Compared to the cities she had seen there, Bhubaneswar appeared dull and antiquated and downright rural.

At the same time, she couldn't understand the utter lack of ambition in her husband and his refusal to join a profession that most of their friends and Indians were switching over to. She became stroppy. The slow fire of discord was raging to be a firestorm.

Time passed by quickly and she was under official pressure to travel or decline the offer. Some days she looked out of the office window and compared her life to a piece of cloth gathering creases that would soon turn into a rag. Her belief slowly hardened. She asked herself, "Why should a woman compromise all the time. What about my desire and my dreams. Where is the place for me to put to use what I learnt? Why should the kitchen be the default option for a woman?"

She also debated, "At least let me go there and utilize the opportunity. Worst case I can still return once the project or the visa gets over and pick up the threads of my life here."

She left once again. Alone.

Apart from his lack of interest to switch his profession, Siddharth never told her the real other reason why he did not want to relocate abroad. His father had returned from USA to be with his grandmother and a certain sense told him not to wander away from them ever.

And Kiran never told him what she had seen when she was cleaning the house one day. An old bag with a brown diary that had pages of hand written poems and few love letters wedged in between them from someone called Hazel.

After she left, the nails of loneliness pierced him. In the bath he would often get lost in the splashing sounds of tap water, oblivious to the overflowing bucket. He remained immersed in her thoughts and pined for her and kept wishing she would be back soon. He dreamt of waiting in the railway station holding a flower for her. The same station where he had met her the first time holding a book.

Initially, they spoke over the phone frequently. But slowly the calls reduced to once weekly and then once monthly and then hardly any. That he did not matter to her anymore dawned on him only after the telephone stopped ringing altogether.

Kiran's parents too were disturbed by the change of events. Whenever he spoke to them he could feel sympathy in their voice and helplessness. Eventually, even they stopped responding to his phone calls.

Two years into this hiatus, still hopeful that Kiran would come back, when he learnt that she was at her parent's house in Kolkata for vacation, he decided to go meet her. He carried a box of 'coconut laddoos' that his grandmother had recently parceled and a novel, 'Fathers and Sons' by the Russian writer Ivan Turgenev.

After a short train journey, he took a taxi to his in-laws house. But a big lock dangling on the front door drained his spirit. Even the windows of the three-storied house were shut.

"The whole family has left for the hills. They won't be back until after two or three weeks," said a neighbor.

With the packet of sweets in one hand and Turgenev's book in the other, he stood there unable to contain the rising ocean of sorrow in his heart, unable to stop his left hand from twitching. He left the book and the packet of sweets with a note at the doorstep.

Then he looked at the busy street unsure how to face his life ahead and made no attempt to hold back the rush of emptiness streaming down his eyes.

Travelling back home in the evening train, he thought about his mother, the faint recollections of her soft hands stroking his cheeks and her lullabies. He yearned for her presence, for her unconditional love and selflessness.

When he heard about Kiran last, she had joined a startup company in California and was chasing the American dream. Another year passed before he finally filed the divorce papers. That evening he walked on the streets aimlessly and then into an open field absent-mindedly stepping into a large puddle that soiled his pants. He picked stones and tossed them at the sun until his hands ached.

When the moon came up few hours later, he was silently trudging back home, dragging his feet and the draggled jeans, his hands and shoulders drooping like broken branches of a tree and the eyes holding the look of a fire-pit that had just perished.

Chapter 14

HAZEL STILL IN COMA

Right before the ICU there was a familiar gathering of Aunt Mary and two other relatives. They were wearing heavy sweaters and gloves. Aunt Mary wore a woolen scarf covering her head and ears. A team of doctors doing rounds, were looking at reports and offering explanations. It was about nine in the morning.

One of the doctors said, "Since it was a case of diffused hemorrhage and edema, we have done repeat examinations for the last several days on how her pupils are reacting, her reflexes and motor functions. The latest MRI reports show that the edema has not yet reduced and the small clots are still present."

"Isn't there any improvement?" asked Aunt Mary.

The doctor shook his head. "Not much. Actually her condition is not encouraging."

As soon as the doctor said that, Aunt Mary broke down and her two relatives immediately held her hands and consoled her.

"What's the plan now doctor?" asked one of the relatives.

"We will continue to monitor and see. And will hope for the best. That's all we can say for now. Please have patience and faith in god. We are doing all we can."

The team of doctors and nurses walked away discussing in a dialect only they understood.

Siddharth had arrived at the hospital when the doctors were talking to Hazel's mom. Standing behind them, he heard parts of the conversation. He felt the moment was not right to talk to Hazel's mom. She had anyway covered her face with a shawl and was sobbing. So he stepped back and walked towards the café. As he had arrived directly from the railway station he wanted to eat something. Also he had to accomplish an important task that morning.

As he was approaching the end of the corridor that led to the staircase, his eyes caught a rapid movement of a man taking a hasty right at the end of the corridor that led to the female ward. It appeared the man was trying to hide from him. Feeling suspicious, Siddharth walked briskly towards the staircase and took a right there. But he saw nothing unusual, only people passing into or out of the ward. He stood there wondering who it could be.

Then he headed towards the cafeteria. After a quick breakfast on cheese sandwich, French fries and tea, he picked up his bag and checked for the Locker key, his Identification card and other details from Hazel's letter. His breathing was heavy and it made him aware of his nervousness. It was an important day for him. It was a day he thought should have come to him many years back.

The 5 kilometers ride to the SSBI bank on the auto-rickshaw was bumpy.

After completing the formalities, an aging man led him to a large dusty room with racks of lockers. He sneezed a lot, almost turning asthmatic, till his nostrils got over the ticklish allergic response. Standing in front of the locker, he wondered what lay inside.

The key turned smoothly inside the key-hole and with a

few clicks the locker door swung open. With his job done, the old-man left. Siddharth extricated a pile of envelopes from the short tunnel of the locker. The covers of each envelope had serial numbers. Before closing the locker, he looked inside to see if there was anything else. It was empty.

Outside the day was still the same. Hordes of people streamed in and out of the bank. The security guard stood erect with a rifle slung from his shoulder, alert. The sun was gentle. Everything was the same. But Siddharth had a feeling that a lot would change for him once he read the letter. He hired another rickshaw for a ride back to the hotel.

The bunch of envelopes made him nervous and his hand began to twitch.

Back at the hotel room he felt more at ease and drank a glass of warm water. Changing into a cotton drawer, he sat on the bed and stacked two pillows in front making a seat for the envelopes. He fanned them out like a pack of cards, so only the sequence number showed at the top. He pulled out the envelope numbered '1', thought about Hazel in the hospital, prayed for her and started reading.

An unknown history, dating seventeen years back, gurgled out.

Chapter 15

THE LETTERS IN THE LOCKER

Letter 1: Dated 01-May-1994

Dear Sidd,

This is my first letter to you that I am placing in the locker. It is special for me as I have finally taken this step. Though it is one sided, it still gives me assurance and strength when I imagine that this will be read someday. And if there is anyone in the world who will read this and the ones that will follow, it would be only you.

This locker is not just a metal box. It houses a chunk of my heart.

Three years have gone by since we left school, since we last met. In between, people and places have changed numerous times. But my eyes kept searching for you. It took me time to realize that I may never see you again. And then it took me time to figure out how to communicate. I am uncomfortable with postal letters and concluded, this is the best way.

Writing, brings a different rhythm to my heart. It is a rhythm of joy. One that makes me believe that the soft vibrations of the pen on paper, as I write, will one day be heard by you like the bold beats of 'dhaks' played during Durga Puja. It is also a recompense of my lost years, my endless tears and my future ahead without you.

Writing to you sets me free. Like a river. It allows my heart to pour freely.

My next letters will bring forward what remained hidden from you and the world.
Love Hazel.

Siddharth felt he would have hugged Hazel if she was with him. He removed the next letter from the second envelope.

Letter 2: Dated 02-May-1994

Dear Sidd,

Today I imagined that somewhere, you are still breathing, dreaming, painting, eating your favorite Hilsa fish and perhaps playing pranks with your friends.

*How can I forget **Valentine's Day in Feb 1991**? It was our last time of togetherness.*

A month later, I could not appear for the High School exams. I am sure you wondered and worried over my sudden absence. There were two reasons. Probably you know one but not the other. One was measles and the other you'll know in the next letter.

Towards the end of my measles, when I went for a checkup to the doctor, we discovered that I had conceived. I was shocked and panicked. I knew it was coming though.

After that, things changed drastically at home. I could barely recognize it as my own.

Mom tried to comfort me. But father went ballistic. He locked us at home. Unable to control his fury, he foul mouthed me and mom repeatedly for days for being careless. He declared you responsible and said that he would settle it with you and your dad.

Father seemed to have lost his mind. He set arbitrary rules that we had to obey. Our movement outside the house was restricted. I was not allowed to meet anyone. Often I thought of somehow meeting Jennifer, Dimple, Neetu or Shankar to let you know about me. But it was impossible. Even without guards the vigil was tight around me. It was just father's roving eyes. Mom and I were like captives under house arrest.

Even my cousins and relatives were turned down when they came visiting me. With that done a message was carefully spread to our relatives that you were the culprit.

In any case within one week of the doctor's announcement we left the town. You probably know this. Father dictated that we should go to Ernakulam in Kerala, for my college and abortion. Mom and I had to quietly follow his instructions as otherwise he threatened us, mostly mom, with dire consequences.

Why would a father behave that way Sidd? Why would so much malice be towards me and you? When you know about the reason for that, it will haunt you as it did to me.

But I need to choose another day to write it down and let you know as I break down frequently when I think about it. I need to stop now before I tear this paper into pieces, which I have done several times already.

With love, Hazel.

Siddharth read and re-read the letter multiple times. He found the tone of the letter direct and revelatory. He was beginning to feel agitated and helpless and wished to go back in time. But the past could not be held. It was amorphous, gone.

This was the first time he was getting to know Hazel's side of the story. In a way it was ironic, he realized, chasing to know something he had ignored earlier.

As he unfolded the next letter, someone knocked at the door.

"Room Service," a voice boomed from outside.

"No need at this time," said Siddharth.

"But you had ordered for tea, Sir," came the reply.

Siddharth remembered ordering tea at the reception after

he arrived from the bank. He opened the door. "Please drop all you have on the table and run," he told the waiter.

The tea remained untouched. After he read the next letter both the tea and he became dead cold.

Letter 3: Dated 5-May-1994

Dear Sidd - I proceed with my story.
Much before the doctor detected that I was carrying, something else had happened.

*We had met last on **Valentine's Day in February 1991**. The next Sunday morning when I woke up I saw two butterflies, tracing a helix together and sometimes a zigzag pattern. They were carefree and intimate like us.*

To remind you Sidd, a week prior, on our way back from school we had stopped at Ravi's 'golgappa' stall and gobbled mouthfuls in a hurry. And you had choked yourself on them so much that it left you coughing the rest of the way back home.

Being Sunday, life seemed rosy. After attending mass at the Church with mom, we had Mom's friends pouring at our house for lunch. After lunch father left to be with his friends. He was supposed to travel the next morning for a business trip. Mom and her friends played cards and then discussed how to spend the evening.

They decided to go for Amitabh's movie 'Hum'. If you recall, that movie was just released and such a taboo for us to watch especially Amitabh's song for Kimi Kathkar.

"I can't go. There is so much work to do," said mom.

"Come on. Get it done once you are back sweetheart," said Mrs. Govia.

"James is leaving town early morning tomorrow. He is with his friends now. I can't leave Hazel alone. It will be 10 pm by the time we are back. And tomorrow is Monday. I have to ready things," insisted mom.

"Hazel is a big girl. And we can inform James on the way."

"Its' ok mom, please go. I'll be fine," I encouraged mom.

After putting up a lot of resistance she finally yielded to their pestering.

Once they left, I began studying for the exams. At around 8 pm or so, I was at the refrigerator pulling out a lemonade bottle and the ice-tray, when the doorbell rang. Father was at the door with Darryl and his father. It was not unusual to see them drop by our house.

"Studying well for your exams sweetie?" said father. His face had a disturbed look.

"We won't bother you Hazel. Just a private talk with your dad," said Darryl's father. Although he forced a smile, even his face was flustered for some reason.

Darryl grinned at me in a manner that made me feel like flinging the bottle at him.

I had noticed that their breath was reeking with the smell of whisky and their gait was unsteady. They dropped a strong stench wherever they paused.

"I am thinking that lemonade would do us good too. Let me make some for all of us," said father. He took the bottle from me and picked up few glasses muttering unkind words about mom and her attitude. Then he went off to his room with Darryl and his dad. They closed the door behind them but their voices streamed through. They seemed to be agitated about something. I walked back to my room and continued studying.

About half an hour later Darryl came back with two glasses of lemonade and said, "Here is your drink. Study well. Dad and I will leave soon." He waited for me to respond. But I looked at him the way I always did. Indifferently. So he went back inside father's room and I heard the door click shut. I sipped the drink and found it too sweetened. The ice cubes tinkled against my glass. And then I pored over the book that terrified me most. History.

Tired of cramming dates of historical events, I switched on the television to watch my favorite serial 'Karamchand'. You know Sidd how much I loved that detective serial.

That night a murder mystery was being telecast.

I pulled out a few pillows from the cupboard and stacked them up to a comfortable position so I could rest my head and my back on them as I watched. It was cold and I spread a quilt over my body. As I lay watching the scary episode, feeling creepy inside, I thought I heard some noise in the hallway, like a door opening and closing. I could make out that it was the front door. I was relieved that Darryl and his dad had finally left.

Halfway through the episode, I felt sleepy and my eyes began watering. It was difficult to keep staring at the television. The lady on the bed was being hit by a masked man. He pounded on her repeatedly until the knife she was holding loosened from her fingers and fell. I had to squint to continue watching.

Karamchand's voice was ringing in my ears. He was chewing his carrot and asking his secretary to shut up. The lady was being tied to the bed and was resisting. I could hear all that but wasn't sure if I could not see clearly. My eyes started playing tricks with me.

Moments later something coiled around the neck. It was as if her throat and mine were being strangled. The hands and legs began to thrash about but something pounced on them and clamped them to the bed, something heavy like the weight of a mountain. The bedspread and the quilt formed tentacles of different shapes and started curling all around, swaddling, suffocating and even dousing the loud cries with the pillow.

The lady was screaming. And so was I. Her screams got suffused with mine and we both screamed in fear till I was unable to breathe and I lost trace of time.

And then, Sidd, I saw your face flash by, followed by the Valentine's Day when you and I held each other tightly, which was to be our last time. Smothered in your tight embrace and crushed by your gentle chest, I had felt so complete and content.

I thought I was under your spell again.

But then my senses warned me that it wasn't you or else why would my body feel spasms of cruelty? Why would it feel betrayed? Why the force, the blur. It was as if I was losing something, something precious like you, like mom, the world, my dreams, myself.

When I woke up next morning mother was shouting at me.

"Hazel get up. You are late for your coaching class. Were you not supposed to get early to study for your exams?" She elbowed me when she was in the room and left.

After sometime she screamed again, "Your exams are just a few weeks away. You did not have dinner as well last night. Get out of bed Hazel for Christ's sake."

But I was drooling. My eyes were heavy and my legs felt clobbered. I wanted to call out but something tied the tongue. My throat was dry, my limbs inert. The best I could do was to raise my left forearm and swing it at the elbow. But mom wasn't nearby to see me wave. So I looked around and saw the television remote. I grabbed it and flung it at the door. It landed on the ground without striking the door or seizing mom's attention.

Mom continued with her loud cries from the kitchen, "You

and your dad slept off before I came last night. Your dad left already for his tour. Now will you get up please?"

A pain speared through my body from the toes to the head and tears gurgled out of my eyes. I knew I had to wait for mom to come by and hold me in her arms.

The wait was not too long......

By the time Siddharth completed reading the letter twice and had taken in the contents, he was fighting his tears. They kept rolling and blinding him. He was far more stunned than he was saddened.

Alternating between wiping his tears and blowing his nose, he went on reading the letter again and again until he lost count of the number of times he read it. It was already late afternoon and past his regular lunchtime. But he did not feel hungry.

Resting his head on the pillow he looked up at the ceiling and the motionless blades of the ceiling-fan. He observed how the fan blades became invisible when they moved fast but could be distinctly seen when they didn't. "What appears," he told himself the ageless adage, "to the eyes can be so different from reality".

Sleep gripped him with the power of a vice and didn't release its hold until late evening. As he splashed water on his face he saw the wall clock in the mirror right above the washbasin. It was eight. He could not drop in at the hospital as the visiting hour was over.

Although he wasn't hungry, he stepped out for dinner. A vendor was selling egg-rolls from a wagon nearby. He bought one. As soon as he started chewing the first bite, all that he read in the afternoon flashed across his eyes. He tossed away the egg-roll and walked away.

The night was cold. He loitered on the streets aimlessly. When he was back at the hotel it was ten o'clock. He looked at the bed and saw the bunch of unread letters tied with the rubber band. They looked neglected and wanting to be rescued from their bondage.

Letter 4: Dated 06-May-1994

Dear Sidd,

Sometimes I doubt if there is any use of writing, as I am unsure when you will read this, and so much would have changed by then? But, on me, it seems to have a miraculous effect. It heals and rinses my charred soul in ways than I cannot list out.

I had told you earlier that within a week's time of my pregnancy being detected, we left Jamshedpur. Both father and mom wanted to get out of town...but for different reasons.

Father had forced us to travel to Ernakulam for getting my abortion done and admitting me into a college there. He wanted to save his face in town, using you as the scapegoat. The train tickets and other arrangements were made in haste.

Mom, on the other hand, wanted to protect me from the trauma and stop the muck flying around. She too wanted the abortion done quickly but she did not believe that Ernakulam was the place for that. Rather she wanted to get it done in a place where there was no interference from father. Nor did she want to send me to a remote college.

But he had become brutal in his ways and threatened me and mom. Often hysterical and drunk, he hurt mom in several ways, both physically and mentally.

"I will never let Hazel out with you, you scum," mom had screamed once.

"If you don't do as I say, I'll use this," he threatened with the kitchen knife. "And after that I will hunt down that bastard Siddharth and drill this into his head."

"It was you and them you sinners," said mom.

"Shut up," he screamed. "I had nothing to do with it. Don't

ever talk to me like that." He cursed and slapped mom. I watched how quickly that man had turned into a monster.

Weakened after the bout of measles and unable to protest, I was spared of his wrangling. But mom took it all, initially by reacting violently and then in utter silence, when father started blatantly using his hands. I saw the fire of mom's hatred for him in her eyes.

When it comes to guarding a child from a threat I saw a mother's fury and resolve. And tact too. On the fourth or fifth day after we were locked in, to my utter disbelief, mom sided with his decision. We started packing our bags to board the train to Ernakulam two days later. I remained disoriented and weak and helped mom with the packing.

"Why are you accepting it?" I whispered to mom, alarmed at the decision.

"Let us first get out of this god forsaken house. I will settle it with him in my way."

Knowing mom, I couldn't doubt her.

Father had brought his cronies to the railway station, lest we create problems. They stayed with us until the train pulled out from the station. It was Jamshedpur-Allepey express. The onward journey details, from Allepey to Ernakulam, was known only to father.

As the train moved, we sat sulking in silence. There was a slight change in mom already. Suddenly, the bones in her face turned rigid, her lips stiffened and her eyes no longer carried the look of a beaten wife.

Mom escorting me to the restroom irked father. "I can take her too," he said.

"If you touch her or get near her even once, I will get help

from the police and the people in the train," threatened mom. Her icy tone and sudden swing of demeanor startled father. He realized that inside the train, he could not wield his authority over her, that he had lost the power to control her by fear.

A day and a half later, as the train was chugging into the Chennai station, mom woke me up, shaking me persistently, and whispered, "Hazel, honey, can you quietly follow me?"

I was too sleepy to move. I was about to say something when mom silenced me. "Do as I say honey. Make no noise. We need to go to the lavatory."

Father was snoring but suddenly shifted his body's bulk in the narrow berth from one side to the other with his face on us. Mom's face hardened and her fingers tightened around my wrists. But slowly father's snoring picked up. Then we tiptoed to the lavatory.

"Hazel, my love, from now on just do what I say. Don't question."

I sensed mom was up to something. She pulled my hand and we crossed several compartments and waited. Just as the train was slowing down we jumped off onto the platform and hurried towards the station exit. Once outside, she immediately hired a taxi.

"To Egmore."

"No meter amma. Fixed rate of hundred rupees."

Mom was in no mood to haggle and we got in quickly.

"Where to amma?"

"Take us to a decent Hotel in Egmore."

On the way mom told me that she had been there during her college days, on a tour to South India. Visiting historic temples in Madras, Madurai and Thanjavur.

For two nights, we stayed in a modest hotel in Egmore. We had to buy new clothes as our luggage was in the train. Mom had carried only her clutch bag.

"We have to save money. I have a rough plan in my mind for what we will do next."

"What's the plan, mom?"

"I will let you know. Just don't worry. I think we will be safe from him now."

And then something remarkable happened. Mom and I went to the 'Langar' in a Gurudwara in Egmore. We ate there for the next two days.

It was my first visit ever to a Gurudwara and it was an amazing experience. I learnt from a staff member about the philosophy of a 'Langar'. He told us that the Gurudwara is open 24 hours a day and free meal is served to whoever walks in. In those small moments, as he was explaining, for the first time my mind was unclogged of its miseries.

I felt proud that such Gurudwaras exist across India and even in other countries.

The third day, mom dropped a few hints about her plan. I wondered why she did not explain all of it at once. It was later I understood why, when she told me that there was no fixed plan and each day she simply toyed with an idea and worked on a possibility.

"Honey, we are heading to Kolkata," said mom before we left the hotel. "I got the tickets from the hotel's travel desk." As the train chugged off from Chennai station, for the first time after weeks, I saw a hair-thin smile emerge on her face and a look besiege her eyes that could match the grit of any damn Olympic runner just before the starting gun is fired.

"Where in Kolkata mom?"

"I will let you know once we are there and only if it works out. Don't worry child."

I spent the time on the train reading books and mom either looked out of the window or was lost in deep thought. Once we reached Kolkata, mom seemed to know exactly where to go. She hired a pre-paid taxi that took us to the outskirts of Kolkata, in a place called, Liluah.

"We are going to a place where, I believe, we will be safe," said mom. The Taxi was already plying the pot-holed roads.

"Which place mom?" I asked eagerly.

"A friend's place," she replied beaming brightly like the daylight.

"Does he know we are coming?"

"No. We haven't met for many years but I am sure he'll recognize me. He welcomes whoever reaches his door for help," said mom. Her confidence snuffed out my worries.

The taxi parked in front of a large iron gate with an overhead arch that housed a Cross in it. A security guard was sitting on a high stool with a stick in hand and stood up as soon as he saw us. Mom walked up to the guard and told him something.

Few minutes later an old slightly bent man with thick white flowing beard, dressed in a white gown, walked with the guard towards us. As soon as he noticed mom he hastened his pace with his arms outstretched slightly. He came over and held her hands at once.

"Look who we have here! Can someone prod me with a hot wire or something? I can't trust my eyes these days," he exclaimed with a soft affectionate voice. Tall and somewhat thin, he had a charming personality and distinctly blue eyes.

"Father Romelo, how are you?" asked mom with a tone of deep respect and sincere delight. She held his hands with reverence.

"Outstanding," he replied. "And how are you my sister?"

"Lately been facing a storm. So I came to you to seek your help Father."

"Come on inside my office. I hope things are okay and who is this young beautiful lady here," he asked looking at me while guiding us to his office.

"She is my daughter. Hazel."

Father Romelo paused for a brief second and took a second look at me, "Has she grown so much since I last saw her, Mary?" he chuckled. "How are you Hazel?"

Before stepping into Father Romelo's office to speak to him in private, mom asked me to view the surroundings. I did not wander and sat in one place. There were sounds from all corners of metal hitting against something hard, of maybe hammer against stone.

She spoke to him for an hour. When they came out, mom's face had turned ashen. Father was holding her arms, almost supporting her, his eyes reflecting the concern in hers.

Father Romelo held a big hoop with a bunch of keys and walked us on a corridor past a row of closed doors. We could make out that each door led to a room. At the end of the corridor, dense bushes and a cluster of banana trees formed a partition, beyond which there was a big clearing with a small house in the center. Father opened the big iron lock hanging on the door and led us inside the house. It had two small rooms with basic furnishings.

"This is our guest room Mary. This is yours now. My boys will attend to you shortly." Father smiled and handed over the keys to mom. Little did I realize then, the small guest house was to be our shelter for half a decade.

We picked up the threads of our life quietly. There was little choice. I had frequent mood swings and mom bore the brunt of my bad moments. She was the only crutch I had. That horrible night flooded my mind every now and then.

For weeks I was asking mom the same question. "How could they do this to me?"

"Do not think about that my dear," replied mom, every time.

But my questioning did not stop. Often I became mercurial and challenged her.

"How can I forget? And dad? How can he turn a blind eye?"

Mom reminded me, that dad had repeatedly been saying that he had left the house with Darryl and his father that night. That there was no one in the house.

"So it was some ghost that night, mom?"

But I could see that she was herself unconvinced with what she said and yet cited them hoping to steer me away from my hurt. Dad's indifference had torn me apart. But I knew it wasn't anyone else apart from them. Exactly who, was like chasing a shadow in the dark. Every day my questions multiplied and each of them sliced a portion out of me.

Mom told me to try and relax as much as possible and focus on different things. She took me to the nearby hills. She brought me novels, took me to the movies, theatres, dinners and anything she could think of. But my questioning went unabated for weeks and then months, especially on dad and his coldness. On even his possible silent involvement.

Finally, mom relented and offered words to quieten me.

"Hazel, first you must get better, much better, than you are now. And then we will talk on this. There is more to what you know. Do not force me to talk about it now. It will only worsen your health. But I will answer you one day. I promise."

When I kept asking mom the same question, I was only expressing my shock and disbelief. I did not expect that her answer would involve peeling layers of an onion whose core was replete with terrible realities. I must tell you that story.

But before I write about that, I must tell what I did not earlier. That Sunday night when mom returned after watching the movie 'Hum', I was a heap of sprawling defeat on bed and father had slept off in his room. He left on his business trip early next morning.

You can imagine when he returned after two weeks, how life would have been in our house. It was a battlefield. Mom accused and threatened him. But he accepted nothing and tried to steer away every talk about Darryl or his father.

Unable to defend them or himself, he left the house again, left his wife and his daughter to deal with the cruel and unbelievable circumstances alone. I missed my board exams. What kind of a person would leave his family behind during such a time?

Mom was numbed. Her world had crumbled overnight. But her eyes were not wet for long. She prayed to the Lord for strength and attended to my needs. Confused at times whether to inform her relatives or the police, troubled at times over the stain my future would carry if she did, finally she didn't allow the matter to go outside the four walls.

From that night for more than a year I was in an endless state of shock. The hurt spread through my body like a germ. Life *became pointless.*

And more than anything else the image of a father was flawed, broken.

At first the shock kept me awake at nights. And then it was my crying spells. And when the tears dried up, there were anxiety attacks. Performing simple daily tasks appeared difficult and I couldn't focus on anything. It was not just the measles that kept me from appearing for the High School exams. How could I?

And when father came back after a month, and heard about my pregnancy, he swung the tables around and started blaming you.

And now Sidd, this is a story my mom told me.

This story is about a young woman. She saw him in College Street, rifling through books at a bookshop. Something prevented her from shifting her eyes off him. Probably it was his sophisticated looks, the broad convex forehead, the curled eyelashes, the simple clothes or his persistent questions to the shopkeeper about a book he was unable to find. His friends urged him to abandon the search in the interest of hitting the Coffee House soon.

Instinctively she followed him with her friends shadowing behind her. They had spent half a day already amidst the sea of books in the College Street, famous for bookshops, and decided to end the hunt with coffee. As her friends regaled themselves at the table, through the rising spirals of coffee steam and tobacco smoke-rings, she observed him.

He was sitting calmly with his loud friends, a rock amidst boisterous waves, both engaged and detached at the same time.

An hour later he rose and told his friends, "I'll meet you guys again next week here. Need to hurry now."

As he left, she felt a vacuum build inside her as if her blood had drained away.

A week later she saw him again. But this time it was in a tram that was taking them both to College Street. He was alone, like her, but while he was staring out of the tram window at the cobbled, crowded streets of Calcutta, she followed his gaze. When they had to get down at the stop, he gave way to her, before stepping out of the tram.

"Do you come here every week?" he asked.

Her heart skipped a beat. "Yes. No. Actually not every week. Sometimes."

"I saw you last week. I had a feeling I'd see you again," he said and smiled.

They met frequently after that. She was studying English Literature in St. Xavier's College and he was a practicing doctor. Two years after her graduation they got married and lived a life seen in dreams. They moved to South Calcutta the year she bore a child.

He had friends around him all the time from different professions, from doctors to engineers, from lawyers to professors, from artists to political thinkers both rightwing and left-liberal. Once he told her, "I guess I am plain lucky to get such accomplished friends."

"It's because of you dear. Your nature. They love you. And you are no amateur in your field," she tried to correct him. For that was the truth.

Every Sunday evening, his friends would arrive in packs, and the tea kettle would stop hissing in the kitchen only after they left. They would discuss politics, arts and football and call out her name as soon as the tea-cups became empty.

"There is no tea in entire Calcutta like yours," was their usual refrain. They openly flirted with her in front of her doctor husband.

"There are no eyes in India like yours," they would tell her.

Some of them even suggested, "You should take to acting. You will have an amazing screen presence. After Suchitra Sen, it will be you." They simply doted on his beautiful wife and he would simply laugh and watch her even more lovingly.

But beautiful things in life have a typical way of ending prematurely.

Shortly after their child turned two, he went missing. Disappeared! Tirelessly, his friends searched for him, yet there was no clue. He had just vanished. Terrible stories were heard. Some said he was killed, some said he was in hiding. She almost lost her mind. Probably the only reason that kept her from turning insane was the tug of motherhood.

It was during the Emergency in Calcutta. Those were bad times.

Slowly the gathering of friends thinned down except for one of the friends who started visiting her more frequently. The visits went on for a year or two. Then, at the behest of her parents and close relatives, she married once again.

It was probably in August or September that year when mom told me this story. Given the details in the story, it took her three days to complete it.

She spoke about the tragic fate, the family breakdown, the struggles of the mom and the child, the trauma, and later the re-establishment of a new family, a new order, a streak of happiness, so to say, touching unfortunate lives.

On the third day, at the end of the story, mom asked me a few simple questions.

"Did you dislike anything about the story Hazel?

"Did you feel the mother was wrong in getting married again?"

"Did you feel negative about the man entering the mother's life for supporting her?"

I thought deeply. For all of them I had a single answer, "No."

And then she carefully placed another question, "Suppose the child in the story is actually you, would your answer still be the same?"

At first I did not understand the implication of that question. "Are you serious?" I asked. But when it dawned on me the ground seemed to have cracked open where I stood. I staggered over to the bed and wept like a girl lost in a dreaded jungle.

My heart had once again become a collection of countless broken pieces.

Mom came by and rubbed her palms over my back and ran her fingers through my hair. She consoled me. We were both awake that night. My questions were infinite and mom answered them patiently. She started putting in more details to the story she told me earlier.

"Your dad was a very handsome, passionate and learned man. He was killed in unknown and mysterious circumstances during the Emergency in Calcutta in 1975. We used to live in South Calcutta then."

Mom brought out two tiny pictures from a holder, the size of a card holder, from her clutch bag. She brought them near my eyes. "I always carry them with me. You have never seen them though," she said and showed me one by one. "This is my favorite one. You are sitting on his lap. The other one where you are kissing him was his favorite."

I was seeing my father for the first time. My real father. Can you believe it Sidd?

"Do you have more photos mom?" I asked.

"Not at this time. But there are more at your granny's place."

I was captivated by the large jet black eyes that had an unusual sparkle in them and were so different from mine. The eyelids were broad and lined with curled eyelashes. His forehead was large and convex and shiny.

"Your dad was a doctor and a fearless man who never tolerated disrespect for the poor. Probably that is why the gods snatched him away from us." Mom rarely cried but that night her eyes were not hers. They had in them, the man in the photos, who I was grappling with to accept as my father. He had once again settled in her eyes and thoughts.

I looked at the pictures again and again and noticed a stark difference in our looks. I did not get his eyes and I told mom about it.

"His eyes were true ambassadors of his kind heart. You got my eyes. But you got his courage, honey," said mom. "I have noted that often. In difficult situations you always reminded me of him."

"Was he a doctor?" I asked to re-affirm.

"Yes. And he was a Bengali. His name was Indranil Ghosh."

That meant I have the blood of a Christian as well as a Hindu Bengali. At that point I thought about you Sidd and how much of me you did not know. There seemed to be so much of my own history that was unwinding before me. I wondered how you would react hearing about this shade of my life.

"Going to the temple on your birthday was something he made compulsory. That is why I always insisted you to follow," said mom.

"But how was he killed mom?"

"That is unknown. He just did not return from office one evening. You were two years old and still breastfed. After several attempts to reach him, we sought police assistance. But they could not help us find him. Theories abounded for his disappearance but no one could get him back. Those were difficult times for people in Calcutta. We had to accept what befell. Everyone had lost the rights to protest. It was the Emergency."

My dad was so handsome that months later, after the fact of my true parentage seeped into my core, I would gaze at those two pictures for hours. I imagined what it might have felt sitting on his lap and playing. A faint bond slowly developed for the man in the picture.

And then that night mom also told me about my step-dad, James. I heard whatever mom told me about him although it no longer mattered.

"James lived in the same locality where we lived and was a frequent visitor to our house. He was many years younger than your dad and was unmarried. After your father's sudden disappearance, he started visiting me more often," said mom. "Finally he proposed to me and vowed to take care of us forever."

She continued after a pause, "Although devastated after I lost your father, with a lot of cajoling and convincing from my relatives I agreed to settle down again and start life afresh. It was not easy even though our religion was the same. You were too young to realize him swap the place of your father. We moved to

Jamshedpur when James changed his job."

At that very moment, whatever attachment was left with my step-dad snapped. In fact the initial disbelief and shock I had experienced turned into hatred and revulsion. I vomited.

Mom also told me that he was running different businesses that kept him away from home for long stretches of time. They were not running well. And that he had taken a huge loan from Darryl's father and considered him his savior. But unable to pay back the loan installments timely had strained their relationship. Yet they held on together as they both agreed on one thing. That I would marry Darryl as soon as I was out of college.

I was shocked to hear that. But mom said that she never agreed to it and never would and had told James to dismiss such thoughts. And they fought over it often.

"Why did you not tell all this earlier to me mom, especially about my early life?"

"It had to be kept away from you my dear. Our true story is known only to our relatives. I had to wait for the right moment to disclose all this to you."

"And what was the right moment mom? Now?" I asked her mockingly.

Mom could see my rising vexation and held my hands.

"We had decided that 21 years of age would be the right time. You wouldn't be too old but mature enough to face your true past and learn about your real father."

"Who is 'we'?"

"Me and my mother, your granny."

I reflected that I was almost the age mom had planned to break the secret. But I guess she never imagined the devastation it would wreak before it ceased to remain a secret.

Sidd I must stop now. I will write more about Father Romelo's beautiful campus and another person I met there.
Love Hazel.

It was late, very late he thought, such discoveries of Hazel's past. Yet it was all in front of him. He could not overlook them anymore. And only he would ever know of such details about her.

Siddharth was grief-stricken and thought of Hazel. He could not resist reading the next letter.

Letter 5: Dated 07-May-1994

Sidd - What I slowly learnt about Father Romelo's institution was incredible.

Over the years, several hundred destitute children, less than ten years old, were rescued from the streets of Kolkata, Howrah and nearby places. They are provided with food, shelter and education for many years before they are given an occupation.

Father Romelo gave them a kind world within a harsh one.

Once their fingers are capable of holding and striking wooden hammers against chisels they receive basic training for two years and slowly start making sculptures which gets sold in the cities at decent prices. The training goes on till they grow up and hone their skills enough to be able to work unaided.

When they reach twenty one years of age they are given a choice to stay and work with Father in the institution *or step out into the world on their own. Many have stayed back and many have chosen to settle elsewhere.*

When we moved in, there were about a hundred members in the age-group of four to thirty. With a fifty acre land, that housed the small rooms for the members, the workshops for sculpture, the slabs of rocks and raw wood kept outside, orchards and vegetable plantations, it looked like a self-sustaining world, a beautiful orchestra of man and nature.

It took time for me to adjust to the place. I missed Jamshedpur and its way of life, it's industrial and cosmopolitan culture but knew there was no option other than staying here until the immediate needs of my abortion and mental well-being were taken care of.

"I know James. He can do anything to harm us," said mom. "I

*will never risk you with him. We will live here till I see another
road ahead of us."*

My gratefulness for mom increased every day, for her will to
remove hurdles in life, for her sacrifice, her grit. For her love for
me. For mothers. For motherhood!

One evening that winter, Father Romelo and I were walking
around the campus. The sun was a bright giant orange. We
conversed about my health and general matters. Then I asked
him a question that was waiting to shoot out once mom had
disclosed my true past.

"Father, how did you and my mother know each other?"

"Through your father, Hazel."

"Really? And how was that?"

"Your father, Doctor Ghosh, was born to serve mankind. And
he did just that. It was easy for me to get attached to such a
gentleman and respect him. Thirty years back, I had to take a
group of my boys to his private clinic as they all suffered from
smallpox and severe cholera and were almost struggling for
life. With the limited means I had at that time it was difficult
for me to get a good doctor to look at them. I took them to the
government hospital but the situation did not improve. So I went
looking for Doctor Ghosh."

"Did you know him that many years back," I asked at that
point?

"Yes. Your dad was actually a reputed doctor in south
Kolkata at that time and I was told that he could treat my boys
for a certain discount. After he learnt about my institution and
understood my challenge to pay the fees, he waived it off entirely.
Moreover, he said that from that day onwards all my children
would receive free treatment from him. His words descended on

me as a shower of rain on parched soil."

I asked him if his boys recovered.

"Yes, almost all of them. His help to me from then on, went a long way in supporting my fledgling institution."

It was really nice to hear all that. But I did not tell him that I learnt about my real father only a few months back and that too in his campus.

I went back to mom, feeling proud of my father as much as I was of Father Romelo.

The same week, when mom and I stepped into the campus, Father Romelo had introduced us to a person called Joydeep, who lived in the campus since his childhood. His humble and soft-spoken nature was quite endearing. He was six years older than me.

"I remember the love and compassion with which Father Romelo had treated me during my growing years. He is like a god to all of us. By learning stone sculpture here I learnt to live," said Joydeep, after a few days of befriending him.

He explained the process of wood carvings and stone sculptures, right from the raw wood and stone slabs that were imported from different places to shipping the finished sculptures to various outlets in India. He showed us the ones that were complete and ready to be shipped and the ones that were still in the making. We passed through blocks of soapstone, limestone, alabaster, marble and granite and he explained what each is used for.

"Generally the new boys are given soapstone to start learning to carve, as it is a soft stone. As they mature they are given the harder stones like limestone, marble, granite. We have good demands from the big corporate houses for sculptures in marble *and granite."*

"And for wood-work?" mom asked him.

"For woodwork," he explained, "Indian rosewood is generally the wood of choice, though teak, mango and ebony are also used. But we are better at stone work."

In few days we learnt a lot about the trade. Throughout the day we heard the sound of mallet against chisel and chisel against stone. Slowly the sounds stopped bothering us as we got used to them. It was almost like getting used to not seeing you.

Joydeep knew my condition from the beginning of our arrival. He was one of the most trusted people of Father Romelo and used to escort us for all the visits to the doctor for my abortion and ill health. All through my worst phases of depression he was by my side, by mom's side, eager to be of any help.

As per Father Romelo's instructions, he enquired if we needed anything once in the morning and once in the afternoon. In between, he toiled away at the workshop with others. In the evenings we walked up to the banyan tree under whose shade tea and snacks were served. Father Romelo and other senior people of the campus would gather as well.

My wounds started healing and it took me about a year to come out of my chronic depression. I lost one year in school and joined back the next year and completed my Class 12 exams from a private school and then joined a local college in 1992. I chose Arts.

One day, two years after I had entered Father Romelo's campus, Joydeep proposed to me in a hand-written letter. He wanted to marry me.

At first I didn't know what to do. Confused and in slight indignation at his nerve for writing that note to me, I hastily showed the letter to mom. No matter how unprepared and unsettled I was to get the letter from Joydeep, I could not remain mad with him for long. His innocent face and sincerity could melt anyone, anything, even granite.

However, I did not reply for several days as I wasn't sure how to respond.

During that time Sidd, my mind remained populated with your thoughts. I wondered if we could meet again and continue from where our lives had split. But when would be the right time I asked myself? I was still trying to come to terms with my reality. And then I had to continue with college and you with yours. And mom was still not ready to come out in the open. The thought of James trying to hurt me and mom or even you bothered us a lot too. I could not convince myself to collect the bits of our broken lives and start over again, yet.

It drew upon me that the path in front did not lead to you. And I did not see it leading to Joydeep either. Somehow my life had altered its course as if a dam was placed in its river.

Instead I found that it was Father Romelo's institution that beckoned me. The urge to serve a caring organization brought peace to my mind.

Although my chronic depression was gone, my inner self was crushed. It did not exist for me anymore and was devoid of any demands. The thought of getting close to a man seemed repulsive and it slowly hardened into a belief. I contemplated being a 'Religious Sister' or a Nun. I think it was my father's footprints that drew me into it.

I spoke about all this with mom and Father Romelo and tried to seek their guidance. Mom was shattered and tried to explain away my misfortunes. Joydeep was downcast. It was only Father

Romelo who seemed to understand me.

"My Child, you must choose what your heart and mind tells you," said Father Romelo. "You are most welcome to live here as long as you want. But first, you must complete your education. I suggest that you give yourself at least a year or two before I take you to the 'Missionary of Charity' in Kolkata for a come-and-see experience in their order. That life is not easy child but again not unattainable."

Thus began the start of my journey into the realm of spirituality and my determination to spend the rest of my life in the service of God. In parallel, encouraged by Father Romelo and almost pushed into it by mom, I had enrolled for the Bachelor of Arts degree.

At that point Sidd, I quietly sought your forgiveness for the path I chose for myself and the silence mom and I had to maintain with you and the world for such a long time.

Love Hazel.

Siddharth continued reading. He could not stop without knowing what happened to Hazel later. The phone rang in the room.

"Hello Sir, do you need a wake-up call," asked the hotel operator.

"Yes at seven, please," said Siddharth.

Letter 6: Dated 08-May-1994

In that one year that Father Romelo had asked me to contemplate if I really wanted to dedicate my life to the service of God, I immersed myself into reading books that Father Romelo gave me. I was especially awed by the history of mother Teresa. While I focused on my studies, I also helped Father Romelo with the finances in his office. Mom took English lessons for everyone in the campus. She became probably the most popular person there.

Joydeep lost his sweet looks to one of perpetual sadness. Like mom he was unable to accept my desire to walk on the spiritual path.

One day, at year end, when mom had gone out with Father Romelo to get some supplies for her classroom, Joydeep knocked at my door. I recall the conversation clearly.

"Hazel it's me," he called out in a soft voice from outside.

I welcomed him after opening the door.

"I need to talk to you Hazel."

I asked him what it was about hoping that it wouldn't be about the proposal he made a year back. His eyes looked intense and alert. A sling-bag hung over his left shoulder.

"I wanted to let you know that soon I have to go to Bombay. For few months."

"Really? Why?" I asked.

"Father wants me to initiate setting up a sales office there."

"When was this discussed? I never heard mom speak about it?"

"It was in the plans for some time. Father is finally convinced that I should go."

"That's good news. So you must be excited."

"Not that much as my heart is rooted here." Saying that he looked at me deeply.

I avoided his eyes and said, "I know how difficult it is to move from a place where one has grown up, even for a few months. When do you have to travel?"

"Maybe next month."

"Hmm. There is not much time left, is there. You will get to see a fast modern city."

He didn't reply. Instead he removed the sling-bag from his shoulders and unzipped it. "I got something for you Hazel." He placed something heavy on the table that was wrapped in layers and layers of newspapers. Then he zipped up his bag again and asked, "Can you remove the covers, please?"

"Sure." I removed the newspapers one by one and rolled them into a ball and as I was about to fling it into the dustbin, from what remained on the table, I saw something staring at me that looked like me.

"Oh Joydeep," I cried out in astonishment. "Where did you get that?"

"I made it," he stammered, sounding apologetic.

"It's unbelievable Joydeep," I cried out loudly.

"I hope you did not mind Hazel…."

"What are you saying Joydeep? It is beyond my imagination. When did you make it?"

"Over a year. Finished it a week back."

I kept staring at it, the beauty of it. It was an incredible replica of my torso and face on stone, exquisitely sculpted.

"What's it made of?"

"Limestone."

I asked him if he showed it to anyone.

"No. I made it in my room, so."

All I could tell him was, "Joydeep, this sculpture will remain one of the best gifts I ever got from anyone."

Although he cheered up, it did not make him entirely happy. Sadly, I could not offer what he wanted to hear from me.

I held his hands and made him sit down on the bed. The enormous effort in making that sculpture was obvious and though I could clearly fathom the motivation behind it, a year later he told it to me himself.

"Hazel, when you had chosen not to respond to my proposal and instead thought of becoming a 'Sister', I had to find a way to stop the poison of sorrow flowing inside me."

When Joydeep left for Bombay for the first time, he went there for three months. Mom said that a dollop of cheerfulness had drained off from my face. Although I had goaded myself into not thinking about Joydeep, the limestone sculpture of my face staring back at me from the tabletop, reminded me of his forlorn face and his soft almost childlike persistence to alter my decision.

Joydeep left in March 1994. It was during this time when mom got the news that James had left Jamshedpur forever and relocated to Kerala. Mom confirmed it from multiple sources. Once convinced, she made immediate plans to visit Jamshedpur. A lot of work related to her bank accounts was pending and she wanted to meet her close relatives too.

My footfall on that soil after three years brought me closer to you once again.

I found you everywhere. In the smell of the eucalyptus leaves, in the sound of the temple chants, in the sight of our school, the trees and hills you painted, in the taste of the 'golgappas' at Ramu's, the market lanes, the streets, in the wind, just about

everywhere.
    Love Hazel.

Siddharth was struck by the sculpture Joydeep had made of Hazel. He recalled the paintings he used to make for her. And how for the last seventeen years he stopped painting completely. In a way, at that moment, he kind of regretted it.

    But he moved quickly on to the next letter which seemed to be a short one.

Letter 7: Dated 09-May-1994

Time ticks fastest here; The feet so restless on what are called streets; and I called them veins. The smell of wind so familiar, the pull of places, temples, markets, lakes, schools, the curves on the roads, the unrushed life of the townspeople. They felt so familiar. The railway station, still composed after a zillion arrival and departures.

It was at this time that I decided to write the letters to you. It was here I was determined to open a bank locker and add you as a joint holder. Filling up the forms was easy as I had your photographs. And you know about my handwriting skills. That is how I had mailed the second key to you hoping one day you must know about me.

I also got your address during this time from Dimple.

In a few days I will leave Jamshedpur once again and get back to Liluah. But this short trip has strengthened me to face the unknowns ahead, especially since now I have a way to reach you. For the last few days I have been writing to you. But it is time for me to go back to Liluah. In a day or two mom and I will travel back.

Siddharth quickly saw that the next letter in sequence was written one year later. He decided that it would be the last letter he would read that night.

Letter 8: Dated 10-Dec-1995

Sidd,

I have come to Jamshedpur again after a year and thought of checking the locker once to see if you have visited. But I found the letters arranged in the same way I had kept them. Few things have happened in the last one year and the urge to write to you today is unforgiving.

So I will continue from where I left. I had to actually read my earlier letters, especially the last one, before I could write further.

When Joydeep returned after three months in Bombay, he brought back his successful stories there of how he was able to negotiate tough situations with the buyers. His return was nothing short of a celebration of victory for everyone. Father Romelo had arranged for a humble party for all the members and announced that Joydeep would have to travel back to Bombay, in a month. But this time the plan was that he would be gone for a longer time.

I became aware that mom was staring at me.

Few months later, one evening, Joydeep and I were strolling around the campus, holding glasses that held our evening tea and the reflection of the fireball in the sky.

"Hazel it's time for me to leave. The last few years, had been quite different for me, since you and your mom stepped into our lives, especially my life. Although I am blessed to have a family within Father Romelo's institution, but to me it became a complete one only after you and your mom arrived."

I thanked him for the words but also reminded him that it was for his help that we had settled there so comfortably.

"But now I will miss the family, as I will be gone for a long

time."

"Don't say it that way Joydeep. Will you not come back in between?"

"Mostly not. I wonder if you will still be here next year, when I come."

"Not sure Joydeep. At this point completing my education is important. College will get over in six months, in the summer of 1995. That's the reason mom decided to be here so my studies don't get interrupted. After that, you know, where I want to go."

"Are you sure Hazel about your decision?" asked Joydeep with a wavering voice and trying hard to find a way to sway my resolve.

Sounding firm and opaque, I said, "I think I am. I don't think I can fulfil the role of a wife." I had to tell this, I had to be brutal and cut all stems of expectations.

"I would be happy with you by my side Hazel. I wouldn't want anything more."

"We will always remain friends Joydeep. You will always remain a part of my life. But I must pursue my innermost desire."

Joydeep squeezed a smile and I saw a young man trying to forcibly accept a condition that his heart vehemently opposed.

Before leaving the following week, he came by for one last meeting and stood in front of me with his head bowed like an obedient pupil. His eyes were moist and they avoided looking into mine. I hugged him as warmly as I could and realized that he wouldn't let go off me. He continued to embrace tightly until I spoke to him and patted his back. I had to make the separation as less painful as I could.

"Joydeep you are a wonderful person. We can never forget what you have done for us here. You will always be in my prayers.

Good luck to you and we will always keep in touch."

Cheering up a bit he looked at me and smiled. "Thanks."

"Actually without you this place will lose its sheen," I said.

"Hazel, I will wait for as long as I can." Those were his final words to me.

The institution Jeep drove him away to the railway station as we all stood waving our hands at him. I was trying hard to swallow the sudden lump in my throat that was growing bigger and bigger. The Jeep took a turn at the bend and became invisible.

As soon as I had completed my B.A in college, I requested Father Romelo to take me to the 'Missionary of Charity', in Kolkata. That it was pointless to try to steer me in a different direction, was a conclusion that mom did not accept easily. She scolded and even begged me to avoid taking such a big step. But I was determined.

I did visit the 'Missionary of Charity' in Kolkata and found the selflessness of Sisters, towards suffering, summoning my distressed soul. I started with the preparations to join.

Mom had decided to stay behind in the campus and teach English. But she had a sudden bout of fever and my determination wavered for the first time. I thought how lonely she would become without me. When the day was nearing for me to leave, her sacrifices, our past and her love stood in front of me not like a wall of imposition but as a teardrop of appeal. And that was something I could not and still cannot surmount.

From that moment I promised to be by mom's side always and never think of pushing myself into her memories. As destiny claimed it, I was never ever able to step back to the 'Missionary of Charity' again. Probably the Lord had planned it that way.

When Joydeep returned after his second trip, the entire crew in the campus was standing at the gate to welcome him. The young boys whistled, blew paper horns and flutes and others beat small drums. There was fanfare. Special dinner was arranged and once again he was absorbed into the campus life as easily as a newborn gets added to a family.

Mom and I was still around.

Joydeep was thrilled to see us. And to say the truth I was glad to see him as well. The winter of sorrows started subsiding in the warmth of relationships, with mom, Joydeep and Father Romelo by my side and the constant sound of stone and wood chipping around.

I felt as if my second phase of life had begun.

Sidd, I hope you are taking good care of yourself and doing well in life. I think you must have graduated already from college and are probably working. You are in my prayers and thoughts always.

Until another day, Love Hazel.

Reading each of the letters several times over slowly, word by word, pausing and thinking and going back in time, took the hands of the clock forward to three in the morning. It appeared that Hazel settled down with Joydeep finally. But he recalled that Shane and Helena had mentioned that she was not married. He was confused. But why that should bother him was equally surprising. The fact was, that although she was a mere shadow of his past life, a sense of possessiveness over Hazel took root in his mind.

There were other envelopes and letters that were yet to be

opened. Reading them all in a day was impossible. Furthermore, the tragic contents that he had read so far had to soak in and settle down. Unable to keep the fatigued eyes open any longer, Siddharth reached a point of oblivion where sleep, dreams and memories merge to become indistinguishable from one another.

Chapter 16

CONFESSIONS

"Chief, if you are not prepared to lose in love, chances are you will never earn it. This is what I learnt the sad way," said Mukund.

"This coming from you? What's the story Mukund?"

"I was head over heels in love with a girl once. As same age kids, we often played together. She was the daughter of my father's colleague and studied in a different school. Somehow we never met after Class Five. And then I saw her in a market when I was in Class Eleven. We spoke at length. She entered my bloodstream and thereafter left me sleepless at nights. I tried a lot to go near her but never reached her," said Mukund.

"Why, what happened?" asked Siddharth.

"From that day, every evening I walked by her house to get a glimpse of her. Only one out of thirty days I saw her at the balcony. It still kept me happy until I saw her next. I spent two years on the same ritual and spoke to her only three times on the streets."

"Why didn't you talk directly instead of chance meetings?"

"Talking to her was really easy, in retrospect. But it appeared to be very tough then."

"So did you let her know about it?"

"Hardly Chief. My heart ached for her for seven years, even when I was into my first job. I relied on fate to unite us. Then one day I heard the news that blew me to bits."

It was one of the Friday nights when Siddharth and his

colleague, Mukund, had hit the Royal Downtown bar. As usual, Mukund had lost his taciturnity by guzzling beer and couldn't hold back his love story that never blossomed.

"What was the news?"

"That she got married. What else."

"Oh shucks. I wonder what stopped you from expressing your feelings."

"Lack of courage and ignorance. The path to approach her was not visible to me and the mound of fear was too big to cross," said Mukund.

"Do you repent?"

"Not after getting married. But Chief, I always felt foolish for not even trying to talk."

"Did it ever happen that you wanted to meet the girl again?"

"That's a delicate question Chief," said Mukund and paused before replying. "On rare occasions when certain smells of seasons and incidents line up together, I must admit, I am swayed over to those days. It lingers for a while, trapping me and pulling me back in time. But then it fades away."

Sitting in the hotel room, Siddharth recalled the old conversation. It was about ten in the morning. He had slept off after 3 a.m. and had woken up late morning. Unable to keep his recent discoveries about Hazel, her condition, the letters he read the previous day, he succumbed to an inner urge to talk to Mukund. So he dialed his phone.

"Good morning Chief. How are you?" replied Mukund.

"There are numerous changes happening in my life in the last few days that I am away from Bhubaneswar. Are you in office already?"

"No. I am getting ready to leave," said Mukund and had just lit a cigarette.

"I need to talk to you now. And it may take some time. But this is important."

Sensing the concern in Siddharth's voice, Mukund relaxed his tie and sat down. "Go on Chief. I hope everything is fine."

"It is something that until a few days back I wasn't aware of."

When Mukund got a detailed account of the two women in Siddharth's life, over the phone, his eyes flickered and flashed with the twists and turns in the narrative.

"Life has been unfair to you, Chief." He took a long drag at the cigarette through a clenched fist and closed his eyes. "And I wasn't even aware that you are under such stress."

"I just wanted to empty out my heart. And also seek your help."

"Sure. Let me know how I can help you."

"I need to extend my leave. Hazel is still in coma. Anything can happen. I just don't feel like getting back to work until probably another week."

"Hmm. No problem Chief. You stay put there. I can understand what you are going through. We'll manage it here."

"A zillion thanks."

Mukund crushed the cigarette butt on the ashtray. "I have a feeling that things will turn better with Hazel. Hold yourself well. What else I can do Chief?"

"A request. Next Friday, you know the delegates are visiting from Durgapur Steel Plant to our office. Can you help manage the meetings?"

"Done Chief. I will cover for you. Take it easy."

Chapter 17

MEETING HAZEL'S MOM

After talking to Mukund and sharing his present turmoil Siddharth felt lighter. But he did not go to the hospital the whole day. He sat in his room and read and re-read all the letters again, until he could not only visualize but also feel what Hazel went through after they had separated. The letters left him deeply saddened and he could barely eat the whole day.

He also read the ones he couldn't read the previous day. Mostly they spoke of the campus life, of her mom and Joydeep and the setting-up of the sales office in Bombay. There were talks too of initiating a fledgling office in Jamshedpur. For all the joys that had been drained off from their lives, a hint of it seemed to have coursed back.

There were in all fifteen letters. Siddharth observed that the first letter was written in 1994 and the last in 1997. There was no letter after that. It was over ten years. He wondered why and looked outside the hotel window.

Next day he decided to reach the hospital by ten thirty and meet Hazel's mom. But before going to the hospital he had planned to talk to her. The thought of getting face to face with her made him nervous. He believed speaking with her over the phone might be less difficult. And he had taken her cell phone number from one of the visitors in the hospital.

The thought of talking to Aunt Mary drew him to the phone repeatedly. He could not wait to call her. But surprisingly, each time he dialed, he aborted the call as well.

Something inside made him weak. So weak that his resolve to talk to Hazel's mom snapped. His weakness stemmed from the guilt he was carrying. And his guilt was rooted in the belief that had Hazel not conceived early in life, then her past would not have been riddled with so much suffering. Finally after few attempts he dialed again and waited.

"Hello." A voice crackled after five rings.

"Hello," said Siddharth almost whispering and trying to rescue his voice.

"Yes?" asked the voice questioningly.

"Is this Hazel's number?" he asked.

"Yes it is. Who is this?" The voice was melancholic but clear and tender.

Without another word he dropped the call. In less than a minute, his phone rang. It was Aunt Mary's number flashing on his mobile. Wavering for a while, whether to accept the call or not, he answered it.

"Hello, I just got a call from this number."

"Who am I speaking to?" asked Siddharth surprised at the hoarseness in his voice, surprised that he was asking a question whose answer he knew already.

"This is her mom. Who is this?"

At that question, Siddharth felt his innards would spill out. It was the first time ever he felt ashamed to even utter his name. He pushed hard to break out of the shell of silence. He meant to somehow yet could not gather enough courage. So he dropped the call again.

A little later after worrying for a while, he thought of an even less difficult way to avoid talking over the phone. He started texting her instead.

"Good morning Aunt Mary. I am Siddharth. Hazel's school friend. I hope you can recall me. I heard about Hazel's accident and could not stop myself from visiting Jamshedpur. I am presently in town and would visit the hospital today. I will see you there."

He waited for a few minutes for a response. The wait stretched for fifteen minutes and then for an hour. But there was no response. It seemed impossible for him to talk to Aunt Mary or go meet her without getting a response to his text. He kept blaming himself for all that happened to Hazel.

Although he believed he was the reason, the letters hadn't blamed him, anywhere anyhow. Yet from his point of view, the trauma she had to pass through, did not diminish his part in her life. It did not exonerate him from his own glare. And he could never forget that he had run away from the situation never pursuing to find out about her, ever.

That stung him like nettles. His timidity, his cowardice.

It was around eleven in the morning when his cell phone rang. It was Aunt Mary. Siddharth grabbed the phone, took a few deep breaths and answered.

"Siddharth dear. Is that you?"

"Yes. Hello Aunt Mary," he said trembling, unable to say anything further.

There was a pause at both ends. His pulse raced. The day was cold but beads of sweat trickled down his neck.

"After so many years?" Her shock was evident even over the phone.

"Yes, Aunt Mary."

"Where were you all these years my son?" she asked quietly.

"Aunt Mary I am…," was all he could say.

"Good Lord," said Hazel's mom still recovering from the initial jolt.

"I am sorry for everything…really…sorry," he started imploring her to forgive him for Hazel's past. The load of anguish that got built inside him after reading Hazel's letters, exploded all at once. But he checked himself immediately as he realized that it must not have made sense to Aunt Mary.

"Sorry for everything? For what?" she asked. "Where are you calling from?"

"From this town. I am in Jamshedpur right now."

"In town? It is nice to hear from you again. How have you been my child?" In spite of her daughter in coma, she spoke like she always did. With the warmth of the winter sun. That relieved him. Tears trickled down his cheeks. He had imagined her to either rebuke him or ignore him. But she did neither. In her affectionate words he found the courage to talk.

"I am fine Aunt Mary."

"And where were you all these years?"

"In Bhubaneswar. I work there."

"You know my Hazel is…"

Before she could complete Siddharth said, "I heard about it Aunt Mary. I will visit the hospital shortly. In fact I was getting ready to meet you there." After the phone-call, Siddharth wiped off the tears from his face.

By noon Siddharth reached the hospital. He felt more confident to meet Hazel's mom. As soon as he neared the ICU he spotted her. Before his inhibitions could sway him, he went straight over to her and hugged her. Her face was red and swollen and sad. Her eyes screamed of pain and helplessness. Yet on seeing him she managed to smile.

"You have grown into a big man," she said softly holding his hands. "You were so young when I saw you last," she indicated by the distance of her hand to the ground.

Siddharth smiled and didn't let go of her waist which he held tightly in compassion and sorrow. He couldn't ask how Hazel was. He couldn't ask how Aunt Mary was. How would a mom be, when her grown up daughter was in deep sleep and no one could tell for sure whether she would ever wake up.

"Why didn't you meet me when you came here few days back?" asked Aunt Mary.

Siddharth was shocked to hear that and failed to respond. He wondered how on earth she knew about his earlier visit. All this while he was hiding from her, fearing her, feeling miserable, finding it difficult to even talk to her over phone. And here she was asking him so casually about his disappearance without meeting her. If at all her voice indicated anything it was one of genuine eagerness. Her poise and serenity surprised him.

"How did you know?" he asked loosening his arms around her waist.

"You met Shane, didn't you? He told me."

"Oh yes. Shane," recalled Siddharth. He had almost forgotten about him. "Actually that day you had just left the hospital. I waited for a while and then left." He fibbed.

"I was surprised to hear about you. And wondered how you left without meeting me." She spoke softly. "I thought Shane must have gotten the name wrong."

"I wanted to meet you Aunt Mary. But I had to travel for some urgent work. So…"

"Well it is good you have come back again. Where are you staying here?"

"I checked into hotel Meghdoot. But I am planning to move to another one tonight."

"You came to meet Hazel? Just to see her?"

Siddharth nodded. They stared at each other. The old fondness for each other growing in their faces.

He looked into her red eyes and tried to read how much they had seen and suffered in a lifetime. Yet the grit and hope in them was not lost. He felt foolish for not meeting her on the first day itself when he landed in Jamshedpur.

They sat down and she introduced him to some of her friends and relatives who were hearing their conversation anyway. They spoke about the old times, bits and pieces of their lives and then about Hazel's accident.

"What is the latest opinion of the doctor's Aunt Mary?"

"Well they are saying that a surgery is possible. They could not confirm the date yet."

"That's good news."

"Some hope. Maybe they will confirm in a day or two. Do pray for her, son."

"I will Aunt Mary."

"So what did you say the reason was for changing your hotel tonight?"

Suddenly Siddharth became aware that he was being watched. Like someone staring at him from behind. He spun around and saw few people and nurses walking across the corridors. And then he saw a man hurrying away down the stairs. He could vaguely see the top half of the man's back before he vanished. For a moment he thought of chasing down the man. But he dropped the idea when he reflected, it was merely a hunch.

He wondered if it was the nameless caller who had informed him about Hazel's accident and handed over the key through Shane. But if it was him why was he hiding?

He continued to talk and explained why he was changing into a new hotel that night.

Chapter 18

THE TAXI RIDE

That night he checked out of the hotel only because it was an expensive one and he reckoned he had to stay on for a few more days. On his way to the new hotel he had planned to visit the Kali Temple to pray for Hazel. It was about eight pm. The wind was gathering speed. It smelt of a shower somewhere. He had noticed that the moon did not come up. The chill was beginning to freeze him slowly as he climbed the hill.

At the temple, the evening prayers were over. More people were leaving the temple gates that coming in. He prayed in silence for Hazel for a long time, his suitcase beside him. By nine pm, most of the people had left. Apart from the priest and him, there were less than a dozen people in the temple premises. As he was about to leave there was a sudden downpour.

Siddharth was stranded. The roof of the temple was the only shelter. He stood there with his luggage worrying about how he would reach the new hotel. It was quite far. The rain lasted for about one hour. When it reduced to a drizzle he climbed down the temple steps. The rains had created puddles and water-logging in many areas. When he reached at the base of the temple he waived at a car standing nearby. The car slowly came near him.

"Taxi *lagega*?" asked the driver with a heavy Bihari accent. He was wearing a monkey-cap and dark spectacles.

"Yes. Hotel Kohinoor."

"That is far. Ten kilometers. I will charge three hundred fifty rupees."

Relieved to find a cab, Siddharth sat in the backseat, without bargaining. The taxi rolled off. No sooner had they reached the bend of the road at the base of the temple, he saw a man waving frantically at them with a sling-bag in his hands. He was completely drenched.

The driver stopped the vehicle and asked, "*Kya hai?*"

"Lift. No taxi. No auto. *Kuch nahin mil raha hai.*"

"*Kahaan tak?*" asked the driver.

"Market area, near petrol pump. Please." He looked pleadingly at the driver.

The driver turned his head half-way to check with Siddharth if he'd allow the additional passenger, "It's on the way to Hotel Kohinoor. Should we pick him up?"

Siddharth hesitated once but looking at the state of the drenched man, agreed.

"Thank you Sir. *Shukriya,*" the man smiled and sat on his right.

"*Theek hai.* No problem," replied Siddharth.

The man was wearing a wet T-Shirt and jeans and placed the sling-bag on his lap. As the taxi sped, they spoke about the bad weather, the forecast and train delays.

"The radio reported sunshine from tomorrow," said the drenched man. "It is strange why it rained at this time of the year. But nowadays anything is happening. The seasons are no longer what they used to be."

He struck a lively conversation with Siddharth and asked him about his work and where he travelled from. The taxi swished through the water logged streets and moved fast as the traffic was nil.

Once they had driven a few kilometers the driver got a call in his cell phone and spoke in a language Siddharth did not understand. The call was over in two or three words and the driver said it was his friend appraising him that he got stuck somewhere.

When they had reached half-way towards Hotel Kohinoor the man with the sling-bag told Siddharth that he would split the fare and asked if he had loose change.

"Do you have five hundred rupees change?"

As Siddharth was pulling out his wallet to check the cash he carried, the taxi swerved at a bend near a bus stand and came to a sudden stop. Before the blink of an eye, a man got inside the car, sat on Siddharth's left and closed the door.

The driver smiled and said, "*Mera dost.* My friend. He's stuck here and needs help."

Siddharth wanted to protest but the taxi gathered speed before he could say a word. Suddenly he felt stupid and fearful for trusting strangers and into the car. But it was not his intuition or stories he heard of thugs that provoked his fears. It was something else.

It was actually the glint of metal.

Within seconds, the man with the sling-bag calmly said, "*Maal nikalo jitna bhi hai.*" He pointed a sharp knife at Siddharth's throat and snatched his wallet. When he tried to resist the man on his left punched him on the face.

They snatched the gold chain around his neck and two rings and demanded all loose cash he had. They gripped his wrists tightly with one hand and swayed the knife with the other. The driver hurled abuses in Hindi. And then he swerved the car off the main road to the right onto a narrow road and accelerated.

"We need to check you thoroughly. If you are caught with any more money, the knife will do what it does best," said the man with the sling-bag, suddenly shouting.

Siddharth cowered and kept saying there was nothing more he had. His throat was dry with fear. Meanwhile the man on his left tied his hands in front, with nylon strings. Once he was done he punched him some more in random corners of the body.

They were hurtling through the road like a rocket.

After covering some distance, the streetlights went missing and all Siddharth could guess was they were moving through a narrow road which had dense trees all around. He lost his sense of direction. The driver sped in spite of the narrow road while the other two tormented him. They frequently boxed him on the face and booted him on the shin.

An hour after the car rolled off from the station, it halted. The rain had stopped. The moonlight showed dense trees around and other than the reverberation of the car engine that was left running there was dead silence. In the illumination of the car headlights, Siddharth was dragged out by one man while the other was busy repeatedly kicking him on his legs. He was made to stand leaning against a nearby tree, the headlights on his face.

"Hand over whatever you have or else it will not be good for you," said the driver.

"I told you I have nothing more except the suitcase."

"What is the password for your ATM card?" one of them asked holding the card he pulled out from the wallet. The other were counting the cash in it with a flashlight.

At first Siddharth did not speak but after the back of the

metal flash-light struck him on his face, he blurted out.

"If the ATM password is not correct then we will slice you into so many pieces that no one can recognize if the flesh is of a human or a forest animal," said the driver, holding a knife at the neck and digging it into the skin.

"Yes the ATM password is correct," replied Siddharth. But he lied. Thinking that the ATM machines were far away he took a chance.

On the other hand, looking at the ruthlessness of the muggers, he thought of owning up the other lie he had told earlier, which would be soon discovered anyway.

"I have some money inside my underpants," said Siddharth. He always kept some cash there, in a hidden pocket, during travels. "If you untie me, I can get it out for you."

"We can do that ourselves," said the driver.

They stripped him and mined out the currency notes from the underpants.

"Five thousand bucks," said the driver. Without any provocation the man with the sling-bag ran the knife over Siddharth's left fore-arm and made a long gash at the fleshy portion, near the elbow.

"Why did you do that," screamed Siddharth enraged and trembling in pain.

"You lied to us the first time. If we find more lies we will cut your throat next," replied the driver in Hindi. "Do not test us."

"Now untie me," demanded Siddharth. "You got all I had."

"Shut the f*** up," yelled the driver and kicked him on the shin again. Siddharth shrieked in pain and fell down. It was then that he noticed that the driver was a big man, taller and broader than him. He was wearing spectacles. He also noticed that he spoke English.

"Get his cell phone as well," the driver almost ordered them. This time he spoke in Hindi again. Pointing the big flashlight at the suitcase they ripped it open and foraged through the contents. They found clothes, books, files and other stuff they felt were valuable like an old watch, a camera and some loose cash.

"Let us take the entire suitcase," said one of them.

When they were almost done the driver saw a bunch of painting books and the brown diary. Curious he started flipping through them and said, "This ass is a painter. So he has all this rubbish." They all laughed at something the driver said. It sounded like a south Indian language. But Siddharth could not exactly tell which one.

"This bastard is not carrying much. Today he will pay with his paintings," said the driver and started tearing each painting one by one.

While they were searching the suitcase Siddharth was trying, in sly, to untie his hands. Although he loosened the cords with some effort, he felt that if he wiggled his hands any more he would be noticed. The car headlights were on him. Instead, with his tied hands he reached out for the buckle of his belt and tried to open it. And he succeeded.

So when the driver started tearing the precious paintings meant for Hazel he pleaded and begged them not to. But one of them came forward and slapped him and went back and started tearing the papers faster. He was frightened and felt miserable and kept pleading repeatedly.

But then at the edge of fear lies courage. At the edge of bondage lies freedom.

Something happened to Siddharth. Something unusual and unexpected. Something that was not his character. Quickly his fright turned to anger and then to fury. And he pulled out his Longhorn leather belt smoothly. It was thick and strong and the buckle was heavy metal. He swung it in the air with both hands, holding the tail of the belt.

"You Mother******," he yelled at the top of his voice and lurched at the three men.

The three muggers were startled to hear the sudden unexpected scream. Before they could turn around, Siddharth swung the belt fast and struck the face of the driver with the metal of the buckle. It almost knocked the driver off with blood spurting out from the check bones where the buckle landed. Siddharth struck him once again on the face. The second strike was more powerful. The driver fell to the ground. His spectacles flew off.

Siddharth turned around with bloodshot eyes. The other two men picked up their knives immediately and came forward. But Siddharth kept on swinging his belt with both hands that kept the two men at bay. Then he stepped forward and struck one of them.

The man ducked and the belt caught his arm and coiled around it. Siddharth yanked the belt hard and the man lost his balance at the jerk and came hurtling head-first in front of him. Immediately Siddharth kicked him with full force on his groin and quickly uncoiled the belt from his arms. The man toppled over in pain exactly at the place where he was standing.

The third man swished the knife close to Siddharth's left arm and made a minor cut. Siddharth kicked him in his stomach and used the belt's buckle to thrash his face. That sent the man stumbling towards the same tree where Siddharth was made to stand.

This was probably the first time in his life when Siddharth was violent and stood up for himself and fought without fear.

The fight went on for some time and Siddharth nearly managed to quash them when his left hand began to flutter and he lost his grip. Then a sudden brutal contact of a metal rod against the back of his head sent streaks of lightning to his eyes, blinding him. At once the three men pounded on him and pinned him down. They tied his hands again, securely.

They picked up the suitcase and the other things that had spilled out of it and dragged him to the car and drove down a dusty path for another fifteen minutes. The car stopped in front of a dilapidated one room concrete house. They pulled him out of the car and shoved him inside the broken house. In his semiconscious state, Siddharth vaguely heard one of them say, "We will be back if the ATM password does not work."

The driver added, "If you have lied to us we will come back and chop you. And if you have not, you will bleed slowly to death anyway."

Saying that, the driver rolled a ball of cloth and shoved it into Siddharth's mouth. Then he sliced the left thumb almost halfway through as if he was slicing chicken liver and left him thrashing his limbs about, screaming for help all night through the ball of cloth.

Outside when the three muggers were getting ready to leave in their car it was still pitch dark and they could hardly hear anything beyond a faint murmur from the room.

"Even the frogs are louder than that ass of a Bengali," said the driver chuckling.

They abused him some more and revved up the engine few times before speeding off.

Chapter 19

THE OLD PAINTINGS AND THE VILLAGE DOCTOR

Before Siddharth regained his consciousness for a brief period of time, he could barely recollect anything. He relapsed into that state again slouching against the wall. In between, only a sparrow and a seven year old child had visited the small room with a tiny grilled window to his right.

The child ran away with his loot of colorful papers and reached home to his mother who was toiling away at the kitchen. She demanded an explanation for his absence for such a long time. Hoping his cooperation would reduce his mother's wrath, the child extended his arms and held his booty for her inspection.

She looked at the papers and was awestruck by the beautiful paintings in them.

"Where did you get them from?"

The child pointed to some place behind him.

"Go show your dad. He was asking for you. He is in the bed-room."

When he entered the room, the child saw his father smoking hookah and was cheerfully chatting on the bed with the village doctor with the beard.

"*Arre chotu* where were you, you imp," scowled his father.

The boy did not speak, afraid of being slapped by his father in front of the respectable village doctor. He simply held out his hands with the paintings.

"Where were you?" asked his father again.

Then he looked at what his son was showing him. He took the papers and spread them across the bed one after the other. There were about five of them. Impressed at what he saw he showed it to the village doctor.

The village doctor looked at them and said, "Beautiful. Who made them?"

"*Arre chotu*, where did you get these from?" asked the father. The child simply pointed somewhere behind him.

"*Arre jaban nahin hai ka?*" asked the father again shaking his son by his shoulders.

The village doctor looked at the paintings closely and seemed impressed.

"Really nice ones. But one or two of these pictures kind of strike me that I have seen them before somewhere."

"Seen them? Maybe in some poster or picture," said the father. "*Arre chotu bol na, kahan mila yeh painting?*"

Finally, overcoming his fear the child said, "In the small house by the pond."

"Why did you go there alone?" asked his father harshly. He was about to strike his son when the village doctor stopped him.

"I am quite sure I have seen these somewhere," said the doctor. He was trying hard to recollect and the more he looked into them the more they seemed closer to being recognized. And then he thought, he kind of remembered.

"Can you take me to the person who gave you these?" asked the doctor to the child.

The child became frightened for he had stolen the paintings. But prodded by his father he agreed. And then through the thicket of coconut trees, mango groves and other wild trees he led them until they reached the pond. Standing there he shot up the right forefinger to point towards the small house on the opposite side of the pond.

The boy ran back home. The doctor and the child's father walked along the periphery of the pond, casually chatting about the thunderstorms and rain the previous night. The sky was clear blue and the air was crisp.

Once they reached the broken house they peeped inside through the rusty door and saw someone lying there. So they knocked the door a couple of times before entering.

As soon as the child's father saw the man splattered with blood he immediately turned around to bolt out of the house. But the doctor was calm and looked straight at the face of the man. For encountering wounded people in the village either due to family feuds, accidents or even snakebites in odd locations was almost routine.

But the more closely the doctor looked at the face the more baffled he became until finally he knew his guess was right.

"I know this man. We need to get him immediate help," said the doctor.

The scared father immediately ran to get help from the local villagers. Within fifteen minutes a group of villagers carried Siddharth to the doctors' shack. The doctor took two hours to clean up the blood clots and stains and apply stitches to the wounds. An IV was injected in his arms and a bottle of saline water was hung overhead from the bed pole.

Finally Siddharth blinked his eyes open and looked around trying to recognize the surrounding. He sat up on the bed to drink water before lying down again.

For the rest of the day he drank like a camel and then slept like a koala.

Next morning when he woke up and stared across the room a puzzled expression flooded his face. The bearded village doctor was darting around the bed he was lying on, calling out to some boys, holding a stethoscope in his hand and inspecting some reports before hurriedly walking out of the room. A young woman in a sari declared herself as a nurse and smiled at him and periodically checked if everything was alright.

His memory was slowly crawling back. The doctor arrived after two hours and checked the pulse. Seeing an improvement, he came closer and smiled and exposed his chipped canine tooth, "Are you feeling better, Siddharth?"

Surprised to hear his name taken so affectionately, he looked keenly at the strange looking doctor and his chipped tooth that looked awkwardly familiar. Then his mind raced backwards into the past through the dense forests he was mugged in, to his company, his home, to his college, to Jamshedpur and then finally stopped at his school.

The bruised lips curved as much as they could into a thin smile of recognition and he called out in a feeble voice, "Sudeep, is that you?"

That evening after the birds reached home and the golden sun sank into the horizon, they exchanged their stories. Sudeep remained speechless as he heard Siddharth's entire past up to the point where he was robbed at knife-point. But it was Sudeep who first recounted the story of his life in the village.

"I was always suspicious about the mainstream ideas of success, a job, a car, a house. And then another job, another car, another house. I realized the chase was endless and at the end meaningless. I decided to listen to my heart rather than what glossy tabloids harped on. Opulence bored me. Fortunes of a few at the disgrace of the collective didn't go well with me. Because in the long run we are all dead."

At that point he lit a cigarette. "After completing M.B.B.S and M.D. and practicing for a few years in Delhi, I returned. Not playing a useful role in society troubled me. Reputation and fortune was easy to achieve, I felt, but I wanted to do something significant."

He took few puffs from the cigarette and continued, "I decided to walk the path that was led by my heart. The safe shell I was living in for ten years had to break. I planned to use my learning in a place that was close to Jamshedpur and yet far away from the reach of modern medicine. For the last five years I have been living and working in this village."

"Why did you choose this place?" asked Siddharth.

"I wanted to be near dad and mom too. It is about 75 kilometers from here."

"Are they happy with your decision to be away from the city," asked Siddharth remembering that Aarif-ji the barber had told him about Dr. Mitra's complaints about his son.

"No, they never approved of it, especially dad. They look at everything as an investment. I am not earning much now," replied Sudeep. "They fail to see the satisfaction I get out of doing this nor do they appreciate the work being done in this village."

"Why do they think that way?"

"They feel it is the government's job to do it. Not mine."

"But it is great as long as you are happy." He looked at Sudeep proudly and thought how wrong Dr. Mitra was in the assessment of his son. "I heard you play the 'tabla' for some local band in Jamshedpur?" asked Siddharth changing the line of conversation slightly.

"Oh yes, that's my other passion," replied Sudeep. "How did you know about it?"

It was then that Siddharth narrated about his visits to Jamshedpur and his accidental discovery of Hazel, her letters, about Kiran and his life. Sudeep felt sorry for him.

Later they sat reminiscing over lost times. It seemed that none of their classmates lived in Jamshedpur anymore. Sudeep was the only one closest to the city.

"What about Shankar? Where is he?" asked Siddharth.

"Shankar the boom-box, has settled in the USA. Got a Green card. He went there years back as an SAP consultant. Last I heard, he was an IT Director in a company…some Office Solutions."

"Really? That's nice to hear."

"Yeah he is doing real well," said Sudeep. "Most of the others moved to IT and then finally to the States or Europe. You know how the IT boom robbed all the bright guys. Boring computers. Not my cup of tea."

"Not mine too.

At night he lay on his bed wishing he could talk to Hazel and appraise her about his condition. He wondered what she was thinking in her deep sleep, whether her surgery had happened, whether she was still alive? The last thought made him shiver.

The next day, which was the third day, Siddharth felt better and asked Sudeep if he could leave. "I'd recommend you stay put here for one more day," replied Sudeep.

"How would I reach Jamshedpur from here?"

"I will escort you tomorrow morning, in the public bus that runs between here and Jamshedpur," said Sudeep. He had relinquished his privilege of driving a car long back.

Siddharth had to borrow money from Sudeep as he was dispossessed of both his wallet and cell-phone.

Chapter 20

THE SURGERY

When Siddharth reached the hospital again, he saw an unusual trace of optimism on the faces of people gathered there. Hazel's surgery was decided on just the previous day and would start in the next few hours. A doctor was explaining the procedures to Shane and Aunt Mary.

"The latest MRI reports show that the edema has reduced and the small clots have disappeared. So we are optimistic of going ahead with the surgery."

"We were waiting for so long to hear that, doctor," said Shane. "We hope everything goes fine after the surgery."

The doctor replied with folded hands, "We will try to remove the big clots in the brain today. We will do our best. But this is a critical operation and a lot depends on how it goes. Please pray to God."

Aunt Mary thanked the doctor as tears of hope rolled off from her eyes.

When the doctor left, Shane turned around and saw Siddharth. He noticed the bandages on Siddharth's hands and head. He walked over to him and asked, "Hey what happened to you?"

"Oh nothing. I just ran into a few muggers few days back."

"Are you alright? It looks serious."

"I am fine now. My friend Sudeep here is a doctor. He took care of me for the last few days." Shane shook hands with Sudeep.

"Hazel's mom was asking about you; that you disappeared again all of a sudden."

"Yeah. I was in his clinic undergoing first aid."

"It was not just first aid. It was more serious than that," pointed out Sudeep.

They walked over to Aunt Mary and her friends. Everyone asked about the bandages on Siddharth. He explained again trying to trivialize the incident as much as he could.

Throughout the duration of the surgery Hazel's mom, Siddharth and Sudeep stayed outside the OT along with Shane and Helena and a few others. Many well-wishers were at the Church at that time, praying for Hazel.

"She will be alright Aunt Mary," said Helena wrapping her arms by her shoulders.

"We will not allow anything to happen to her," said Shane.

Aunt Mary sat motionless, sleep starved and groggy eyed. Once in a while she broke into a shiver, imagining her daughter at the site of accident, crushed by the car.

"Everything seems over for me."

"Please don't cry Aunt Mary. We have to hope for the best," said Siddharth.

"She never listened to me. I told her to stop working so hard…"

"Have faith in the Lord," said Shane. "She will come out fine."

"I always suspected that she would end up like her father," she sobbed.

Siddharth figured out that it was her real father that she was referring to. Not the brutal James. He wondered where James was.

"Don't say like that. She is a brave girl...," said Helena.

"Hazel will fight back and recover, Aunt Mary," said Siddharth, almost choking on his words and closed his eyes.

She got him small gifts from time to time. In school, she got him mints and Cadburys. After the Christmas and New Year holidays were over, she would bring a large cake for the entire class. And while everyone was busy nibbling at their share of the cake, she would quietly slip a bar of candy inside his trouser pocket. Once she even gave him a Parker pen. She always gave him something extra than she gave to the rest of her friends.

She made him feel what he was to her. Special. Extraordinary.

Once they had giggled uncontrollably over a silly joke during the Hindi class and the offended teacher turned them out of the classroom. They were made to stand at the door. They stood looking into each other's eyes and made a game out of it.

"Whoever stares longer without blinking would be the winner," she told him.

"Okay what will the winner get?" asked Siddharth.

"If you win, I'll buy you a Russian novel of your choice. Say 'War and Peace'?"

"Okay great," he said sounding elated as he always flipped through the pages of that book by Tolstoy in book-fairs but was deterred by the price to buy it. "And if you win?"

"You will buy me a 'Mills and Boons."

"Done."

She had tricked him in the game. When they stared at each other, she rolled and bounced her eyes and twisted her lips, flared her nostrils, changed her facial expressions from anger, to comic, to sadness, to steamy, all without batting her eyelids even once. And poor Siddharth burst out laughing and failed to keep his eyes open. Obviously, Hazel won.

Next day in class she thrust something into his hands that was hard for him to imagine. "After our war of eyes yesterday here is a flag for peace."

Holding the glossy paperback in his hands he could not help exclaiming, "But you won Hazel. I was supposed to get you your book."

"The winner calls the shots and decides what to do," said Hazel with an air.

"This is not fair," he said looking at the novel with delight.

"This is settled now. I won't hear a word on this anymore."

Sitting outside the OT, Siddharth recalled more such incidents that had made him so fond of and attached to Hazel in school.

The surgery lasted for over four hours. When the surgeon walked out of the OT his face showed was neutral. He simply said, "It was positive. She gets a new life today."

Those who were present there and nearby heard the hall resounding with cries of joy.

"Thank you doctor," cried Hazel's mom. "We will remain forever indebted to you."

"It was all God's will," said the surgeon. "But emerging from a coma is a gradual process of becoming more responsive and aware of people and surroundings. We need to take extreme care of her even now."

Hazel was kept in the ICU for next two days and then shifted to the private ward. One of Aunt Mary's friend said, "I have heard that coma patients may have difficulty recognizing people. It might help if we bring in something familiar, such as a picture, favorite dress or tape of a special song." So Aunty Mary brought in similar objects and items from home.

Siddharth would sit beside Hazel for hours during the day, especially when Aunt Mary and her relatives had to leave after a tiring night by her bedside. He sat beside her for hours and looked at her staring blankly at him, her eye-contact not revealing if she recognized him. Mostly she stared at the ceiling or outside the window, silent, unconcerned. She was no longer the childhood photocopy image that Siddharth remembered when he had seen her last. She looked different, yet her face had the contours of a sweet and loving person.

A day or two later, as he looked at her in the ward, his fingers became fidgety. Something stirred them. Like the sudden resurgence of an old habit. It was a familiar urge that had abandoned the fingers long ago, a sweeping desire to hold, lift and move something. Something that was an integral part of him once.

That afternoon, with the loaned money from Sudeep, he bought large sheets of papers, canvases, palettes, colors, paintbrushes and also stood up an easel in the cabin room. When Hazel woke up next morning, she saw the canvases slowly gain color and life.

Once again after nearly two decades he mixed paints in the palette.

It was for her. Hoping fervently that his paintings would provoke her, rouse her, bring her in to the world, he drew the town, the temple, their school, the classroom, the stadium, the market, the hills and all such places where he and Hazel used to visit. He painted feverishly and also made a dozen sketches, using symbols and sceneries that Hazel had seen in her childhood. Her eyes followed his moving hands as they swept over the canvas.

And when people came to meet Hazel they looked at Siddharth's beautiful paintings and gasped in wonder. For they looked so photographic and surreal at the same time, yet so touching, unlike anything they had seen before.

"Thank you son for filling this room with the dazzle of these gems. Their purity will surely touch my daughter," said Aunt Mary.

"I had no clue you had a genius inside you, man," said Shane patting his back and almost embracing him. "You seem to be deeply attached with this town. Real classy stuff."

"I am short of words Sidd. The temple in the moonlight is so romantic," said Helena.

People lauded and praised Siddharth. They asked Aunt Mary about him, where he lived and what relationship he had with her. Everyone who came to visit Hazel, marveled at the paintings and left the hospital wonderstruck.

But beneath the brilliance of the paintings ran a dead language. A language that had once bound Sidd and Hazel together. And later got buried. Though it was lost it was not forgotten. It had to be excavated. It had to be revived. Through it he wanted to reach out to her soul again. Only she could recall the scenes, the sceneries and the strange symbols in them. He wanted to talk to her through them.

After finishing each painting he motioned her to examine

them, especially the symbols that had fascinated her in childhood. But she looked at them as if they were nothing beyond eye candy. The sceneries did not touch her, the symbols no longer intrigued her.

One afternoon, after a few days, while he was painting and Hazel was asleep, someone came inside the room stealthily and stood behind him. Suddenly he saw a blob of black liquid splash on the canvas he was painting on, messing it up totally.

He turned around and saw a tall and broadly built unshaven man watching him with scorn and anger. He was dressed in brown corduroys and a brown jacket over a black high-neck T-shirt and was wearing black winter gloves. Even his eyes were covered with sunglasses. There was a sudden whiff of hostility in the room.

He smiled sarcastically and said in a low voice, "So you are back again."

Siddharth could not recognize the man as not an inch of his skin was visible.

"It is a wonder. How you disappear and reappear. Again and again like a stubborn wart. It puzzles me and it irritates me." His voice was cold and vindictive.

Quickly the man removed a brass knuckle from his jacket and slipped his fingers in them and clenched his fist. And then he pulled out a cycle chain from the jacket.

"I swore to kill you but could not. You escaped."

Siddharth's mind raced to identify the man but he could not. He said, "Hey who the hell are you? Step back. This is a hospital. The patient is sleeping."

"And guess who will need another bed here after I am done

with you. Last time you slipped away but this time…" he swung his hand as his words trailed off.

In a flash, Siddharth felt the sting of a barb-wire coil around his face and throat.

The man yanked the cycle-chain and pulled Siddharth towards him and then struck him on his face. Blood spewed inside his mouth. Unable to understand what was happening he stood immobile. He suspected the man to be one of the muggers he had lied to about the ATM card password. Probably he had come back to square up the unfinished business.

"Stop it, else I'll call the police." Siddharth leapt forward towards the exit door but got blocked on the way.

"Try now," said the man and elbowed Siddharth hard on the ribs that sent him stumbling back to the window. "Few days back we thought we had dealt with you well and that you would go back to where you came from. But I was wrong. It looks like today I will get another chance today to redeem my vow."

Siddharth tried to go towards the door but he was stopped again. "So you are one of the muggers who tried to kill me after robbing?"

"No. Not me. My hands wouldn't want to touch your dirty skin. They were my men. But obviously they didn't do a good job or didn't scare you enough. Sounds interesting?"

For a moment, Siddharth felt if it was a trap set by the mysterious caller who called him there to meet Hazel. He said, "Get out from here whoever you are."

"Sorry I can't. Since my men didn't leave a lasting impression on you, I had to come. I must do a better job now. Oh that limb? I can work on it." The man struck him on his bandaged left hand and it began twitching.

"Why are you after me? You already got all that I had. Now get out of the room," howled Siddharth raising his arms in defense.

"Who said I got all I wanted." The man struck him again on his left hand. "You lied. The ATM password was fake. But that's just one reason. It is not the real reason."

"Real reason? What reason?"

"Long back someone had lost his eye because of you." He rapped Siddharth's arm.

"Oh shut the crap," said Siddharth and then suddenly, in anger, he slapped the man hard right across his face that sent the sunglasses flying across the room before it crashed against the wall.

And then he saw the eyes.

Siddharth's face turned severe. The room fell silent for a while. The man grinned.

"Looks like you have recognized me. The eyes of an artist are sharp indeed. But my art is not inferior. I can split walnuts and bricks with my hands. No one will know who cracked you up after I leave."

"You were the one following me all these days here? Weren't you?"

"True. I am always on the prowl. I don't waste opportunities."

Siddharth tried to look around the room for something stronger than his hands, something that could counter the cycle chain and the brass knuckles. But other than plastic water bottles and medicine pouches there was nothing. The saline bottle stand would be too heavy to lift and strike with.

"Years back something had happened to this lady," he

pointed at Hazel, "but no one could do much. They couldn't pinpoint the culprit. You see I work smart."

The man paused and held his breath. His lips quivered and his face flushed with sudden rage, "And you were the reason for all that happened to us. If you weren't in the town, things would've been so different, so much better for me. But then no. You distracted her. You distracted all of us. Split our families apart. You ass of a Bengali. And when you left you left someone with a damaged eye for life."

"What damaged eye? What do you mean?"

"Oh, you want to play the Saint now? The day you left this town you had stoned someone, right after slipping a note under our door, like a chicken that you are. Remember? He lay there bleeding for a long time. But we recognized it was you 'cos you left that silly note. If he had not stopped me I'd have butchered you. But you left the town the next day like a coward. Today it is payback time. 'Cos the man you stoned was my dad."

Siddharth got goose bumps after hearing that and was about to say something. "You…."

"I wasn't sure she'd survive," the man said pointing at Hazel. "So I thought it okay to scare you with my men. But her destiny is different. She's gotten better. And I cannot see a mouse like you beside her. But don't worry I won't kill you. I'll reduce you to a shape that won't interest her anymore when she wakes up. An eye for an eye." The man started swinging the chain with his left hand and was about to strike Siddharth's right eye with the brass knuckle. But Siddharth ducked right in time and pushed him away.

"So you want to fight me."

Right at that point somebody tapped at the man's shoulder from behind and spoke with a roaring voice. "He doesn't need to. I will."

As the intruder turned, a severe blow landed on his head that sent him crashing to the floor. When he looked up he saw a pale-skinned tall muscular man with golden strands of hair loom over him. He had a body of a bouncer.

"We have met before buddy. You know we aren't fond of you. And you dared to touch my good friend here," said Shane. At that moment, Helena had also stepped in carrying fruits and flowers in a plastic bag. She went over to Siddharth quickly, wrapping her hand around his waist.

Then with lightning speed Shane pulled up the man by his throat and twisted his arm behind him and said, "If I see or hear you are near these two gentle people ever again, I will show you how to snap a spine like a twig." The man squealed in pain as Shane twisted his arms further behind his back and pushed him out of the cabin door.

"Sidd, you continue with your good work. It is about time now that I take this nuisance to the police station and settle this incident in the right way. Aunt Mary had told me few things after I met you." He winked at Siddharth and dragged the man away.

Helena patted him and said, "You need first aid. I hope you are okay."

"Yes I am," he said and drank water from the flask. Then he went over to Hazel and looked at her deeply. She was stirring on the bed and coming out of her sleep but her eyes were not open yet. He placed his hand over her forehead and stayed that way.

"Let's not say anything to Aunt Mary about what happened now," said Helena. "I'll tell her later on."

"I agree," he said. "I didn't know that Darryl still lives in the town."

He recalled the night before he left Jamshedpur for good when in fright he had stoned a man chasing him, after slipping a note under the door of Darryl's house. He had no clue that it was Darryl's father. And then a question posed itself in front of him. If it was Darryl who was shadowing him all this while in the hospital, then who was the damn anonymous caller?

For the next few days Siddharth painted furiously and even read poems for Hazel from his books. Even Sudeep visited her frequently and talked about their school days and the incidents that could never be wiped out of their memories. Hazel heard them but mostly remained silent. She spoke only if was necessary like asking for water or if she needed help to walk to the attached restroom.

A week later, for the first time, Hazel batted her eyelids at one of the paintings.

The same day the doctor instilled hope too, "She came out of coma last week and was in a minimally conscious state. But now she is coming out of the post-traumatic amnesia, and we think she will recover. It can be slow though. So we must hope for the best."

Overjoyed to hear that Aunt Mary and Siddharth squeezed each other's hands. Seeing that Hazel's lips curved into a smile too for the first time after she came out of coma. After the doctor left Siddharth took Aunt Mary outside the cabin and held her hands gently.

"This is incredible news. Your prayers and dedication has worked. I think I must plan to go back to Bhubaneshwar now."

"You must son. You've been here long enough, leaving your office and home and everything behind."

"But I promise to come back soon Aunt Mary."

"It will be great to see again soon my son. We will never forget the concern you showed. I will tell Hazel about your selfless support once she has recovered."

Though it would take more time for her to recover as per the doctor, the first signs were visible. And as a thread holds a bouquet of flowers, Hazel's improving health held the colors of a beautiful radiant dawn about to hatch open, once again.

Chapter 21

THE CALLER

It was a Sunday afternoon, a few days after Siddharth returned from Jamshedpur. He had finished his lunch and was sitting on the sofa in the drawing room, with the sketchbook on his lap. He was working on a series of sketches on Hazel and about his impressions of the village where Sudeep was practicing medicine. An array of pencils lay on the sofa beside him. The chairs and coffee table were disarranged. The house was messy. Dust had gathered along the window sills and furniture. Babban, the domestic help, was missing as he went to his village for fixing up his marriage. Only the bed and bed-sheet was still bright and clean.

Around four in the afternoon, as he was sharpening one of the pencils and dropping the curly shavings on the floor, the phone rang.

"Hello Siddharth." It was a tender voice.

"Yes."

"This is me. I had called you up few weeks back."

"Who?"

"The one who had informed you about Hazel's accident."

Siddharth sat up in alarm and triumph. "Hello there. I was expecting your call long back. Why didn't you meet me or call me back again?"

"I should have. I failed to. By the grace of God I heard Hazel is fine now."

"Yes she is. I wanted to thank you," said Siddharth allowing his gratefulness to be heard, "for letting me know about her."

"Aunt Mary told me that you were a pillar of support during the crisis. Thank you."

"She was a close school friend of mine. I had to."

"I know. My respect to you for that. Also Shane told me that he gave you the packet that had the key. With that I assume you were able to fetch Hazel's old letters."

To that Siddharth's curiosity soared. He was dying to know few things and said, "Yes I did. But I had many questions. How did the key reach you? How are you related to Hazel? I didn't see you at all when Hazel was in hospital. Were you not there?"

"No I wasn't. You see I don't live there. But I kept checking on her situation every day from Aunt Mary. I had a feeling that by the grace of God everything will be alright. And when I heard you were there I didn't go back."

"Why? What's your going there to do with me?"

There was a brief silence and then he started slowly. His voice suddenly sounded regretful. "I must tell you something now that will probably answer the questions you just asked. Something which I didn't know how to say before. You may be wondering who I am."

"Yes…obviously…"

"Situations weaken us sometimes. We end up doing the same things that we are dead against, things that are against our values and beliefs. Yet we do them. There are moments of irrationality. They have no basis, no logic, even no need. And later we repent for years. The mirror becomes critical of the image it holds. We cannot escape the regret imprisoned within us. We cannot abandon it. And so it was with me. I carried that repentance for many years."

The man paused and couple of breaths later he resumed.

"But when I saw that Hazel was almost at the end of her life, I couldn't take it any longer. I knew I had to find you. So I traced you down and called you on 15 November. That date is important because after I spoke to you about the key, not only was I relieved, I felt courage flow in my veins after a long time. I felt like a new person." Towards the end his voice gathered confidence and strength.

"But what was it that you had done?" asked Siddharth confused.

"Something irrational. Senseless. Cruel. It was for love. Love is irrational. It makes you do foolish things. It made me do such things. A lot may have been different between you and Hazel, had I not done that."

"What? What has this to do with Hazel?"

"My friend, Hazel was to me what she was to you once upon a time." He stopped talking and coughed and moved his face away from the phone. It sounded like he was drinking water. Then he got back to the phone and said, "Sorry I had to clear my throat."

"What's your name? Can I get that now please?"

"Yes. I am JD."

"JD?"

"Joydeep."

"Joydeep?" asked Siddharth flummoxed. "From Father's Romelo's institution?"

"So you know about me already and about Father Romelo as well."

"Very little."

"Then you may know that years back when Hazel came to

live in Father Romelo's campus, I was there as well. Her entry to our simple lives had a magical effect on me. It seeded a sense of belongingness in me. And that sense deepened into a feeling of attachment and finally without realizing how or when it happened, I was in pursuit to attain her. But those were my feelings. Not hers. When the truth dawned on me, I grappled with the realization that she was not mine. That she was only a visiting dream. I was shattered. But I had earned her trust. Considerable trust. And that proved to be the poison as well."

"You sound very critical of yourself."

"For true reasons. One day Hazel wanted to courier the letter with the key. She told me it was for you. And that it was an important step she had taken. She got your college address from somewhere. She and I were to go to the post office together. But Father Romelo had called her to send her to some place urgently. So she asked me to courier it. After she left, when I held the packet in my hands, I couldn't stop myself from reading the letter inside. Hazel had told me about you long back, and that awareness played the role of a Devil in my head. It argued and debated and forced me to commit a sin. It made me remove the box with the key. It infused hope that the link with you would be broken."

Joydeep stopped talking and simply let the moments slip by. Siddharth did not interrupt and he felt a rush of blood in him. Joydeep continued, "I realized my mistake after a few years. And when I learnt about Hazel's accident and that the chances of her survival were low, I felt the dagger of regret pierce deep in me. So I called you."

Once again Joydeep paused for a while. Siddharth felt a surge of rage sweep across his body and then slowly ebb as soon as it came. He was quick to realize that at this stage, with Hazel safe and back in his life again, the past didn't matter. In fact he could feel the anguish of Joydeep. The same anguish had besieged him completely after his separation with Hazel. In that way he felt bad for Joydeep.

"I have nothing more to say. Having said this much I feel a huge block of guilt has been removed from my body. By the grace of God Hazel got a new life. I hope one day you both can forgive me. But I can't imagine what she will think of me if she gets to know."

"Didn't you guys ever marry?" asked Siddharth.

Joydeep coughed a couple of times again and said, "If that had happened why would I be calling you here, my friend."

"Sorry. It was just a poor guess then. If you ever come to this part of the world then do visit me." He spoke some more and then hung up. Joydeep's words echoed in his mind for a long time, "I can't imagine what she will think of me if she gets to know."

Chapter 22

MEETING HAZEL

15 March 2009

A few months later, when Hazel was back on her feet, Siddharth decided to visit her. In between, they had spoken on the phone several times but only for a few minutes each time as he was careful not to strain her. They talked mostly about her health and the advice the doctors had given her. When she heard of his possible visit she was elated. After that, the only thing they discussed was to choose the right meeting place.

They picked their old spot. The Kali temple on the hilltop.

The thought of meeting her made him nervous with excitement. He contemplated carrying something special for her and decided on his old salvaged paintings. On Sunday morning, the day of their meeting, he was all colors, in blue jeans, a V-necked green sweater over a black T-shirt and brown shoes. At the hundredth step of the temple stairs, his eyes traversed around the flat hill top expecting to see a certain silhouette against the back-drop of the temple. But there was no one outside.

Even inside the temple he did not see her. Then he gazed at Goddess Kali in reverence, slowly closing his eyes to pray. He prayed for his dad, his deceased mom, his grandmother and for giving him strength to face Hazel and the moments to follow.

As he opened his eyes, two large eyes with thick lashes

were staring back at him. They were dry and dreamy and kohl-rimmed. A green 'bindi' glowed between the long arches of the dark eyebrows and the lightly colored lips had an undecided smile on them.

The eyes did not blink even once. Instead they slowly turned moist until beads of teardrops clung precariously at the dark edges of the eyes, threatening to fall off.

But they didn't. She wouldn't allow them to fall.

Glued by the thoughts of a shared past, of a time when they could not live without each other even for a moment, of a time when blood surged inside their veins at the touch of a finger, they looked at each other dazed and clasped each other's hands impulsively. They remained that way for a long time, oblivious to the people passing by, unmindful of the inappropriateness of a deep and extended gaze, forgetful of a traumatic past.

The clang of the temple bell broke the trance and their joined hands. Their faces had the glow of hundred light bulbs. It was an impossible reunion.

"Sidd," she said, staring at him and dabbed her moist eyes with a handkerchief.

"Hazel." He looked at her face as if he was in a dream.

With strings of white flowers streaming along her loose long hair and draped in a bottle green cotton sari bordered in dark green, she looked mature and elegant. The tragic years and her accident did not tarnish her charm, except for her eyes that spoke volumes of the hurt they had seen.

"Let's go to that corner," said Hazel clearing her throat. "There is good shade and less noise." She was pointing to a wooden bench under a Peepal tree at the center of the temple compound. They walked over and sat staring at each other.

The soft breeze on their face and gentle swish of leaves was comforting. The priest was tinkling a hand bell inside.

"Most of my paintings were destroyed when you were in the hospital," he said pointing at the rolls he was carrying. "Our old friend and his henchmen couldn't stand them."

"That was a terrible assault. Shane told me about it. That Darryl…"

"Forget him. Look. I got these," he said unfurling the rolls of painting sheets. "Do they look familiar?" Hazel looked at them and at him and at the paintings again and at him again. They brought an endearing smile on her face.

"I remember them," she said softly.

Desperate to hear the words again, he asked deliberately, "Do you Hazel?"

"Quite well." She looked at him and asked, "Is it true you had quit painting Sidd?"

"Ya. But I held the brush again after many years in the hospital."

"The paintings you made in the hospital are at home. You must continue. You must."

"I have a feeling I'll never stop it again."

After looking at the paintings they gazed at the temple and the people around. They barely spoke, unable to honestly articulate their feelings, unable to come to terms with a reality that seemed unreal. In a way, the distance of time had made them strangers too.

"How is your health now Hazel?" asked Siddharth breaking the silence.

"Better." After another pause in the conversation, she asked, "I know which college you went to after school. Beyond that it's a blank slate."

"You want me to write something on that slate?"

She nodded. The hunger to know more of each other's past was evident on their faces.

And then as he honestly laid out his past, she heard him patiently. She learnt under what conditions he had left the town, his vow to never return, his father's trip to Detroit, his college days, about his failed marriage and the court case he was battling for a long time.

"I am so sorry," she said after listening to his long story. The only information he withheld from her were the ones related to Joydeep, especially the removal of the box with the key from the courier. He only said, "I also read the letters you had left for me in the locker."

"Did you? When?"

"Many years after you had written them."

He expected her to ask for the reason for delay but strangely all she said was, "Those are old memories Sidd. I've moved on. I chose to look at the brighter side of my past."

"Why did you stop dropping letters into the locker?"

"No particular reason. I think it just ended as I didn't have more to say. Possibly because I never saw you writing back. I wasn't even sure if you ever read them Sidd."

He didn't know what to say. He didn't want to tell about Joydeep's wicked act of pilfering the locker key. He also realized that possibly she wouldn't believe him if he had told her about it. Because if Joydeep denied it there was no way anyone could prove who was guilty. The conversation he had with Joydeep was only between the two of them. In fact, it was not even possible to prove that the packet that Shane had handed over to him had the missing key. No one had seen what was inside the packet. Not even Shane. And he reflected, the moment was not appropriate to appraise her with such petty details.

Instead he said, "Circumstances slowed me down. But I'll talk about it another day."

While narrating his story, he felt, she was attentive yet somewhat remote. The eyes showed concern as he spoke but they didn't have the admiration in them that they once had. She didn't look at him like she used to in school. And she didn't dig into his past any more than what he offered to tell. Probably the moments muted her. Possibly it was her health.

After a while they walked inside the temple to avoid the growing heat.

Her voice was still soft but her pace of talking slower like her movements. She had gained weight. He told her about Sudeep and his work in the village. She seemed excited.

Siddharth was happy to have her beside him. It was almost like reviving the old days when he used to sit with her for hours together at the temple top, poking her, story-telling about his favorite painters, dreaming of a future together, watching the sun sink into its bed.

Hazel was happy too but in a different way. She watched his dimple chin and droopy eyelids that she was so fond of ages back. She was observing the changes in him and how life kept turning and twisting and throwing surprises at her. Though she was cheerful, when compared to her bubbly nature in school she was relatively more composed and silent.

They were both connected by their past, not their present. And that brought in an air of formality in their conversation. Though their love had receded, the affection and fondness still remained. And that was visible. In their stares, in their smiles, in their gestures and movements.

"Mom told me about all that you have done for us when I was in coma. I can't thank you enough Sidd." She patted his hand and asked, "By the way, how did you learn about my accident. I asked mom about it but she had no clue."

"Let's just say that someone informed me in time. That's all that matters I guess," said Siddharth and left it at that. "Actually, that kind of news travels fast. Even the barber at Azad Bazaar knew about your accident."

"Really? Maybe you are right, as Dimple and Jennifer also called me the other day." She took a deep breath and asked, "How long are you here by the way?"

"At least till tomorrow."

"Then you must have dinner tonight in my house. Mom insisted."

"Sure. I want to know more about your world that is outside the letters I read."

"You know a lot of it already. But we'll talk more about me later."

She didn't volunteer to talk about herself. But he was burning to know more. So they talked some more about her job and his. In her free time, she taught in a school called 'Asha Kiran' for special children, especially autistic. She found her work inspiring. Then they also talked about Father Romelo and his campus.

After one hour they decided to leave. She gave him a ride in her car when she learnt that he would stay at Hotel Jenny's, which was close to her house. In the car, they spoke of their school friends and teachers. When they reached the hotel, she smiled at him and said, "Mom will be delighted to see you Sidd. We'll talk more tonight."

"Sure." They stared at each other. It was obvious that they didn't want to disperse. "Want to come to my hotel room? It's basic but decent. I can serve coffee."

She shook her head. "Maybe another day. I need to take some rest. Come early."

Chapter 23

DINNER AT HAZEL'S HOUSE

After relaxing for the rest of the day Siddharth went to Hazel's house for dinner at eight. The door was ajar and it opened directly into the drawing room. As he pushed it gently, sweet sounds of piano drifted out. Someone was softly playing the 'Moonlight Sonata'. He removed his long overcoat and cap and knocked the door instead of ringing the door-bell wishing not to interrupt the piano playing.

Hazel's mom opened the door. She embraced him and holding his arms walked him inside. She was wearing a long black skirt and a fluffy bright blue cardigan that made her face even more radiant and cheerful. Her hair was dyed black.

The modest apartment did not have the disturbing presence of Uncle James.

"We were expecting you earlier Siddharth," said Aunt Mary beaming. "And I can't help exclaiming again that you have grown into such a big man."

"You still look the same Aunt Mary. As beautiful as you always were."

"Now you are trying to deceive me child. I am a hag now. But thank you."

The weight of sorrow that Siddharth had seen in her face at the hospital had disappeared, got replaced with the exuberance of a bright day. During the initial pleasantries he handed her a pot of 'rosogollas' which he had bought from Azaad bazaar. The piano playing stopped inside.

"How is Mr. Banerjee your father and where is he these days?"

"He is in our ancestral house with granny and is doing well."

"I heard he was in the USA for some time, is that true?"

"Yes, he worked in Detroit for many years before retiring."

"How wonderful. Have a seat child."

Sitting on the sofa in the drawing room, he noticed pictures of Fathers and Sisters strung on the wall and sculptures kept on shelves and alcoves. He surmised that they would have been from Father Romelo's institution. A stone sculpture of Hazel was kept on a table. It was a replica of her face. He guessed it would be the one Joydeep had sculpted for her.

"I am so glad that you escaped from that rascal Darryl and his crooked gang. I was shocked when I heard about it. Hazel mentioned about Sudeep discovering you in the village. Looks like he was like a godsend for you there."

At that moment Hazel stepped into the room beaming. She came forward and hugged him. She seemed more relaxed and cheerful than she was in the morning. But her eyes had the same entrenched melancholy in them. She was dressed in blue jeans and a red full sleeved turtle-neck top. Her long hair was left open.

"Let me first pop a 'rosogolla', although the doctor advised me to keep away from sweets," said Hazel. She stuffed one and relished the sweet juices flooding the walls of her mouth with her eyes closed. "Delicious."

"Were you at the piano Hazel?"

"Yeah. Though I am at it quite irregularly."

"It was sounding cool. The last I heard anyone play it was our school music teacher."

"Mom is a lot better at it. Actually I am learning from her now."

At that point Shane and Helena walked in from the room where Hazel had come from. They were holding each other's hands and on seeing Siddharth they loosened the hold.

"How are you, my artist buddy?" asked Shane hugging Siddharth.

"Great. How about yourself and Helena?"

Shane and Helena sat on the sofa sticking to each other. Hazel sat on a high chair. "We are doing well," said Helena.

"Do you work here?" asked Siddharth, his gaze shifting to Shane's bulging biceps.

"Yes, at the Truck factory as an Engineer. Been here for five years," said Shane.

"Say you live in the factory," said Helena emphatically. "Through some miracle he came with me here today. Otherwise you can only find him at the factory, never at home."

"Oh come on that's not true," said Shane laughing loudly.

"And is it not true that last month you ditched home for three nights together?"

"That was for a problem at the assembly line. That's my job, honey," said Shane guffawing this time. Though he spoke little, he seemed to laugh aloud at everything. Helena was talkative and for the rest of the evening was telling on Shane lightheartedly. Everyone was relaxed and cheerful and appeared different from what they had been in the hospital.

"Now that's a great husband and wife conversation to have. You people carry on while I get the snacks," said Aunt Mary.

"You must be very excited to meet your old friend Hazel after so many years?" asked Helena looking at Siddharth.

KEY TO MY SOUL

"Of course. It is special," he replied. He reflected on his own words and realized how terrific it actually felt. Discovering Hazel and seeing her come out of the deathbed was like seeing a rebirth. "Where are you both from?" asked Siddharth. "I had meant to ask you in the hospital itself but never found the right moment I guess."

"Assansol. We moved here five years back. I work with Hazel," said Helena.

"Let's go to my study room. I want to show Sidd something," said Hazel.

Inside the room, huge racks lined the walls and were stuffed with a dizzying number of books. Siddharth started leafing through a few of them. He was pleasantly surprised. They sat on the wicker chairs that were lying around.

While they were chatting, Hazel's mom came back with tea and a tray-full of snacks. "Dinner is also ready, whenever you guys are, okay? Let me know." Before leaving for the kitchen again she gave her enigmatic and contagious smile. Beneath it, her past struggles, her bravery, the sacrifices she made were hidden neatly.

Hazel poured tea for all in small china cups, the ones without handles.

"You seem to have a big passion for books huh," asked Siddharth.

"Yes. After school they became my oxygen," replied Hazel slowly.

"Hazel, you both talk. Shane and I will go help your mom with the plates," she winked at Hazel and pulled Shane by his arm. "Come with me. Be of some help."

After they left Hazel pulled out a few picture albums from

one of the racks and gave them to Siddharth. "Have a look at these."

"Is it your picture album?"

"Yes. It also has Father Romelo and his campus and Joydeep."

Hearing the last name Sidd hiccupped. He reached for the tea to moisten his throat.

Joydeep had a thin long face and clear bright eyes. There was definitely an endearing and honest quality in them that Hazel had written about. In the pictures he appeared lanky and slightly taller than Hazel. Although in many pictures Hazel and Joydeep were seen together, he noted, they were never seen holding hands in any of them.

Flipping through the rest of the pages he was able to relate to the pictures based on the descriptions he had read in the letters.

"Great. I wish I could have met Joydeep."

"Mom told me that he was here during my initial days in the hospital. He may visit us again soon."

"Maybe next time we will meet. Who are they?" he asked pointing to a group picture.

"They are my office colleagues."

"I was about to ask you more about your job. Where do you work?"

"I look after the sales of sculptures from Father Romelo's in Jamshedpur and nearby districts. We have a small office and a warehouse as well."

Hazel's mom walked in at that point. She sat on a wicker chair beside them, wiping her hands with a soft white kitchen towel. Shane and Helena joined them too. They talked about a lot of other things, especially about the town and their simple lives as it used to be two decades back. Finally they walked over to the dinner table.

"Remember last time you over-ate and couldn't sleep the whole night," said Helena tapping Shane's shoulder.

"Well the tongue never stops lolling at Aunt Mary's," said Shane and giggled.

"Thank you dear. Please help yourselves with my modest menu," said Aunt Mary pointing at the laden table. At the center was Chicken rotisserie and around it Mulligatawny soup with diced lamb, rice pilaf, cauliflower curry, potato wedges and raw salads.

"This is anything but a modest menu," said Siddharth after filling his plate.

"Mouthwatering as always," said Shane chewing a chunk of chicken and closing his eyes. Helena nudged him with her elbow.

"Mom conducts piano classes sometimes in our old school, Sidd."

"Really. That's nice. Can we hear you play tonight Aunt Mary?" asked Siddharth.

"Sure I will. But I see you are not eating much child. Not liking?"

"I am loving every bit of it. The food is just delicious Aunt Mary and the roasted Chicken is out of this world," said Siddharth munching. He became aware that Hazel was staring at him. He glanced at her to find an odd look that was nearly the same as when they were in school. It was one of dislike and irritation but now moderated with a polite smile. He realized that he was making the characteristic noise as he chewed that had always annoyed Hazel. So he immediately muffled it up.

"Totally agree," said Shane. "After a long time I am eating such delicious food."

Helena was about to say something, but checked herself. She didn't seem too pleased with her husband's comment.

Shane had brought two bottles of wine as gifts and poured a glass each for everyone. It tasted sweet and almost medicinal.

After dinner Aunt Mary was getting ready at the piano. It was kept in her bedroom adjacent to Hazel's. Everyone sat around her. As she ran her fingers over the keys, she said that it belonged to her late father. It was a black colored console piano.

"I could not lay my hands on this for many years. Finally when I moved back with Hazel to this town again, I got it transported."

Once she started the romantic *Tchaikovsky Opus 72 Number 5*, there was a shift in the mood and everyone cheered up. Along with the wine it eased wrought muscles. She played more sonatas, some melancholy some foot-tapping. Everyone clapped with admiration.

Siddharth smiled at Hazel appreciating her mother's virtuosity. And then every now and then he tried to hold her look and traverse deeper into her eyes. But she restrained. Every time his gaze lingered, she looked away smiling, almost casually, but gently, without hurting yet without approving.

Finally, few renditions later, as if telegraphed by the same thought, Hazel and Siddharth looked at each other and walked out of the room into the attached verandah. They stood looking at the night sky lit by a gibbous moon. An occasional draft of wind made the night chilly. She stood a couple of feet away resting her elbows on the railing.

The music honeyed the moments and sprinkled the air with romance.

He imagined her to be the same girl he was once mad about and remembered their carefree and intimate moments. That made him suddenly long for her. Although her looks had somewhat roughened with time he could not deny that he was still attracted to her. The curves of her body were pronounced, her skin looked butter soft. He stared at her long neck that was half covered by the fall of silky hair. As the wine flowed into the corners of the body the years of separation narrowed down.

It was as if he was separated from her by only a few months.

"Can I ask you something?"

She smiled and said, "Only if it's nothing serious."

"Are you happy?"

"Now that's a really serious question." She giggled.

"I mean it," he persisted

"Yes I am Sidd. Why do you ask?"

"I had the impression that you are married."

Hazel paused at the sudden and direct question. She looked at him deeply, as if she was pondering over something, and asked, "Is marriage the key to happiness?"

"For some it maybe. It does have a positive impact where it is smooth and goes well. But not always," he replied reflecting on his own condition.

"I was never married."

"Hmm. I thought you were after reading your letters. I heard in the hospital though that you were never married. Yet I just can't seem to believe that it's true."

A brief silence fell on them and then she added, "We lived together, with mom, for a couple of years before moving here.

I did consider marrying Joydeep. But I don't think I was ever ready completely. We had a deep understanding and affection for each other and finally left it that way, unharmed."

"Hmm. Where is he now?"

"In my old world. In Father Romelo's campus. Married to a lady worker in the same organization there. He is happy. And so am I."

Siddharth watched the moon in silence. The night was running out fast. A sudden desire awoke in him to find out if any corner of her soul was still lit by the flame of their lost love. Did any part of her heart still preserve a part of him?

But he was afraid to ask and afraid to know.

"Don't you think of having a family of your own?"

"I haven't really desired one."

"Are you determined not to marry?"

"I'm not sure."

"Why not?"

She didn't reply and kept staring at the moonlit road. The breeze stirred her hair.

Unable to hold himself any longer he moved sideways along the railing till he stood near her, his right arm almost brushing her left. The years of depravity without a loving woman by his side had made him a loner. He had forgotten what it was to feel the softness and delicateness of a woman. Yet he remembered how in his arms she had sought refuge so many times. He recalled her sweet breath, her submission, her surrender.

But standing there with the weight of his past on his chest, it was he who wanted to yield, to be smothered in her arms, to be subdued, overpowered and even quelled. He wished Hazel would admonish and rebuke him for giving up on her and for his follies and then cuddle him, in an act of compassion. He sought her forgiveness so and felt the stab of guilt pierce him once again.

"You have been through so much. If I could bend time backwards, I would have done things so differently," he began. "After reading your letters I felt like waking out of a bad dream. Actually, I started hating myself."

"Why'd you hate yourself?" she asked.

"I ran away without trying to seek you, without trying to know the truth."

"How would you know about us? We had left the town in haste. We absconded."

"I still could have. I could have." Something was starting to break inside him.

"No you couldn't."

"At least I could have tried to do something. You don't know how I feel about myself today. When I think about my past I only see myself taking easy decisions. Be it my job, my failed marriage, my paper-thin resolve to find you. I realize now that it's easy to run away. That's what I have been doing. I've been running all my life. Running away from everything and everyone in my life."

"Don't loathe yourself like that."

"But that's true. I ran away from the town. I ran away from reality in college. I ran away from what gave me joy in life, painting. In many ways I ran away from my marriage as well. I ran away from you and your thoughts. And the reason is one…only one fucking…" his voice started rising and he started shaking and shivering in anguish. It seemed that he was about to blow himself up.

"Stop it Sidd."

"No listen, listen. The reason is that I have always been a fucking timid person." He knew even without the locker key, if he really wanted to, he could have traced down Hazel. Somehow. The errors of his past decisions and judgments pricked his eyes until they watered.

"No that's not true."

"Maybe that is why love, true love, has always eluded me," he blurted out and stopped talking. Slowly, very slowly, did his shivering fade away.

Hazel watched him but remained composed. She heard his heavy breathing and understood his turmoil. There was no one else who had understood him as easily as her. That being so much in history did not seem to lessen the ability. She placed her left hand on his shoulder and comforted him, albeit formally. "It's okay Sidd. Take it easy. Know that my past doesn't bother me anymore. Seriously."

The piano was roaring at times and pensive at others and Shane and Helena clapped after the end of each crescendo.

"And you have nothing to blame yourself for. You couldn't have done much. At least I think so." Those words gave him more comfort and strength than the wine had.

"Father Romelo once told me, that one way to defeat our miseries is by trying to reduce another person's. Or by having goals in life that are beyond the self. That's what my father did, who I never met. That's what I have tried to do. It has rescued me from my past. We often try to run away from reality. That's natural I guess. I did it too few times for there is so much to be sad about in our lives. But at the same time there is so much to be happy and proud about. Why not choose to look at them instead?"

He blew his stuffy nose and didn't deny what he heard. The sweetness in her voice was still intact and so was the strength of reasoning. As they stared into the moonlit night, listening to the piano, small incidents from school days came to his mind and he pined for her, for her touch, for that deep inexpressibly sweet love she had showered on him once.

He held her hands. He wanted to ask her, "Can we become the friends we were once? Can we be in love again?" But he couldn't say it. It was too much to ask for and too soon. In some ways it seemed incorrect as well as he was technically still married. They stood in silence till his eyes dried up.

"You didn't answer my question. Why don't you want to marry, Hazel?"

"Probably because I don't have an answer. I am not averse to it as I was in the past. I've come a long way to accept it as normal. But I don't know what's in my destiny."

In the back of his mind he was trying to visualize having Hazel by his side as his companion for life. Somewhere deep inside him he tried to argue with himself if he should tell her about his feelings right there. He was tempted to. But he checked himself and decided to think over it again. Standing by her side, on the verandah, one thing was clear in his mind, that Hazel's presence unlike anyone else he met in his life, electrified him, filled his heart with a longing to celebrate life, a longing to fall in love again and again many times over.

However, deeply aggrieved by the failure of his first marriage he backed off and instead asked, "Where is James, your step-dad?"

She shrugged her shoulders and frowned. "I don't know. I

don't care. He had left the town long back and was suffering from some illness."

"One thing I learnt is no one really forgets old obsessions and dislikes."

"What do you mean?"

"That Darryl. He still has so much venom against me."

"Ya. What he tried to do to you is unnerving. When he came to know that we were back in town he started his old tricks again. He tried to corner me several times. In fact he spoke to mom to get me to marry him. Can you imagine? After all that had happened in the past he had the nerve to ask for my hand. Such a shameless pig. Luckily, because of Shane he couldn't do much. One person he fears is Shane."

"What does he do for a living?"

"Owns a few car garages. You know repair and stuff."

"So even he isn't married?"

"Who will marry a ruffian like him?"

"What happened to him after Shane pulled him out of the hospital. You know about that incident, right?"

"Of course. We talked about it almost every day after I was back on my feet again. Shane had registered a police case against him. I am planning to lodge a case against him too for his past sins. It may be too late. But I still want to see the end of it. From what I heard he is maintaining a low profile now." She emptied the wine glass.

They remained silent for a while and listened to the soulful melodies oozing from the piano. "And what else occupies you outside of work, Hazel?"

"The world of letters." She gave him a look that was at once serious and not.

Siddharth was not sure if he understood her words. At that moment the piano stopped and Aunt Mary called out, "Hazel can you guys come inside please? It's time for dessert."

More conversation flowed over honey-coated banana-split ice-cream and applesauce.

"You play so beautifully. Hearing you is so inspiring," said Shane.

"Absolutely. Do you give performances anywhere?" asked Siddharth.

"Except at the church choir and school functions, nowhere else," replied Aunt Mary.

"I was thinking probably you could play at our office parties," said Shane. "Although I heard you so many times, I never thought of this possibility earlier."

"You are great Aunt Mary. From the balcony it sounded richer," added Siddharth.

After a while he went to the study room once again and browsed through the book racks. The collecttion of books and authors amazed him and he found his favorite ones as well.

"Are you still fond of poetry, Sidd?" asked Hazel.

"Yes. I stopped writing for the right reasons, and instead became a reader."

Close to midnight, the get together came to an end. Everyone thanked Hazel and her mom for the lovely time. They spoke some more at the door and hugged each other.

"I will send you a surprise soon Sidd. I have something in mind, but will let you know about it later," said Hazel.

At that point Shane, Helena, Hazel and Aunt Mary

exchanged naughty smiles that left Siddharth guessing of a secret he was being shielded from, one which they all knew about. Something not trivial.

"Surprise. Surprise. See how good a friend Hazel is. And you?" said Helena to Shane.

"Why last year didn't I give you a surprise on Halloween night?"

"You call that a surprise? That was a shock mister. Not a surprise."

"What was it child?" asked Aunt Mary curiously.

"He dressed up as a vampire and woke me up from sleep in the dead of the night with a dagger in hand and white fangs piercing out from his red mouth. I almost fainted."

They exited into the moonlit street amidst giggles and laughter. The cold was piercing. Shane pulled up the zipper of his leather jacket and put on a helmet and gloves. Helena put on a thick woolen sweater and ear muffs. Then Shane kick-started his motorcycle parked by the curb and Helena hopped behind him. The bike leapt forward and sped away.

Siddharth wore his long overcoat and walked back to his hotel. By the time he reached there it was midnight and the silence of the night was merely scratched by the faint dongs of a church bell faraway.

Chapter 24

FATHER AND SON

Once again he entered his house, like any other day, navigated the dark rooms, the curtains still shut, the noncompliance of Babban still visible, the only sounds if any were of his feet. Yet the stillness didn't sting, the darkness didn't dampen him. After a wash, he unhooked the window curtains and kept them aside for a rarely done activity. Laundering.

Sunshine flooded the east facing rooms like a sense of serenity that eased his soul.

Meeting Hazel had calmed him. The inner burning subsided and the shackles of guilt split apart. A tiny shift of perspective was breeding inside. It was spawned by his awe for Hazel, for the way she rose from her inner turmoil. His unsteady life that was meandering without a destination, got somewhat fortified. The possibility, even if remote, of getting closer again to Hazel filled him with hope and purpose.

Even the defunct yet deliberate knots with Kiran did not bother him anymore. It took some time before his old life reclaimed him back to its old ways.

For the next three months the frequent work related tours kept him busy. Yet he was in touch with Hazel, Shane, Aunt Mary and Sudeep over phone. His life started sailing again. He completed a series of sketches on Hazel, her face and full portrait.

One day, talking to his father on the phone he learnt that he had just recovered from a bout of fever. "No need to worry," said his father. "I am alright now."

But the conversation left him restless and he planned for a quick but short visit.

After reaching Baharampur he found that his father had not yet recovered; That he had lied to him. The family doctor was beside his father's bed and said, "It was an enlargement of the prostate gland. He passed blood in his urine. It will be in control soon with the medicines he is taking."

After the doctor left, he asked, "*Baba*, why didn't you tell me about this?"

"It isn't anything serious. And what could you have done remotely, except worrying," said Mr. Banerjee unable to get up from the bed without some support.

"Slowly," said Siddharth helping his father sit up.

"It is good you have come *babu*," said his grandmother. "It is always good to have you here. It's probably time you started looking after your dad once in a while."

Those words echoed in his mind for a long time.

During his stay, Siddharth started going to the market daily for groceries and vegetables. He queued up at the pharmacies for his father's medicines, patiently evaluated the fish and vegetables in the market before buying them and ran errands. At night he took over his father's duty to massage his grandmother's feet with hot mustard oil and garlic.

Something drove him to be responsible for things he was blind to earlier.

He chatted with them for hours and when the electricity went off he fanned them with the hand-fans made of palm leaves. But in all his conversations till then he had omitted the trips to Jamshedpur, Hazel's coma and miraculous recovery, Aunt Mary, the incident with Darryl and his accidental discovery of childhood buddy Sudeep.

One afternoon as he was passing by his father's room he saw him trying to get off the bed. Quickly, he walked over to support him. In the process his father' shirt rolled up to the chest, revealing a long scar on the right side, just above the waist-line. It started from the navel, winding up to the back and almost touched the spine. On a closer look he saw there were two scars.

"What's this *baba*?" he asked surprised.

His father immediately rolled down his shirt, "Oh nothing, just an old scratch."

But as far as Siddharth could recall he had never seen it ever before. So he insisted in knowing more about it, fearing something grave was being kept hidden from him.

"Did you get hurt somehow here?"

"*Arre na*. This is an old scar from wild thorns," Mr. Banerjee fibbed.

"*Thakuma*," Siddharth called out to his grandmother unconvinced that thorns could create such a deep mark. "What's this?"

"Oh I have seen this on him for many years now. He never told me about it either."

"Alright so it's not new. That's nice to hear. So how did you get the cut?"

Mr. Banerjee started laughing. "Why are you behind this scar? Leave it alone."

"No I won't. You got to tell me." Siddharth was dogged in

his inquiry.

There was something different that Mr. Banerjee noticed in his son, in his voice that had become more serious and demanding, yet sincere and concerned. It was not the usual casual voice he was accustomed to hearing of his son.

"Unless you let me know *baba*, I am not leaving this room."

"Forget it boy. Stop pestering."

"Did you have a surgery or an accident?"

"No."

"Then why these stitch marks?"

Never before had he seen so much persistence in his son. The tone and behavior surprised Mr. Banerjee. He knew his son as a calm and aloof boy, undisturbed by the world around, immersed in his private thoughts. Even during his painful separation with Kiran, he never saw him reacting or bad-mouthing. Although he knew that his son was shattered inside, he never saw the thorns of anguish surface.

"No surgery *babu*. There was a minor cut once. So the doctors stitched it."

"Very well. When was this?"

Mr. Banerjee tried to pass it off with a suppressed smile like a child cornered for stealing and trying to dodge interrogation by faking an innocent smile. "*Ma*, when will we have lunch?" He asked his mother.

"It is ready. I am soaking the rice. But come over. I got drumstick leaves braised with garlic for the start. I know *babu* will love it."

"Stop all that. Don't try to change the topic *baba*."

Seeing no way out of his son's persistent interrogation, Mr. Banerjee relented. "Well if you must know it then I will tell you.

It's an old story."

What Siddharth heard rocked him for days.

"It was a cut I got from her dad."

"What cut? Whose dad?"

"Hazel's."

"What?" shrieked Siddharth, "when?"

"When you joined college in 1991. Few weeks later."

Mr. Banerjee recounted that one night when he was coming from Azaad Bazaar, he was stopped and forced into an argument. "James accused me and you of playing around with his daughter. I did not accept all the dirt he spoke. It seemed to anger him. He struck me. I didn't leave him either. We fisted each other a couple of times and then one of his friends who seemed to be waiting nearby, pulled James away and drove off in a car. James was insisting on one thing."

"You never told me all this. What was he insisting on?"

"To get out of Jamshedpur for good."

"And what about the scar?"

"A day after, while I was driving back home from office, he stopped me at the area near the water tank. You know it was the desolate stretch on the way home." Mr. Banerjee looked around to confirm that his mother was out of hearing range and then proceeded.

"He got into the same argument. A little later someone else came out of the car. It was Darryl's father. James pointed at the man's eyes and said that you had done that to him. I saw stitch marks around his left eye. Darryl's father said that you had stoned him. I denied. That annoyed James and he knifed me few times."

"Oh no."

"He did not anticipate what I'd do next. Probably he thought I would retaliate, but I simply ignored him and somehow got into my car and drove off. He kept chasing me up to a certain point and turned away as soon as he realized that I neared the police station."

"And then?"

"The police admitted me to the hospital and later I filed an FIR. Since I had to relocate to Detroit in a month, the company assisted me. James was rounded up in the police station and asked to leave the town. He was still trying to do business outside Jamshedpur for a while but later I heard he left the town forever."

Siddharth flared up, "That bloody James. You don't know what kind of a devil he is. I will tell you more about him later."

After lunch while his grandmother ground areca nuts and betel leaf in her bedroom, he shared nuggets of his story about Hazel, her letters, the accident, her coma and recovery and his visits to the hospital and town to be with her, Darryl's encounter and the truth behind Darryl's father losing his eye. Mr. Banerjee was shaken to the core when he heard it all and especially about James and his actual character.

In the evening, around sunset, Mr. Banerjee asked Siddharth out for a stroll around the lake. After listening to a part his son's life that was eclipsed from him, he felt he needed to talk to him about an important matter.

They spoke about various things from poetry to local politics, developmental plans of Baharampur, old friends and relatives. It was already dark when Mr. Banerjee actually spoke about what he had in mind.

"Do you like Hazel?" asked Mr. Banerjee.

"What? Why are you asking?" asked Siddharth, taken aback at the direct question.

"Just wanted to know if you like her in the same way as before?"

Siddharth didn't know what to say and blurted, "Actually, I'm not sure."

"I think you do. It is not difficult to see that. And it is great to have strong feelings for someone. You must seriously think about Hazel."

"About what?"

"We are all lonely in the world, son. I realized early in my life that we need someone beside us to defeat the tragedies of life, when they strike. Someone close. It helps. Each time I lost someone dear, I could deal with the loss only because I had a family. When I lost my father, I had my mother, my brothers and sisters, you, your mother. When your mom left us, it was shattering. It was like building the bricks of life one by one again. I was hardly able to do it. But I had you. And I guess that gave me enough strength to bear the tragic loss."

"But you didn't marry again."

He took a pause and then continued, "At times I did consider looking for someone to lead my life with again. I managed to move on somehow. But your case is different. You have no children from your marriage."

"But I don't need to get into a relationship now. I have you, I have *thakuma*. I don't think anyone can give that kind of love to me."

"You are missing a vital point here, son. What is love? It is one word alright. But it brings out different feelings and emotions in different relationships. We all need food to stay healthy and survive. It's one word, food. But our body needs different types of food. So it is with love. Love for the nation, for a sport, for a flower, for parents, for children are quite different from each other. And so is the love for one's partner. We cannot experience the different emotions from one person or thing. We need them all to blossom."

"Maybe I am disillusioned. My marriage didn't work."

"You have seen a dark shade earlier but all women are not the same. I strongly feel you must look forward now."

"I don't know if it is the right thing to do at this point in my life."

"There are no rights or wrongs in a world, if it doesn't hurt anyone. You have a life ahead of you. The past cannot decide your future. Only your present can. Give it another try."

"But how do I know if she is the right one for me?"

"Think about it this way and see if it makes sense...one day I'll be gone too. With all that has happened between you and Hazel, if you believe that she is the one you'd like to have beside you when I am gone, your *thakuma* is gone, when you are all alone in this world, then she is the right person for you."

Siddharth thought about it. He took a long time to answer. It was difficult for him to open up and admit such thoughts to his dad. But in front of the honesty and strength in his dad's words he knew he had to tell the truth. At least he had to try to and he said, "Yes I guess I do see her that way."

"Good."

"But then I don't know if she will agree."

"Let her know about your feelings and see. Take your time but not a whole lot."

He patted his son's back and they walked back home. Before entering the house-gate he said suddenly, "Oh before I forget, remember to take the poetry books you left last time."

"Oh those. Let them be here. Once I come back I'll read them. I am not finding much time these days to read poetry. I kind of started painting again."

"Oh is it?" exclaimed Mr. Banerjee beaming. "That is so wonderful. That is a great news I heard after a long time." He patted his son again. "Don't stop it ever again."

That night when he thought about his father, his sacrifice, his love for his son, it moved him. But it was his father's silence about the encounter with James that baffled him the most. It brought him closer to understanding his father, closer to understanding a father's love for his child, closer to understanding the meaning of fatherhood.

Two days later when he was leaving for Bhubaneswar, he hugged his father and held him tightly for a long time and said, what his dad had told him once in Detroit, "You may think I am so many hours away but I am just a phone call away."

He came as a concerned son to meet his father and returned as a proud one.

With the changes he saw in his son, Mr. Banerjee also felt likewise. The distance certainly had narrowed between them. Mr. Banerjee felt lighter and more fulfilled in life and prayed for his son and Hazel.

Chapter 25

INDRA

The courier guy came as a startlingly bright spring morning. It was a few weeks after Siddharth met his father and had no clue of what the courier contained. When he tore open the packet he found three poetry books and a handwritten note.

He looked at the books and turned them around. They were glossy paperbacks. The back cover of each book arrested his pulse. From within the delimiting lines of a square, a face was staring back at him. It looked too familiar to be true. He could not look away.

He thought about the same set of books that lay by his bedside for months wrapped in gift packing without being opened. And after that they got accidentally misplaced at his father's house to be forgotten altogether. He hurriedly read the note.

"Sidd, I had told you that I would send you a surprise. This is it! I had asked mom, Shane and Helena not to disclose this to you, on the night you had dinner with us.

You may not know I have written three books of poetry using the pen-name INDRA. That is my father's nickname who as you know is no longer with us. I used his name as a tribute to him. It is for our unaccustomed love.

Next time you come to Jamshedpur I have to tell you many more things. I wish we could meet more often."

One by one he went through the books and the poems in them and to his disbelief he found his name in the dedication page of the second book published in 2004.

"For Sidd Banerjee who is still in my mind as the melody of a sweet song that lingers eternally, long after it is no longer heard. For what he showed me with his painting brush, I have tried to sketch in words."

His eyes couldn't resist from blinking and watering, as if stray sparks from a firecracker had singed them. The torrent of tears blinded him. After mopping his eyes with the back of his hand he called up Hazel right away.

"So this was your surprise gift."

"So the courier service was reliable." She chuckled.

"You never told me about it, you prankster."

"I was waiting to tell you, Sidd. When I got to know about your interest in poetry I thought I should surprise you but not immediately."

"Shane, Helena, your mom and you conspired that night." He blew his nose.

"Sort of," giggled Hazel, biting her tongue. "Sorry."

"I want to pinch your cheeks for that and then pull your hair and then …."

"And then?"

"Then poke your ribs and tickle you where it rattles you the most and then…" he stopped and wiped his eyes dry with the sleeve of his shirt.

"Go on. Go on. And then?"

"And then blow air on your eyelids and hold your hands and tug them forward…"

"And…"

"And then hold you like a doll and hug you and then twist your ears for the surprise."

"Ha ha ha," laughed Hazel. "Sweet."

"Now can we plan to meet?"

"Hmm. It's been a while."

"It's over four months that we met. I wish we lived within a mile."

"Come over to your old town."

"If only wishes were horses. So much work to do and getting time off from office is difficult. Isn't there a way you can come over instead?"

"Hey, hey...not so fast." She paused for a moment and then said slowly word by word as if she was meditating and pondering as she spoke, "But I may. If I ever go to meet you in Bhubaneshwar will you do few things for me? Two things in fact."

"I hope you won't ask me to leave the city or the country."

"Oh please. Am I that cruel?"

"I hope not. What two things?"

"First, you need to make less sound while eating."

"Come on. Don't pick on me that way Hazel. I can buy ear plugs for you."

"Ear plug is not an option, Siddy boy. You agree or not."

"Ok for now. What's the other one?"

"I assume you'll pick me up from the railway station?"

"That, without question I will."

"And you have to greet me with something. Remember."

"With what thing?"

"I had told you that several years back. Think and tell."

Siddharth thought for a while and gave up.

"They are the original keys to my soul."

Siddharth thought about the locker keys. But this sounded different. He had no clue.

Hazel admonished him playfully. "Roses."

"Big red roses," said Siddharth remembering their ancient talk. "Oh that! That's easy. I'll stand at the platform with a big smile holding roses for you. How about tomorrow?"

They both laughed.

"For the time being Mr. Painter, its better you keep coming down here."

"I'll try Miss Poetess. And I hope you've got out of your infatuation with cigarettes."

"Of all the things is this the only one that you recalled about me, you silly? That and I walked out of our teens, together. It was that long back."

"Then I look forward to the day when I'll have a reason to buy roses. Big red roses."

That night there was an acute silence in the room, except for the sounds of his fingers dancing rhythm-less over an old scraggy daisy-wheel typewriter, along with the golden swirls of a wind-harassed candle. Power outage and a faulty generator had plunged the house into darkness. The air from the front window bent the steady flame of the candle.

At a time when computers were still alien and he was fifteen and fancied writing a chapbook of poems, he had begged his father into buying him the type-writer. Incited by friends and inspired by Hazel, he wanted to possess one. But soon his fascination wore away when he found it did not aid in producing better poems. So he locked it away for good.

That night he wanted to paint his past in words. He toyed with the idea of writing his love story. Though he wasn't sure how it would end he felt the end didn't matter. He was happy that for him, Hazel was no longer a shadow of his past and that she existed as much as her poems and his paintings. So his fingers once again sought the keys of the old type-writer and he wrote nonstop for three hours. The time was one in the morning.

After a lot of indecisiveness his forefinger hit the dot-key for lack of words. His ideas were thinning down with each sleepy breath. Tired of typing he rubbed his over-used eyes and fell into a long soundless yawn. Then he swung his arms back and with clenched fists kneaded the aching lower back and love handles till they felt supple again.

To oust the heat in the room he opened the second window that was behind him.

Through it he saw the dark outlines of an ample 'peepul' nearby and thick tree-hugging creepers tightly coiled around its trunk like a serpent around its prey. It showed the silhouettes of the moon, partially eclipsed by the branches and a curvy road that flowed like a silver ribbon across a black canvas. The cool air greeted him with a faint smell of jackfruit.

Unbuttoning his shirt, he drank the musky air.

The candle was still tall and unbent but lost its regal glow and flickered more due to the cross-winds in the house. It would burn till it melted into a puddle and harden. Such wax spreads on the table were many and gave the table-top a corrugated and an unclean look.

He slipped into his pajamas and slid under the mosquito net. As his spine straightened along the lines of the smooth

KEY TO MY SOUL

pinstriped spotless bed-sheet, a sliver of smile showed on his face.

A gecko darted after an insect on the ceiling and gobbled it. He was reminded of Hazel chasing him one evening at the temple base in their home town, for he was unaware that it was her birthday.

The candle would burn until it was snuffed out by the breeze from the ceiling fan. By the time the power returned and the ceiling fan turned he was fast asleep, reading one of Hazel's poems in his dreams.

I collect, one by one, my memories,
that lay scattered, inert,
in the open fields of childhood, where
we vowed never to look beyond,
and now half-way as I have stacked
each bit, an unmindful wind whisks
them off like pollen,
and I run behind, in frenzy,
to re-collect,
only to tumble on a thirsty weed,
which slurps a teardrop,
that rolls out in pain, robbing
a bit of you from my eyes.

I lay static, jaded, parched,
hoping to reconstruct you again,
from dreams we once saw here, as
the distant temple-chime from the hilltop
ushers twilight, and the birds in the sky
trace a pattern that I recognize,
is your dimple-chinned innocent face.

FOUR YEARS LATER - NOVEMBER 2013

The news of the severe cyclone Phallin that had hit Orissa few weeks back was being telecast on the overhead television sets. It was one of the biggest evacuations done in the world and the Orissa government managed it successfully with minimum damage to lives. The affected people were slowly regaining normalcy in their daily existence.

The train was visible but as a dot. It was approaching the station. The loud speakers announced its arrival. After a while the platform rumbled and the sound of the engine got louder and louder until it was deafening. Some people covered their ears with their palms.

As soon as the wheels screeched to a halt, the crowd on the platform broke in all directions. People climbed the wagons as if they were fleeing away from the city. Passengers getting down had the typical grumpy look of those held hostage for no reason.

When the din had settled and the sense of equilibrium returned in the platform, two feet in sneakers stepped out of the train and stood still. The head, covered with a shawl, turned in the direction of the engine and then towards the rear end. And then a smile as big and as beautiful as a rainbow flashed across the face and reached the kohl-rimmed eyes.

A tall, dark and dimple-chinned man with droopy eyelids was waiting eagerly to see the face that had been visiting him a million times of late, in his dreams and in daylight. Unable to restrain himself, he dashed across the platform, holding a bush of big red roses in his right hand and a few pencil sketches he had finally made of her face.

Dressed in a crepe big collared white full-shirt tucked inside a smart fit deep blue jeans, he looked stylish. The sleeves were rolled up to the elbow. As he neared her, he extended his arm and said, "Welcome to the City of Temples."

She held the roses first and then the pencil sketches and hugged him and said, "Am I dreaming or is this real?"

They stared at each other like they used to, many years ago. Their lives were no less cyclonic. But after every devastation the dust settles down, after every thunderstorm there is silence. After every war peace returns. After every dark night the sun rises to light the path of hope. It gives conviction that there are still many things to look forward to in life.

My love is like ether. It will survive winds or fires, flooding waters or a barren earth. My love will exist like the fifth element.

Outside the Bhubaneshwar railway station, the place was bustling with people hurrying to and fro, chasing their dreams and destinations. The sun was going down in the west and the cool November air felt like anodyne caressing souls. They walked hand in hand, feeling the pull of the future, imagining the new life waiting to open its doors, chirping like merry birds about to build a new nest, until they were swallowed by the evening crowd.

"My love will shine like the moon when the light in the lanterns fade away."

Acknowledgement

Writing "Key To My Soul", was like a trek up an unknown hill on a sunny morning with a spread of blue winter sky overhead. Maybe it was the allure of the hill or the sting of a series of tough days that pushed me towards the adventure. It led me not only to the discovery of the story but eventually to a sense of self-discovery as well. On the uneven path, I saw forgotten memories sprout as wild flowers on the wayside.

After reaching the hilltop, I saw the completed book staring back at me. Now as I walk downhill and continue to look at the beauty of the skies above and the depths below, few faces sail across like cheerful clouds. They are the faces of grand people who I had met on the way up. Some known, some unknown. They stopped to chit-chat or show me the path ahead or simply patted my back. Some filled me with hope and others with strength. It is now my time to thank them!

I must start with my wife, Sudeshna, who patiently read the early versions of the book and provided the initial manure and sunshine it required for an independent growth. She also bore the brunt of my wild writing schedules, silently and sometimes not so silently.

To my cousin, Shayonee for a thorough and critical analysis of the storyline and motion. She almost missed her wedding date reading my book.

For Surojit Chakrabarty, my friend for many years who went out of the way to review and provide his sincere and valuable comments. And in the process, lost more hair.

For Namrata Madhira (@PrivyTrifles) for being the constant rock of reassurance and making me feel like a rock-star and the book like a masterpiece, for offering the title of the book and for her constant guidance.

Sujata Rajpal (author), who appeared as a surge of electricity and welded me to the right network of people.

Dr. Arun Kumar Mohapatra, for blessing the portions related to medicine and surgery.

Mr. Prakash Behera for his guidance and insight into the non-biological aspects of giving birth to a book. Binay Dutta for bearing with my stubborn calls and ultimately showing me the goalpost.

Nandan Singh (Maple Press), who, I must have turned half-mad by repeatedly asking him spools of questions and later again asking the same set of questions.

My cousin Paromita, for reading a portion of the initial manuscript.

Kuntal Paul, a shutterbug, for clicking my pictures on the book.

Ronny Sequeira, ace lensman and my friend, who guided me in every other way.

To Ma, Bapi, Dada, Sudeshna, Prithvi and all my dear ones for being there and for loving me always, with or without this book.

ABOUT THE AUTHOR

PROBAL usually writes poetry/short stories. Through them he reflects on the delicate transformations of relationships with time and the often overlooked beauty and vulnerability of nature. Probal's poems have appeared in various Indian and International journals like Wasafiri, Acumen, Indian Literature (Sahitya Akademi), amongst others.

He was awarded the FIRST prize in the All India Poetry Competition, 2014, conducted by Poetry Society of India.

"Key to My Soul" is his debut novel.

Occasionally he goes out for a stroll in:

Facebook: https://www.facebook.com/probalmazumdar.official.page/

Instagram: probalmazumdar99

Twitter: Coral @ probalmazumdarJ

Website: www.probalmazumdar.com

Key to My Soul

PROBAL MAZUMDAR

Did you like the book

Email your
queries, experiences, and suggestions
to the author at
probalmazumdar99@**gmail.com**